BLACK SAILS, DISCO INFERNO

A novel by ANDREZ BERGEN

with RENEE ASHER PICKUP (Chapters 7-8)

For Cocoa, Yoko, Fée and Des
—*Andrez*

For Jonathan
—*Renee*

PERSONS OF THE DRAMA

Issy Holt: Playboy heir to the Holt family fortune

Trista Rivalen: Business advisor, friend & heir to Marcella Cornwall

Isidor 'Anguish' Holt: Patriarch of the Holt criminal empire

Alaina Holt: Issy's mother, wife to Isidor, respected surgeon

Marcella Cornwall: Grand dame of Cornwall crime family

Governal: Trista Rivalen's mentor and loyal lieutenant

Brangien: Issy's best friend and confidante

Geoffrey: Marcella Cornwall's secretary & servant

Al Rivalen: Marcella's brother-in-law, Trista's father

Blanche Rohault: Trista's mother and Marcella's sister

Moore Holt: Brother-in-law to 'Anguish' Holt

Marshal 'DuBois' Rohault: Adoptive father to Trista

Ronnie & Reggie Mudbug: Lower-echelon gunsels

Captain O'Dar: Corrupt city cop in thrall to the Cornwalls

'Duke' Morgan: A rising gangland rival

The Norwegian: The Holt family's notorious hatchet man

Daniels, Thomas & Béroul: Minor racketeers with the Cornwalls

Lou Holden: Driver and minder for the Holt family

Alex Shulgin: Hospital chemist with a bent for MDMA

Sergeant Tusk: A police officer with unknown loyalties

Elton McMurphy: Heads Catholic charity & volunteer workforce

Chris Destroys: Punk and amphetamine drug distributor

Mary: The Holts' talkative replacement driver

Andred: Issy's cat

1

TRISTA

[KAREOL HEIGHTS, ROOM 503—EARLY THIS MORNING]

*T*he sweat caught in Trista's eye.

She'd been listening to the fire brigade sirens across town for something like three hours. They bothered her. Made the woman sense something had changed, and she didn't mean just the architectural landscape surrounding a building aflame.

Hence an inability to sleep.

Even the abrasive sounds of Miles Davis's *Agharta* over on the hi-fi had no chance in Hades of drowning out the ruckus, let alone edging her in the direction of La La Land.

Had been partially aflame herself, lying on the single bed in nothing aside from a brassiere, underpants, a necklace, and a film of perspiration.

Heat was killing her, like always in this city every summer.

So, when the phone rang at two a.m., Trista lunged across the room to scoop up the thing.

Person on the other end?

Panicked.

Though failing basic manners—no self-introduction—after a few seconds' histrionics she was able to recognize the caller as Siggie Eisner. Persona non grata in Marcella's inner circle ever since she could recall, stationed at one of their subsidiary holdings.

"Mm-hmm," Trista squeezed in between flighty sentences. "Yeah. Mm." She waited for another gap. "So—getting back to the point. Who was killed?"

"Thomas and Béroul! I already told you already."

"Huh." Phone receiver held under her ear by the right shoulder, the woman adjusted her left bra-strap in a nearby mirror. "Did you? *Already?* Sorry. Zoning out."

This was the moment the speaker on the receiver seriously impaired her hearing: "How can someone zone out when two of our people've been murdered!"

Très ouch, she thought, flinching.

Eisner was being out-of-line. Trista remained nonplussed, however, skirting flexible. She'd already sussed that this man was under rat-bag emotional duress.

"Be serious," her voice crooned, even while distracted and racing on with notions inside the old head. "Tommy and Berry aren't a priority." Like Eisner's own fine self—something better not mentioned. "I mean Béroul could scarcely say boo-hoo."

More pointless gushing choked up the telephone line.

Time to wrap.

"Anyway. Shhh, listen, I've got to go. Call me when you have more."

Waiting for a response in that kind of moment is for chumps. Straight after 'more' kicked out through the woman's lips, she tucked the receiver back into its cradle.

"Bugger," she muttered, understanding what was now required, regardless of the ungodly hour.

Trista crossed carpet to the dresser, rifled through unkempt drawers for a fresh pair of undies; the Cross Your Heart bra she already had on would do.

Dress-wise, knew she had a clean BH Wragge in the closet. While functional and neat, it was hardly the kind of haute couture expected where she was off to. Not that Trista gave much of a damn. She threw the thing on and zipped it, chucked on some tights and pumps that thankfully matched one another, reapplied a bit of pearl-pink lippy, and stared at the face looking back in the mirror.

Noted a guarded expression behind the damp, flushed face, glanced down at the annoying duck's bill mouth, back up to those hazel eyes—the redeeming feature, since they belonged to her papa.

"Bugger," she said again.

They'd found Tommy's ancient fedora. The only recognizable thing discovered in the wreckage of a ten-story operation that'd had the bejesus blown out of it. A single hat with a hole seared through.

Some kind of lucky souvenir for the clean-up crew.

And while Malory Thomas was more nobody than Eisner in the el grando Cornwall scheme of earthly things, he and Trista shared something in common: their fathers had both been murdered in the same ambush fourteen years before.

Leveraging a cigarette from a bent pack, she lit up, at the same time pouring a healthy-sized tumbler of bourbon.

What this boiled down to was dealing with Marcey—a potentially bigger explosion, since it was pretty obvious someone had lit the fuse.

Trista finished her glass in seconds, butting out the ciggie straight after.

No way to be passed off as an accident when the entire city block was rubble, though she'd require a reliable person to corroborate Eisner's version.

No one better than Governal, who anyway occupied

rooms on the same floor of this building.

The woman neatened hair, squirted Mystère on her left wrist, rubbed both wrists together, popped a couple of mints—no need to come off either as an ad hoc ashtray or ring-in brewery—and ventured next door.

***

Governal had been awake.

Sometimes Trista doubted the man truly slept, though the notion piped through less often now than during her childhood—since once or twice she'd caught him napping.

"I think better with my eyes closed, you know that," he'd protested.

When he answered the door, Governal was immaculately dressed in a steel-grey suit matching his hair, aside from lighter silver patches that had lately sprouted around the temples. He did not look uncomfortable in this heat, so she figured he'd surreptitiously invested in an air conditioner after they shifted to these premises.

The two shared a quick illycaffè espresso he brewed (to perfection), half-listening to the Cat Stevens LP *Mona Bone Jakon* that she'd gifted him the previous Christmas, before returning to Trista's apartment.

While Governal then used the phone, she took opportunity to brush teeth, wash up, reapply make-up (twice; the first time was a disaster), comb, curl, and hold everything back from her face with faux tortoiseshell, barrette-style hair clips. She kind of hoped these'd offset the ho-hum dress.

Also stole an occasional glance through the gap between door and wall to watch Governal pace the living room, telephone in hand, talking quietly. In the soft lighting he reminded her of an oddball fusion of Patrick McGoohan's character Number 6—from British series *The Prisoner* (he used to religiously watch this)—and sexy French actor Jean-Paul Belmondo.

Well, Trista found Belmondo sexy. She wasn't sure Governal knew he existed.

The man dressed shades of more obvious idol McGoohan too, like he'd lifted his wardrobe from the '60s TV show. Most of these clothes had a label reading 'Portmeirion' on them (she'd checked, though had yet to pinpoint where exactly this manufacturer or tailor might be).

With some pomade and spray, Trista fixed the last remaining unruly hair.

Hurrah.

That was when Governal chose to knock at the bedroom door. "Car's downstairs, waiting. You all ready?"

Having checked the looking glass one last time, Trista screwed up her face out of sight of her handsome, middle-aged guest. "Sure," she fibbed.

***

It was dark and warm outside when Trista stepped into the Cadillac de Ville, deathly quiet aside from those sirens off in the distance. There was a vague orange glow over the buildings to the north as the car eased onto an empty street.

"Straight to the boss's place, ma'am?" asked the driver, a young man whose name Trista couldn't place. Too tired and too stressed.

"Yeah, Tintagel it is." She flopped back, partially pressed against a door, put up feet on the adjoining passenger seat, and then exhaled long and slowly. Breathed again. Did the same.

Something Governal had taught her to relax.

As they passed through a green light and still met no other vehicle on the roads, Trista noted that their car had picked up pace.

"Mind the speed, love."

MALORY
[THE CAXTON BUILDING—LAST NIGHT]

*W*eren't Friday nights rumoured to be the bomb?

That's what stupid kids on the street were saying these days.

While an older dickwad'd likely recite that nugget, "Thank God it's (Friday)", for our whiner Thomas there existed zero cool about Fridays, nothing in the vicinity of relief. The day meant f-all in his line of work.

Instead, this man feels bile steep in the gut alongside some mismanaged, half-digested potato salad—the goddamned wife's idea of a healthy dinner.

A nearby clock says, 'TICK, TOCK'.

This here was one of Queenie's places, a miniature boardroom shoo-in stuck on the ninth floor of a 1940s office building. Hot and sticky, it was a rank-smelling joint, mostly sweat and cheap cologne beyond a stale, second-hand incense from fags and cigar smoke.

Evening might've held sway without, yet in that space, day or night, there was a pale lamp in one corner, with its material shade—likely white in origin—turned its own shade of emphysematous-brown. Go thank years of proximity to tobacco-chuffers for a decorative miracle.

The overhead light fixture lacked an active globe for years, and all four walls were laced with a spider web of cracks where mildew sprouted. The solitary window? Dressed in a tightly closed tobacco-stained blind he'd never once seen open. It looked the same here either side of a 24-hour cycle.

A shit-hole, in other words.

TOCK, TICK.

Malory Thomas, marginally better known to the rank-and-file as just plain Tommy, wipes his brow with a shirtsleeve.

He then adds fresh aroma to the room by lighting up a

Salem the opposite side of a green formica-and-chrome table from Norman 'Berry' Béroul.

Before doing so, he'd stuck his threadbare grey fedora (carelessly) on an empty shelf next to that loud timepiece.

TICK, TOCK.

To be honest, Tommy was careless because he didn't give a rat's arse about the hat.

Thing belonged to his dad—the respected, if very dead, former Cornwall family enforcer Johnny 'Justice of the Peace' Thomas. Tommy adopted the faded thing at age seventeen after the old man was killed, not so much as a sign of respect but in an attempt to clutch onto the J.P.'s coattails of success. Before he carked it, anyway.

TOCK, TICK.

Clearly this old-fashioned bonnet possessed none of that paternal fortune.

Tommy remained slap-bang on the bottom rung at thirty-one, an errand boy forced to kiss the rear-end of those with less brains than brawn. Now, however, things were set to change—for the first time, at least so far as he could recall, in his favour.

Berry had a notion.

One that'd win them both a higher standing, so long as neither screwed up—or so Berry implied, in less vocabulary, over the phone.

TICK, TOCK.

Yet still Tommy has his doubts.

Niggling ones that cloud the edge of vision, as he pokes a glance at the twin-bell clock beside his hat.

An archaic, wind-up appliance with a greasy glass face that lacked the finesse of its modern brethren—those brightly lit, Jap-made, flip-digit doohickeys currently on the market. Sure, they made a racket too, but nary second-by-second clatter. Instead, the blighters emitted a whirring sound once a minute when the numbers clicked over.

TOCK, TICK.

Tommy has begun to air out one of his doubts, "Well,

you know what, Bez?" and then pauses to fan the ciggie in his gob, enticing the cherry to flourish. Breathes in a little, clears his throat, exhales a plume in the direction of a pitch-black ceiling. Could kill for a drink, but knew from experience that the single faucet here gave out only water rusty and foul.

Fanning himself a little, he decides to continue:

"Honest-like, I dunno if Marcey will be in on this."

TICK, TOCK.

Norm Béroul, eldest and largest of these two occupants, says nothing.

Embalmed in a cheap black suit and ill-fitting woollen coat—in this heat?—the other man is marinated in gloom and Old Spice his side of the rickety diner. Béroul additionally fiddles with a matchstick like it might in fact be a cigarette.

Often, the other boys, Tommy recalls, they joked that Berry resembled one of those bloated mob extras in a film three or four years back, *The Godfather*. You know, the ones that had no line in the script and didn't fit on the end credits.

Resting on the table proper between them is a large, earthenware pot of sand turned grey by vast quantities of discarded ash. Across this apocalyptic setting in miniature, brown butts litter the diorama like fallen trees.

Shrugging to himself almost as much as to his dead old man, Tommy leans back, more certain now. "Dead-set. She ain't gonna dig it."

Still no verbal response emerged from his erstwhile partner, the man that suggested this meeting out of earshot of their bosses. Didn't a parley require at least two persons' confab?

TOCK, TICK.

Says Tommy, "I mean it," eyes half-closed to ward off smoke and a feeling of frustrated claustrophobia. *Talk, damn you.*

Berry then grunts.

At least, Tommy thinks the man grunted. Béroul didn't have a fine way with words on the best of occasions, and with nighttime traffic outside in the city running interference, Tommy hasn't a clue.

"Still," he adds, bedazzled, "be blown if we don't give it a shot. Right?"

TICK, TOCK.

A continued lack of aural response, aside from the timepiece, is plain aggravating. "Well, don't get all excited or nothin', you git," Tommy rattles on, wiping moist palms on his pants.

CLICK.

He doesn't have opportunity to glance at the clock, but enough of it to squeeze out something short—"Eh?"—when a timer goes off and the entire ninth floor explodes to the tune of four-and-twenty sticks of dynamite.

The hat that belonged to Tommy's father survives the experience—unlike its second owner. A little frayed and scorched, it sails three hundred feet into the sky after passing through a ceiling conveniently rendered Swiss cheese.

Not that gentle descent to terra firma marks a switch from careless hoodlum to a more deserving man's crown. No, this particular headwear is destined to collect mites in a police evidence room locker, and later still to be incinerated with the other unloved trash.

TRISTA
[TINTAGEL—AROUND DAWN]

As the sun fought a shimmering haze on the horizon, the de Ville idled by a kerb in a plush area of town.

Having hopped out before the driver could attempt a shot at chivalry—all that opening of doors, kowtowing, and other nonsense—Trista leaned through his window to place a five-dollar bill on the dash.

"Go get yourself some brekky," she said. "Should be done by eight."

The man's eyes bulged. Probably couldn't believe he'd be eating like a king this time of morning.

Trista checked her watch as the car drifted away. Almost five in the a.m.

So. Heigh-ho.

Checking for still non-existent traffic, the woman walked up a slope toward an elaborate ironwork gate wrapped in bright pink, organized and cared-for climbing roses.

Marcella Cornwall, better known as 'Queenie' outside the family's upper ranks—a coinage she resented—lived atop Church Hill in this better part of the city, close to its eastern heart.

The matriarch and her entourage took up all three floors of Tintagel Apartments, which had therefore become an apartment singular. Making the building, a huge Gothic Revival place, again the mansion it was intended to be when built by extravagant, English-born confectioner Conan Merry.

This was back in the late nineteenth century, prior to Merry finances going belly-up once his hapless grandson took on the show.

The place was abandoned, their family relegated to a rumpled page of local history.

In 1928, after a dozen years of unoccupancy, Tintagel got purchased by a group of Czarist Russians.

They resurrected some of the former glory: turned the ground-floor ballroom into a nightclub called Dark Age, and used the upper floors for meeting rooms. The house became known informally as the 'Russian Embassy', up until a number of its residents were deported in 1948—some kind of communist conspiracy charge—and the state requisitioned their property.

To be sold at auction in 1949, and straight after? Subdivided for more profit, as well as to satisfy an uppity middle class longing for life in a fraction of a manor.

Trista knew these details because Governal had once handed her the background paper trail as homework.

He had his reasons for same, and as usual failed to share them.

According to those books, in the mid '50s Tintagel was then leveraged from all separate title holders—some (there had been eleven people) vanishing completely—and the new owners added the house and adjoining ten acres of land to a ballooning Cornwall Trust of real estate holdings.

Marcella'd been holding court here since.

All that was missing was a qualified jester. Trista felt if she'd been blessed with better punch lines, and was available, this would be a serious job opportunity.

Before reaching the front entrance to Tintagel—a pillared portico with stained glass windows set in leadlight behind the porch—she noticed an elderly man in the elegant ensemble of tuxedo, bowtie and polished dress-shoes coming out to stand to one side.

He mimicked deferential.

While uniform, footwear and posture were immaculate, this smooth-faced individual, sixty-odd, boasted rowdy, snow-white hair that circumnavigated his scalp, yet made no impression up top.

"Miss Rivalen," he purred, hands clasped behind the back, and gave a slight nod.

"Geoffrey." Trista smiled in reply.

"You're expected."

"Thought so."

"As I suspected you would. Upstairs, in the library. Marcella will be along shortly."

This 'library', situated on the third floor, called for a route following Geoffrey via a ballroom.

No longer the White Russian club, it'd become glitzy circus instead.

Trista had dug three rings when she was a toddler, but at her ripe age (nineteen), and in this place, the concept grated. Chiefly, its performers were the usual suspects—hangers-on, sponges, leaches—clutching to Marcey in gaudy get-ups.

These people called it high fashion: threads conjured up by designers with names like Kenzo Takada and Sonia Rykiel, bearing price tags that pushed into the thousands of dollars for a single gold-lamé necktie. Flared, check-pattern suits with over-large lapels, belted double-knit sweaters (even in summer), the odd denim leisure suit, and male ponchos were de rigueur.

Highlighting all was an over-abundance of necklaces, long hair, chest curls, fat ties, and other hideous things aplenty—though there was the odd exception.

The ever-sceptical Eddie Leighton had bucked current fashion-trends to dress like a Pre-Raphaelite dandy, strapping a corset beneath his frock coat, with lace-cuffed, starched linen shirts highlighted by an elaborately knotted cravat.

Herb Draper, forever decked out in sparkling gems on all nine fingers (one pinkie was missing, taken as recompense in a gambling con), laboured under the weight of a diamond-encrusted medallion he wore outside his high-buttoned velvet jackets.

If strolling beside her, which he wasn't, Governal would've tut-tutted.

"Don't be so judgmental," he'd intone. "Watch. Listen. Learn."

The expression had become a silly mantra over the years. Trista considered making armbands, proudly emblazoned with the initials 'W.L.L.', that they could wear while wearing down the competition. Made her laugh inside. One day, she'd be proved right. On that day, people would mock this decade's dress code.

Trista smiled demurely to each clotheshorse. All coy-like. Couldn't trust a single one.

They performed the merry meet-and-greet routine beneath a high, gabled ceiling with an enormous chandelier that lit the space in a yellow hue. While no trapezes could be spied, there were couches and armchairs scattered around—patched-up, leather-bound relics of the building's inglorious past—and about thirty people milling about them, men who acted like boys.

On a colour television in one corner a football game was in progress, volume too loud, that grabbed their attention. Wads of cash changed hands each time a goal was scored.

Oh, the pleasantries did apply, and everyone was charming to one another. Their acting skills pushed superlative.

And at least this house offered refrigerated bliss at the height of summer—which could partially account for why Trista felt a baker's dozen ice picks in the upper back.

She knew these people hated her: Marcella's clown-prince lieutenants, most part of the peeling paintwork before Trista signed on. Jilted and aggrieved that she, a girl, so quickly pushed in.

Between waves, handshakes and fist-bumps, while aping jolly, Trista could sense what they really thought. Understood that the commentary, once she headed upstairs, would revolve around an eyelash out of place, or her cheap, frumpy choice of wardrobe.

And to hell with them.

Not her fault she'd done a better job over the past few months, or that Marcella thereby trusted her more.

These idiots decided it was an unfair blood advantage, Trista being the Queenie's niece. Ended up crying into their boutique beers.

Still, whatever made them pliable.

This time round performances were thankfully abridged, since Geoffrey whisked Trista through their ranks, thence upstairs to Marcella's den—a room that smelled like old socks and doubled as a study.

"You'll need to wait here," the man said, prior to scuttling off someplace else in this ridiculously large fortress.

At least she liked and trusted Geoffrey, to a degree. He might've been an international creature of (some) mystery, but it was clear the man felt equally obliged in looking out for Marcey's best interests—and he didn't dress quite so much like a damned spectacle.

Trista turned one circle in the large, musty space. Was feeling tired—the strong coffee had worn off ages ago—and considered chewing on a nail. Thought better, and focused on deportment.

Finally, there came the sound of footfall in the corridor outside the door.

These footsteps could be heard fifty yards away, thanks to slate flooring with hollow pockets beneath, something Trista assumed intentional so no one could hope to sneak up on anybody else.

In this case, the woman felt little need to fret—she recognized the particular walking style that approached.

Time to sham preoccupied and a fraction blasé.

She turned to face one wall stacked with books and the occasional misplaced bric-à-brac or stray toiletry, like a half-empty bottle of Anaïs Anaïs that Trista knew was her aunt's favourite fragrance.

Otherwise, dusty hardbacks crammed the shelves. Their spines showcased faded gold lettering that read *Mabinogion*, *Fidelitas usque ad mortem*, *Marie de France*. Trista wasn't certain at first glance whether these were names or titles.

Having placed a finger atop one book, it came away speckled with lint and something that looked like a stray pubic hair.

She quickly wiped the hand on her dress.

Did Marcella read any of these tomes, were they there for show, or would the books be empty, their purpose to house secret documents—dirty little truths about politicos, union bigwigs, cops, city officials, media and judiciary types currently in this woman's sizeable pocket?

The footsteps now ceased.

The door handle rattled, and turned.

And then *she* entered: Trista's mother's sister, her boss, her life. Any semblance of tranquillity always fated to suffer.

"What the fuck is going on out there, Trista?!"

Marcella's riff filled the room before she'd crossed the threshold. It was so loud and so thoroughly incensed that Trista was certain there remained a trace echo of animosity.

Signalling the start of a classic Marcella rant.

This fifty-nine-year-old dowager with faded blue eyes kept her greying hair (once honey-blonde) reasonably short on the back and sides, but longer and wavy on top. An overall look that lately never failed to remind her niece of actress Angela Lansbury in the film *Death on the Nile*.

She had on an ostrich-feather blouse with navy slacks, and fluffy room slippers made from something like mink.

The woman stood shorter than Trista and looked fragile—one way in which Marcella deceived enemies and intimidated friends.

The wrath of this grande dame, with a miraculously conjured imposing presence, was the stuff of legend, yet the minor details could lead you astray.

Such as three of the fingers on her left hand being crooked, thanks to an automobile accident she had while car racing when young.

Above a jutting jaw line, her face bordered timeworn, weathered, wrinkled—and handsome all the same. Most of the lines there added colour to moods, joy through to fury. Trista had witnessed both within a five-minute time bracket.

Marcella paced the study, tossing her head about in one of those rages.

Hardly seeing the younger woman or the rows of suspect books, she spat out complaints with components like "Goddamn, it's all wrong—", "For flying fuck's sake—", "—but, seriously, can we *take* this kind of shitty hit?", "*Whoever* did this is going to pay big time!", and a surprisingly thoughtful "Thank God you're safe."

Trista let the woman waffle on, offering time to get it out of the system as much as a demonstration of respect. In biding that time, she allowed eyes to wander paintings in the room: reproductions of medieval courtly lovers, and people playing harps in armour. For just one moment, she wondered if her aunt had had Moses in to do the home furnishings.

When Marcella hammered down on the writing desk in a corner of the room, creating a little cloud of dust particles just as she announced that, "This ends now!", the other woman believed things were about to wrap.

"You hear me, Trista?"

"Sure, boss."

"Don't call me that. You know I don't like it."

Trista inclined her head.

Marcella's response was to wash steely eyes over her visitor. "And what on earth are you wearing?"

"Didn't think anyone would notice this time of morning."

"Well, I did. Wear something classier next time I see you."

"Yes, ma'am."

"Anyway—this is *not* going to stand."

Marcella now bore a snarl, wardrobe faux pas a subject of the distant past. In a fit of this kind, all comparisons with Angela Lansbury vanished.

"I tell you, I'm going to rip out someone's vital organs. I ought to piss on the shit-for-brains responsible. I'm thinking—"

So, while Trista partially listened to an encore one-way oratory of extraordinary projected violence, she began compiling mental lists of anyone and everybody that could've organized the bombing. The crims, low-lives, gunsels and/or disgruntled police officers who hated their

Queenie enough to kill two men and take on the undisputed ruler of the south west.

Then she switched attention on one very oily dime to another thought: what if this wasn't an act of revenge, but of attrition?

Who would benefit most from attacking Marcella Cornwall right where it hurt most? To kick her in the balls, embarrass the woman, pinch her falsies, show a weak-spot—and thereby undermine the Queenie's control of these parts?

Someone wanting to wrest mojo from the family, like those peacocks in the ballroom? Yet in degrading Marcella's powerbase and authority, they'd have to know this would impact on any future coup—leaving them equally disabled.

The throne'd be weaker.

The more she thought, the deeper the frown. Trista glanced at her aunt to let the woman know she was, indeed, paying attention to the tirade, even if not.

Getting back to the crew downstairs, she couldn't see a single bastard having the gumption to challenge Marcella. As individuals they were wallflowers, hardly made of the right stuff to go toppling tyrannical leaders.

Which left another option: somebody from outside the clan, making a play. A person or group seeking to expand and create a kingdom by knocking over theirs.

One name stood out in that field. A moniker Trista had no love for in the first place.

Meanwhile, Marcella's sizzling passion began to burn out.

"I demand answers!" she shouted to no one in particular, waffled on a tad more, drifted into self-pitying remarks, swung back into anger. Threw something into the mix in Italian, and then tacked-on what could've been Russian; Trista wasn't sure. Didn't 'moodak' mean arsehole in Russian?

More yelling ensued, followed by a tear, or a bead of

sweat. Hard to tell.

Finally? Resolve—the Marcella that Trista admired most. Orders, demands for appropriate action, a clearing of the throat.

This meant Trista's turn to speak. She wondered if Governal would be happy with what was going to be suggested.

"I think we seriously," she said slowly, clearly, gazing into her aunt's eyes, "seriously need to look closer at Isidor 'Anguish' Holt."

ISSY
[DISCO INFERNO—TO THE WEST, ACROSS THE MUIR ÈIREANN RIVER]

No need to strain his brain appreciating this—Isidor Holt, Jr., had more of a blast at Disco Inferno than any other nightclub in the world.

Most evenings lately, for the Holt family heir, started the same.

He'd have a quarrelsome, frosty dinner with the folks, thereafter throwing care to the wind via a series of rapidly mixed drinks, tuning in to Gloria Gaynor.

Put on a suit and kipper tie, make a request for the Mercedes limo, and lastly get Lou to drive downtown and deposit him up front.

Issy dug hopping out of the car to ogle a ridiculously long line, four people abreast, of dripping hopefuls who braved the summer nights but would never get in. There were usually ambulance staff nearby to treat people suffering heat exhaustion almost as much as alcohol poisoning.

And the man would waltz by them all, to be ushered through a briefly opened velvet rope by Steve and Ian. It felt good—people staring, waving and taking pictures of those who were admitted, thinking if you got in you must be somebody.

And Issy supposed he *was* a somebody. He happened to be the son of the owner of the fucking club.

That 'fucking club' had a Laurence O'Toole-designed interior that boasted 10,000-square-feet of dance floor and, above, an eighty-two-feet high ceiling with three massive mirror balls. Capacity was two thousand people, yet often they shoehorned in two-and-a-half.

A marble staircase off the entrance hall led to the plush mezzanine lounge, followed by a second bar blessed with its own private mirror ball, and thence to a broad, curving balcony with rising rows of velvet theatre chairs—from which you could perv on the dancers crammed below.

Any given night of the week was an opportunity to schmooze with, or share lines alongside, visiting celebrities like Gina Lollabrigida, James Caan, Bianca Jagger, Truman Capote and Cher. Then there were regular Transatlantic visits from Valentino or Karl Lagerfeld, bringing huge entourages.

Surprisingly, Issy's dad—Isidor 'Anguish' Holt, who had christened Disco Inferno himself—said the name didn't come from The Trammps song. He claimed it was a joint reference to Dante's poem the *Divine Comedy*, and someone named Joe Mengele.

Issy didn't know Mengele, guessed him to be one of his father's many silent business partners.

Anyway, the old man had an artisan put Dante's famous spiel above the entrance foyer, carved into the granite with a mother-of-pearl inlay: *Abandon all hope, ye who enter here.* Beneath that, in finer print, was another line in a lingo Issy couldn't get his head around: *Abandon orice speranţă, voi care intra aici.*

Being the owner's kid, and having finally hurdled the legal drinking age in this puritanical state (twenty-one), meant that Issy had free range of the club. He often spent daylight hours there too, after partying all-night and sleeping in till midday(ish). He did so-called office chores.

Made some of his better pocket money absconding with stuff that addled clientele left behind: jewels, pills, cash, cashmere scarves, watches, gold chains, a camera or two, the odd hair dryer.

Hocked the goods, and carefully set aside thirty-three percent.

He'd then repeat the cycle: head into the club for several hours after opening time to find someone called Diane or Brigid, Tina or Jamie, and leave, since it doubled as a pickup joint.

More often than not you'd exit Disco Inferno accompanied.

Still, sometimes the thing hanging onto your elbow wasn't a member of the opposite sex, nor your own kind, but one of those bushwhackers Demon Drink or Malignant Spirits.

Hence, you'd get hammered, go a wee bit too far, and wind up in the dunnies—like Issy was right now, throwing up in a grotesque, supposedly stainless-steel cistern to the sounds of 'I Feel Love'.

He felt less love than that he was going to die. Pulled disparate parts of nausea together, tried to ignore the smell of piss and shit and spew, and flushed his head in one of the sinks.

That was when Lou Holden, the family driver, poked his head through the door, causing the musical swagger of Donna Summer and Giorgio Moroder—colluding in a second disco showstopper—to come through louder.

"Mr. Holt, you in here?" asked Lou, though he was staring straight at his charge. "You okey?"

Taking time, having splashed more cold water across his face, and then slapping cheeks and forehead to remove some of the moisture and get the blood flowing, Issy eyed himself off in a filthy mirror.

"Sure, Lou," he finally said, disappointed.

In the reflection, Issy could've sworn something similar coloured the chauffeur's demeanour. "You look terrible, so you do," the man remarked, with trademark Irishness, a deeper flavour still than Isidor Senior's.

Issy managed a smile. "Yeah, I have been better."

"I bet. So. Your father's expecting me in at the office—an', therefore, you'll have to make your own way home. Sorry, mate."

"Shit."

Holden softened his expression. "C'mon, boyo. Get the crap outta here."

After patting his boss's son's shoulder, Holden peeled away in a crowded corridor, pushing in the direction of the rear entrance. Isidor Junior headed for the front door—through fragmented lights, strobe effects, an overactive smoke-machine, and people still more inebriated. Eased through sweaty office workers, sidestepped a tall black male model dancing away in a beautiful Giorgio di Sant' Angelo white dress, and brushed by a Grace Jones wannabe wearing a T-shirt with suspender-braces, jeans, and a straw hat.

Or maybe that *was* Grace?

Near the exit, Issy passed a group of bored-looking Holt family thugs. These men were collectively dressed in black, off-the-rack suits that fitted poorly—though one had panache enough to wear a trilby, adding Sinatra-style class.

He nodded. "Boys."

"Junior." They collectively smirked.

Thank God, pre-dawn ruled outside the club.

In the distance, over dark rooftops and flashing neon billboards, was a vaguely orange glow. Issy blinked, wiping his chin with a handkerchief. That couldn't be right. Despite his state, he knew this site and time well. The glow came from the wrong direction.

And then he remembered the dare made with his best friend to wear a pair of currently fashionable boys' school shoes—Bata Scouts; he'd had to pay extra getting them made up in his size—onto the dance floor of Disco

Inferno, to see if anyone in the club noticed.

They didn't.

Issy crouched down on the cement, carefully removed a right shoe caked in specks of vomit, and checked the toy compass built into the sole. According to that, the glow came from slightly east of the north.

He sighed, placing the shoe on the ground. Didn't the sun rise directly east?

"Hey, you."

Leaning over the roof of her ancient purple VW Beetle appeared Brangien.

A nursing cap sat jauntily atop her head of bouncy, coppery-blonde curls—ones that mimicked, in their way, puffs of cotton candy.

She also wore a set of false lashes hanging in precarious fashion, and above these had shaved the eyebrows, to draw on a pair. They made the pretty woman resemble Joan Crawford—if she'd been a bottle-blonde with a perm, at any rate.

Over her shoulders was wrapped a hot-pink feather boa which hurt Issy's already suffering vision.

"Can you take that off?" he whined.

Brangien mugged his way. "What part?"

She skipped round the vehicle to graciously open the passenger door. It groaned loudly, causing Issy more trauma.

"Come on then, darlin'," she laughed. "I'll give you a lift."

Now he could see what else the woman had on, which didn't amount to much.

She was clad in a tight, mini-skirted nurse's uniform (courtesy of the job at St. Maignenn's) and a pair of black stockings. Setting these off were glossy white, knee-high vinyl granny boots.

No doubt about it, she looked sexy—Brangien always did. And without someone hanging off his arm, Issy found himself switch to a smile.

"Brangien, did I ever tell you I love you?"
"All the time. Don't forget your shoe."

2

ISSY

[CHAPELIZOD HOUSE—THE HOLT FAMILY MANSION]

*I*ssy had this recurrent dream.

In it, there existed a gleaming harp up on a mountain outcrop. The thing came across desperately symbolic, like it was trying to fill in for the Holy Grail, or the Ark of the Covenant.

Twisted and distorted words that made no sense—should've lived instead on blackboards—surfed the edges. Chitchat like 'mabinogion', 'chevrefoil', 'baucis', and 'rāmin'—whatever that was. A noodle soup?

Sometimes he wondered if his mother'd force-fed him too many picture books illustrated by Beardsley when he was a child. That, or his choice of college curriculum ought to be held responsible.

While not owning a religious bone in his body, Issy was majoring in the Christianization of Europe and had, over the past few months, boned up on the First Crusade from 1096—a major assignment that'd snatched years off his life.

His da did not approve.

"Why're you wasting time on the Old World?" was a regular complaint, usually uttered at the dinner table when the family found nothing else to talk about.

Meaning a nightly discussion, since Issy was on summer vacation.

"This country is the here and now," the old man'd slug on, raising the ceiling, "a right land of opportunity and adventure. Bad enough that they transplanted European place-names. The real Muir Èireann is a vast sea between Ireland and Britain, one hundred and fifty miles wide, not some pissy f'n urban stream."

Issy one time decided to push the envelope.

Putting down the *Anna Karenina* in his hands, he said, "You know, Dad, I have a feeling you would've shared a lot in common with Peter the Hermit."

Anguish's response had been to glare, like he felt slapped by his son. "The *craic* is that?" he'd demanded.

It seemed odd, Issy reflected later, the way in which his father deployed the word 'craic'. Lou and the other Irish émigrés he knew used it with a positive, at times mischievous spin. Isidor Senior spat the thing out in menacing, threatening fashion.

"Nobody," was all he muttered in reply.

"What? Are you saying *I'm* nobody?"

Issy tried hard not to roll eyes, shook his head instead. "That wasn't my intention."

"I thought not. Pfft. You wouldn't have the balls to imply such a thing."

Opting for silence also hardly pacified the old man.

"How can you be my son?" he muttered. The way in

which his da pronounced 'how' made it sound more like another *who* question.

Anyway, better to ignore his family and get back to the dream.

In it, there were ring-in medieval knights, along with a riotous pack of playing cards better left to Alice—a comingling of pointless junk that absconded with the hung-over sleep he would've preferred.

And, typically, an ill-timed VW Beetle burst through it all to demoralize him with a loud 'beep-beep'.

Usually the point he woke up, hopefully on his own king-size waterbed.

If so, there to be first greeted by an overhead original poster of *M*A*S*H* that his mam got personally signed by actors Donald Sutherland and Elliott Gould. On the shelf directly next to the bed were copies of *Wuthering Heights*, *Nineteen Eighty-Four*, *Madame Bovary*, and Peter Abelard's *Historia Calamitatum*.

Once in a sitting position he could see, on the distant other side of this very large room, a flashing a neon advertising sign that read 'Merry and Bright' (his dad's first company), and the formidable Komet TV-and-stereo ensemble.

Between these two large things fretted a small Theremin on a pedestal—gifted to Isidor Senior by an appreciative Lev Sergeyevich Termen.

Issy's crimson velvet drapes were usually sensibly closed, and to top the lot off—on this particular occasion—there was one rather sinister glowing lava lamp next to the door.

Where'd that come from?

So entranced by said orange lamp, he didn't straight away cotton on to the fact he had company.

"Omigod... it lives!" reaches out and smacks Issy's ears from behind. He fathoms the source despite post-kip bleariness: best friend Brangien, enthroned upon the nearby cane peacock chair. She has a treacherous tabby feline purring atop her knee—Andred, who belonged to him.

Thankfully the girl had scrubbed her face, losing the false lashes and excessive make-up, and was wearing one of Issy's t-shirts—too large for her—along with a pair of someone else's tracksuit pants.

It's the trackies that make him frown. "Crap. You."

"Well, try not to get too excited," she says.

"Try isn't the word I'd use." Issy wipes sleep from his eyes, annoyed.

"You have a better one, then?"

"Honestly? I'm not in the mood for hijinx."

"Since when?"

"Since now."

The woman blows out her cheeks. "Well, that's inconvenient."

"Bee—please."

"Okay, lemme guess. *That* dream."

"Obvious?" he asks.

"Relatively."

"You kidding?"

"Never."

"Yeah, okay."

"Spooky reruns?" suggests she.

"Mm. It really psyches me out." That, and the fact the slumber obviously wasn't sufficient. He finds himself shoving the balls of his hands against his eye-sockets. "Man, I need quality sleep."

"Hah!" Brangien chortles, not the more melodic of sounds. "Thought you would've forgotten all about that by now." A blessed moment's silence prevails, before the harpy goes on: "You are Issy, right? Not some evil doppelganger?"

Having climbed out of bed, the man stands before her in white singlet and white boxer shorts—his port-of-call pyjamas—and Issy feels somehow proud. "Gee. I hope so," he's saying before he knows it.

"Debatable." Brangien started toying with her lower lip, tugging at the thing, and after a few seconds allows it to snap back into her teeth. She did this a lot.

Issy ceased to find it endearing in second grade.

"So, what've we got planned for today? Another fine jaunt of adventure and derring-do? ...Actually, I don't even know what time it is, and my watch's stopped."

Shaking the stupid timepiece doesn't get it working again. So much for the reliability of Patek Philippe. Tossing the thing aside, Issy pulls on a fresh shirt and suit, not worrying about undies, and rises triumphant.

"There. All dressed, and ready to rumble."

"You couldn't fight your way out of a wet paper bag."

"That's why we have henchmen."

Brangien, however, had remembered a more important detail, holding up shoes. "Don't forget your princely footwear."

He takes them with a grimace. "Enough with the Bata Scouts. Give me proper ones. And I still want to know what time it is."

"Yes, yes, all right. Hold your horses!" Having pulled up her sleeve, the girl nods. "There. It's just past four."

"In the p.m.?"

She holds aloft her wrist. "Read and weep. So what else is new?"

The metal hands there are definitely close to the four and the twelve. "I guess."

Reclining across Issy's bed, causing ripples, Brangien looks more cat than Andred—who'd scarpered at some point in the conversation. That was the moment that the woman chose to rifle through a stack of his 45s and 33s.

"Don't you have anything low-key to fit the mood?"

"What mood? The cranky one I'm in right now?"

Brangien stops flipping and produces apparent gold: the Brian Eno record *Another Green World*, a borrowing from Issy's friend Ollie O (a disc jockey at Disco Inferno) that he'd failed as yet to listen to.

"This is what I'm talking," the woman says, as she goes to the record player and places the stylus on a song called 'Sky Saw'—ambient music rather than pop, still melodic and rhythmic. "*And* you take more of that time to get ready than me," she decides above the music.

"Well, you're not ready."

"Soon will be." That's when she pulls Issy's spare t-shirt off herself, revealing absolutely nothing worn beneath— then starts yanking down the pants.

Yeah, like we mentioned, Brangien was Isidor Junior's best chum. Had been since they started primary school together, on the same day, in the same class.

She nursed him when he was ill and otherwise tended to be bossy, but this girl was his confidante—and he'd never lie to her. Lie *with* her, maybe. But not the other.

Naked now, aside from a skimpy piece of pink satin material between her legs that passed for underwear, Brangien places herself facedown and stretched out across Issy's bed quilt, her right hand supporting her face as she peers up at him.

There's an unexpected vulnerability to her eyes.

"Even enough time for a quickie before we go," she says—so of course Issy gives in.

***

He knew what Brangien was going to utter as soon as they climbed into the rear of the black Mercedes-Benz 600 limo: her favourite line from a dumb bath-soap commercial—for Imperial Leather—that was popular on the box.

"Simon—Tahiti!" she announces.

Thing being, the driver's name wasn't Simon (he went by Lou Holden) and their destination was the Disco Inferno. They couldn't find somewhere better to party hearty.

Certainly not Tahiti.

Issy had been there once for a Holt family getaway, and was bored stiff inside of twenty-four hours.

Issy spies Lou's eyes in the rear-vision mirror, and the way in which he lifts them Heavenward, without Word, while pulling out from the kerb.

A good-looking man despite his middling age—somewhere around the same as his dad, yet in better shape and less creases lined the face—Lou still worked-out, had a fine head of brown salt-and-pepper hair trimmed short.

The guy drove the family ever since Issy could remember, and though they shared few words, he implicitly had trust.

A bottle of Charbaut Certificate rested in a chrome bucket of ice on the bench seat opposite the two passengers, and within seconds Issy has popped the cork and poured a couple of flutes. He once tried offering a glass to their driver, but the man declined with a stern look. Straighter than an arrow, it appeared.

"Play this, will you, Simon?" Brangien requests, handing a cassette over the seat. Lou palms the tape and shoves it into the car hi-fi without a by your leave. Seconds later, they were blessed with 'S-S-S-Single Bed' by British band Fox.

The vehicular sound track had segued on into ABBA's 'Take a Chance on Me', which made Lou curse brutally, when they arrived at the club.

"Alright, kiddos," the driver growls, tossing the cassette into Brangien's lap, "get the hell out."

Seconds after they exit, the vehicle careers into heavy night time traffic, like Lou had somewhere he needed to be post haste.

Before them, swarming the sidewalk an entire block was more than the usual swell of hundreds of punters. Spotlights continuously sweep the crowd, and a party atmosphere prevails—streamers, balloons, and outrageous costumes.

Having stepped out before Issy, clad as she is

in chunky platform shoes and a Diane Von Fürstenberg polka dot wrap dress, Brangien confronts the multitude with mouth wide open.

"Oh. Okay," she mumbles. "It's chockers."

***

A full twenty-five minutes later, having passed through Customs (the door staff), checked coats, and obtained free sloe gin fizzes—followed by much pushing, shoving and cajoling—Issy and Brangien found a position on the mezzanine. They stood before a writhing dance floor, mirror balls spinning above, as the disc jockey mixed in a pounding rendition of 'C'est Chic' by Le Freak.

"Déjà vu," Issy puts out there.

"Ohhh, yeah," agrees his partner-in-crime.

Which is when some Joe sidles up to Issy, pressing close, to whisper in his ear, above loud music, that, "Junior, the Mudbug brothers are expecting you. Below."

Excusing himself several times (Brangien couldn't hear), the man detoured via a separate set of stairs that were quieter, past a sign reading *We've Got Crabs Downstairs*.

Entered a subterranean part of the club where the plebs were not allowed. This staircase descending before him was dark, menacing almost, and when the door closes, it's almost impossible to see. Yet he'd been up and down dozens of times, and intuitively knew most steps.

In the crypt—a dimly lit den decorated with framed stills from old mobster flicks, a large refrigerator, and bargain basement chipboard furnishings—the disco above is barely a muffle.

Seated at a small round table covered in encaustic tiles and several bottles are two identical men, ruggedly handsome, in carbon copy tan boiler suits.

Ronald and Reginald Mudbug, unofficial guardians of the Disco Inferno, are the guzzlers.

At least a dozen long-necked brown bottles of

imported British lager decorate the table, most empty, their red labels bearing a caricature of Bonnie Prince Charlie.

The age of the gentlemen drinkers? Late-twenties, perhaps, though hard living made then look more like forty. They were not twins. One was older than the other, though—to look at—people couldn't tell which.

Issy's da called them just in casers. Issy didn't.

The thing was, while Isidor Holt, Sr., refused to pay these brothers much heed, let alone respect, sometimes small fry knew more than supposed bigger fish. And Issy liked the boys. So once an evening, or every second one, he paid the two a visit.

"Well, well," declares Reggie, between swigs, "if it ain't our junior guv." He holds a current bottle higher, a kind of salute, and inclines his head. "Here's to your beneficent gent of a pop." And then he drains the flagon, at least half a litre in one shot.

"Yeah, cheers for the beers," chimes in Ronnie, before following suit.

Of the two, Reggie was the talker. Ronnie watched everything with ale-hungry eyes.

Isidor Holt, Sr., told his son absolutely nothing about the business. Everything Issy knew, he learned from this duo of raging slushes.

"You hear about the bombing of the Queenie's establishment two nights back?" Reggie inquires. He and his sibling tended to drop hs at the beginning of words, and the g on any verb ending with ~ing.

Issy had been staring at a large, violent poster on one wall that showcased a gangland slaying—a man, on his knees, about to be shot in the head in a dark alley, blood-red letters that announced 'Legend!' above the scene—and, glancing back at the men, his blank look leads Reggie to continue.

"Blew shit out of the place, killed a couple'a their people, and word on the street is your old man authorized the hit."

"Did he?" asked Issy.

"Did he what?"

"Authorize it?"

"You tell me. We're nothing more than clean-forgot hired help."

"Innat true," Ronnie says.

When Reggie focused—really thought, put on his glasses, and stopped drinking for half a second—he was a wealth of knowledge and insight. He had those spectacles, horn-rimmed ones, on now, though they sat slightly askew.

They also helped to tell one Mudbug from the other. Ronnie never wore glasses.

"Well," Issy muses. "You think this could be dangerous to us?"

"By 'us', you mean *us* us? Or you and the family jewels?"

"Both?"

Fixing his tie, Reggie shrugs. "Could be, young sir."

That's when his brother pipes up, all loud-mouthed and clearly inebriated. "But, serious-like, whadda we know?"

"Shush, Ronnie."

"Gimme another brew, bruv, and I'll shut me gob."

"Volta," says Reggie, sliding a freshly opened bottle before his sibling.

"Oi. What's 'volta' mean?" asks Ronnie.

"It's French, innit?"

"Classy."

Trying not to smile, Issy finds himself impatient to get back up to the club, the music, and a prospective pull. "So—I might see you boys back upstairs?"

Having adjusted glasses, Reggie nods. "Sure."

Isidor Holt, Jr., then really does smile as he hands over a fistful of notes. "Buy yourselves a slab of McKrays."

Taking the money, Reggie returns the expression, albeit a vaguely bland variant. "Don't mind if we do."

And with that, Issy takes his leave.

Heads back up darkened stairs toward Brangien and

the Disco Inferno. This little chat meant he had a wee bit to think about—above and beyond partying hearty.

LOU
[EN ROUTE, HERBERT DRAPER DRIVE]

Sure, Lou had things to do, but were thinking instead about the package he'd just delivered in a bow—Issy, doing himself no favours as usual—at the dancehall he liked to frequent.

This 'feckin decade had a lot to answer for. Lou wanted to give out about this fact, but mostly kept his gob shut. The suit Issy'd been wearing (a raw silk plaid number made in limited numbers by a Frog named Pierre some-wanker-or-other) was an eyesore, with ridiculously wide lapels and flared pants.

Plus the chiseller needed a haircut.

In spite of these things, he were a fine thing.

A handsome lad, the owner of strong features beyond that girly full mouth, though Paul Newman had one of those—and there went a man's man.

Definitely had his mother's looks in him, except his eyes were blue to her brown. Very little of his da, sad to say, aside from that eye-colour and light brown hair, and tended to act the maggot.

Might've been twenty-one—yet behaved like a complete bowsie. More often than not, Lou had to prise him up out of the gutter, escort him home in the backseat, bowdlerize that skull of the alcohol and chemicals and other nonsense.

Still, unlike Anguish, Lou saw potential here.

The kid had heart. He'd witnessed that himself. And while Isidor Holt, Jr., often played the fop—a Zorro trick Anguish and Alaina Holt fell for—Lou spied intelligence, a deeper understanding in the occasional glance or uneven grin that toyed with Issy's lips.

Thing was, as a dauphin Issy remained a woose, one hardly capable of running the family biz. Not that Anguish would be happy to relinquish control of this kingdom he'd built himself from scratch.

Built himself.

Lou rubbed his chin.

Seemed like even he was beginning to believe the lie. But, then, he'd been back peddled into this inferior position twenty years before.

Bloody Alaina.

Two blocks from the club, Lou switched on the left indicator, checked traffic behind, and pulled over close to a shuttered art deco building that still had signage up reading Cuvilliés Theatre. Tried to focus on what he was going to do. No one close by, so he opened the glove box before him, and sighed.

Wondered what his old lady in Castlehaven, Country Cork, would say knowing the antics her only son were up to now.

Reckoned the old duck'd spin a Derry jig in her coffin.

TRISTA
[CORNER OF STRENGLEIKAR & GERBERT]

*M*idnight.

The city feeling like a blast furnace, two blocks down from the Disco Inferno.

From this position on the sidewalk, outside a closed delicatessen called Sam's, she could hear beats from the club, an electronic-affected voice asking something about being taken to Funky Town.

Whatever.

Police were arriving in droves, and their wailing sirens began to drown out cheesy disco. Luckily, O'Dar was

officer in charge, handling things here. He was one of
Marcella's.

Think a short, stubby man with overly thick neck, aged
in early fifties, who liked to parade in dress-uniform on the
city streets.

Divorced once, and then wed a woman half his age.
Girl exhibited expensive taste, judging by what Trista had
heard. Plus, O'Dar carried a boy from the first marriage
who had to be supported through college—hence
additional wages, under the cuff, courtesy of the Cornwall
family.

From previous meetings conducted during daylight
hours, Trista knew Captain O'Dar had a ruddy, unhealthy
complexion. There were folds of skin in that fat neck,
tricky areas to shave, where clumps of silver whiskers
poked out.

"Hey, Trista," he said as he approached, tipping the hat
a fraction. "Sorry to have to drag you down this time of
night, this side of the river."

The girl produced a smile she felt sufficient. "No
problem. Can't sleep in this heat, anyway."

"There is that."

"How's the family, Harv?"

O'Dar's eyes shifted uneasily. "Swell. They're swell."

"I hear your son's doing big things."

"So he is. About to graduate, actually."

"Studying criminology."

"That's right."

"Must run in the family." Trista deliberately injected
warmth into the comment, wanted the man to feel at ease.
Having reminded him who paid the bills, she needed
O'Dar on the ball.

Still, she thought: *Taylor, what were you doing over here, on
Holt turf?*

Without further need for pleasantries, the captain took
Trista past a narrow corner, under a signpost reading
'Gerbert Street', and down an alley not so well lit by

surrounding fluorescent advertising in this area. The police, however, had set up a tripod with a bright lantern dangling beneath. A uniform was placing yellow tape across the other end of the lane, where a small crowd had gathered.

O'Dar looked seriously unhappy about that.

He waved over two other subordinates. "Lode, Tusk—get those people back! This isn't some goddamn public spectacle!"

Placing hands in her pockets, Trista waited for the police to get themselves organized. A minute later, O'Dar returned to take her closer to the tripod and its well of light—which showcased a corpse.

"Here he is in all his glory: Taylor Daniels. Laid out before us in a forgotten back-way I don't even know the name of."

"It's Strengleikar Lane, sir," said a nearby flatfoot, the one O'Dar had called Tusk, a lanky individual Trista hadn't met before. She made mental note of the name.

"Thank you, sergeant." O'Dar was put out, and his exhalation made him sound like he'd deflated a pound. "Anyhoo—Daniels has been shot three times, from what we can tell. Hard to. Tell, I mean. We have a medical examiner en route."

"Witnesses?" Trista asked, while crouching to get a closer look at the body.

"Nope," said Tusk.

"Apparently not," agreed O'Dar, eyeing his colleague.

Trista didn't care.

This was a bald, obese man before her, larger in girth than O'Dar, lying flat on his back on cobblestones. His mouth ajar, tongue peeking out, a trio of gaping holes in the chest, and most of his innards lying up round the head.

Taylor was old school, a gentleman; one of Marcella's few cronies Trista actually had time for. It was awful seeing him in this state.

"Didn't know the guy," O'Dar went on, shuffling feet.

"Only by reputation. Yet it's a fucked way to end your days."

"Mmm."

"Queenie ain't doing a spot of spring-cleaning I ought to know about—is she?"

Trista glanced up. "That isn't your business, Harvey. But, no." Her eyes dropped to the level of the man's crotch. "Looks to me like you've got your pocket full already."

O'Dar performed another odd shuffle, twisting slightly away. "Just asking. Got to follow up all possibilities."

"I get that. Still, I'd be more focused on Isidor Holt. Or do you Irish drink out of the same bottle, despite loyalties?"

The copper scowled, said under his breath, "He's about as Irish a pineapple," but Trista heard the remark. It made her frown.

"This is his backyard," she said.

"Yeah, about that." Leaning closer, again with the lowered voice, O'Dar seemed nervous. "What would a man like Daniels be doing on the wrong side of the Muir Èireann? He's bound to have enemies here."

"Mm-hmm." Distracted, Trista returned attention to the scenario at her feet.

A beaver-like toupée rested three or four feet distant. She never realized Taylor wore a hairpiece—but, then again, he went everywhere in a homburg. What remained of the man's polyester cardigan, much too warm for this temperature, was still zipped. This inferred he hadn't been reaching for another piece, or was caught unawares.

"Guy was packing," O'Dar confirmed, apparently catching Trista's train of thought.

"Taylor always carried two."

"That's how many we found."

"Recently fired?"

"Nada."

"Huh. For someone as cautious as Taylor to be caught

napping is... odd," Trista said.

"More odd," interrupted Tusk again, "is that over there."

The woman stood and looked in the direction this officer indicated with a flashlight. On the redbrick wall were scrawled two large words. Whoever did it was no artist—but the paint hadn't yet dried.

Beside her, O'Dar also studied the sloppy missive. "So. 'One Down'. Think it means anything?"

"Doubtful." Pushing bangs out of her eyes, Trista frowned. "Then again, this might be supposed to throw us off the scent of the murders the other night, you know, of Thomas and Béroul."

"Reckon they're related?"

"I haven't the faintest idea." That was the point Trista noticed something extra—or, rather, something amiss. "Huh. Any idea where his hat is?"

O'DAR
[CORNER OF HERBERT DRAPER AND LEIGHTON]

*H*is hands shook while he slowly peeled the clear cellophane off a cheroot, and then lit up on a street corner away from the crime scene.

Damn her eyes.

The police captain didn't like this girly. Couldn't put a finger on exactly why.

He drew hard and exhaled, at the same moment dropping the plastic wrapper to the pavement. So arrest me for littering, he thought.

There was no denying Trista Rivalen offered eye-candy, and she was nothing if not charming. First time he met her, he didn't know if he should pull out his service revolver or fall in love.

Possibly a natural golden blonde—you never could

tell—with reasonably thick eyebrows several shades darker than that. A pillowy pout, suggesting sultriness or sulkiness, yet probably neither. While sparing on the make-up, she applied winged eyeliner to create that perfect cat eye flick—and therefore, over all, bore a passing resemblance to Brigitte Bardot in her prime, twenty years ago, whom O'Dar had worshipped.

The man loosened his collar.

What was the film he always thought of when he crossed paths with Trista?

The Limey doctor one. *Doctor at Sea*, that was it.

Brigitte would've been the same age as Marcella's young emissary—Twenty? Twenty-one?—Though B.B.'s character was that of a brunette, not a blonde, and a sexy young French nightclub singer to boot.

Hardly the watchful, distant pain in the neck.

This Cornwall tramp was not cut from similar cloth, no bloody way, despite tonight's off-the-shoulder top tucked into a belted skirt, wearing a pair of leopard-print low-heels.

Yet the familiarity remained in the back of his mind, paralyzed better judgment.

O'Dar found it further disconcerting that she knew too many little details, and didn't pay the respect he felt he deserved.

Passers-by glanced at this police officer as they walked along the sidewalk, quickly averting eyes. So they fucking well should this time of night.

Two decades later, he still wore the memory like a badge of shame: he'd secretly masturbated beneath his jacket at the movie theatre that time he saw *Doctor at Sea*. Trista's continual expression whenever he met her seemed to contain some knowledge of what he had done.

Worse still, the captain suffered the ignominy of a hard-on whenever she prowled close by.

O'Dar shook his head. This was ridiculous. This child was barely out of her teens. He had put away hundreds of crims before she'd been born.

That thought made him puff harder.

His son offered a different pot of bother, though again it boiled down to respect.

Frank forever had his mitt out, demanding more money, didn't care where this came from or appreciate how lucky his life was. O'Dar had zip-all chance to attend a posh goddamned college, had put up with an alcoholic father who never held down any kind of reliable work and half-starved the family of six.

He'd suffered to work his way up the ranks, from beat-cop fresh out of the academy.

So what if one took the occasional bribe? These perks any good officer-of-the-law accepted when they dangled his way.

Ever the moralist, Frank took his father to task every which way he moved. Said O'Dar was a 'dirty' cop, pulled the bonus shame card on a regular basis.

Too much his fucking mamma's boy.

TRISTA
[ELSEWHERE ON LEIGHTON]

*T*rista had left the dead-zone on foot.

She needed air, no matter that this, here, belonged to the Holts. Walked along an unsurprisingly crowded thoroughfare, beside peepshows and strip joints still popular going on one in the a.m.

Thoughts running through her brain, none sensible. Like, who in their right mind got an erection beside a corpse?

She wagged her head to clear the thing, and same moment saw a drunk ahead, one of many, but this gent snags her attention.

Elderly, in a ruffled navy suit, loosened red tie thrown over the left shoulder. Possibly, he's Japanese.

There's a lyrical poignancy to the lost look in his eyes, his rosy cheeks, the way in which he has arms up and sways, doing his best to bypass others, or perhaps affect a little dance.

An additional sadness pushes through there too, a kind of melancholia she mirrors deep within while watching.

So Trista reacts immediately once a beat cop intercepts, and then shoves the businessman against a shop-front, already reaching for cuffs.

"Get your hands off him!" she shouts into the police officer's ear, nearly deafening him, judging by his reaction.

He jerks about, pissed off, to look her up and down, and she can see he's contemplating arresting her too—right when a shadow comes between.

"Wouldn't do that if I were you," this shade tells the cop. "We're here on behalf of Marcella Cornwall."

A sneer forming on his face, the officer slides his right hand in the direction of the holster on his hip. "You're in the wrong jurisdiction, arsehole."

"Tell that to your widow," says the shadow.

That's the moment Trista notices a wedding band on the ring finger of the cop's leftie. Good call, Governal. He always was the master of those little details.

Within seconds, the police officer has stomped off in one direction, the drunk weaves in the other, and Trista stands outside a closed pornographic bookstore with her ring-in father.

The man has a slight smile that annoys her.

"What?" she mutters.

"You're a good girl, you know that?"

"I'm nineteen. I'm not some juvenile delinquent anymore." Refusing to look up at him, she's lit a cigarette.

"Even so."

"You getting mushy on me, Gov?"

"Never." He slides an arm round her waist. "I have a car over there."

Not certain why, Trista feels the need to physically

disengage from her mentor. "That's okay," she says, doing the manoeuvre in a gentle way, so as not to cause any fuss. "I think I'm going to walk."

"Sure?"

"I am. I have cobwebs to clear." It was an old line they shared, meaning a spot of thinking to work things through. Now, however, Trista really does feel like her head is full of the stuff.

"This part of the city isn't safe," Governal insists.

"For us?"

"In general."

She pats her purse. "Don't worry. I have insurance."

3

TRISTA

*K*areol Heights, unlike Tintagel, was a genuine apartment block built for that specific purpose—smaller, in terms of room size, with cheaper fixtures, a relatively uncared-for brownstone needing a paint job. But the place edged into otherwise functional, had fairly decent amenities, and was suitably low-key.

It also boasted two redeeming qualities Governal had insisted upon: a hefty security door at the entrance, and no fire escape either side. Trista wasn't confident this second thing should seal the deal, but still.

Her flat, on the fifth floor, consisted of one tiny bedroom, a living room marginally larger, the windowless bathroom with its toilet and shower, and a kitchenette snatched from a trailer catalogue. Nothing decorated the

45

walls, leaving rumpled wallpaper to sun abstract shapes across a pale olive-green background.

Spinning on the record player she had a new EP by Cabaret Voltaire called *Extended Play*—which sadly wasn't so extended (only two tracks a side)—and she had to keep flipping it over.

Still, seated on her living room window sill, between flips, Trista looked not at the quiet, pre-dawn Penzance district street below—usually so crowded in daylight hours—nor St. Mary's Church across the way, but at a large full moon hanging in the sky, distorted by clouds.

She had an electric fan pointed her way.

It was hot and, again, Trista parked herself in the bare minimum bra and undies, along with a pair of Cendrillon ballet flats by French footwear brand Repetto. They were the few things (aside from an expensive hobby) on which she was willing to spend money.

Luckily, Governal carried the tab on her pricey, work-related wardrobe—meaning Marcella eventually paid.

Propped on the ledge beside her sat an open manila folder, clippings fluttering in the artificial breeze.

That air felt sweltering and heavy, like the sleazy, male-only Turkish sauna Trista once went to, dressed as a boy, when tailing Moore Holt to find out information about him.

That'd been an enlightening fiasco—Governal interrogated the girl-in-drag as soon as she set foot back over the threshold: "What do you now know about Moore?"

"He's mad," she'd said, throwing off clothes to get changed into something feminine.

"Mad earns you no kudos. Everyone in this town, their spouses, kids, and likely their respective dogs, knows that."

"Well, he's also Anguish's brother-in-law."

"Do tell. Are you trying to send me to sleep while standing up?"

"Funny. But hang on, I have a question."

"Heaven forbid."

"Enough with the sarcasm—seriously. I mean if he's just an in-law, why the creepy use of the same last name? And don't tell me it's my next assignment to find out."

"Very well." Governal had relaxed back against a wall, legs crossed, while Trista searched chaotic drawers for clean undies. "Moore was adopted into the Holt family after his sister Alaina married Isidor. I presume you know this already, or would like to assume so. Word is he took the Holt moniker since his surname, Ohn, didn't sit overly well with Moore. 'Moore Ohn'—get it?"

"Huh. That's a fizzer."

"I never promised otherwise."

"Whatever."

"Now, surprise me. What did *you* learn?"

Having located underwear reasonably pretty in pink, Trista now hunted down a frock. "Okay. How about him playing both sides of the street—has a girl living above Sheila's Flowers on Rye, and a boy out in Ballsbridge?"

"Moore's private kinks are not the issue."

Turning around in a clean dress, she'd indicated with her head that Governal ought to pull up the zip. "I think they raise some issues," she murmured, during this process.

"I raised you better than to be a prude."

"Really?"

"Well, I'd like to believe so."

In the here and now, away from touching memories, Trista had a layer of sweat on her forehead and in the armpits. Felt claustrophobic, hassled out by things she could not name.

The barely furnished flat was illuminated only by a tiny, white glass standing-lamp in an opposite corner of the room, so as not to spotlight the woman's lack of wardrobe to any outside peeping tom.

Even so, turning attention from lunar observations, turning records, and a frustrating attempt at paperwork,

Trista proceeded to apply a layer of nail polish to each finger.

What she thought about had nothing to do with cuticles.

She tried remembering her papa.

Recalled so much about him: his dress-sense, long hair, and the favoured Persol Ratti sunglasses. Lately, however, his face had begun to blur. The cheeky glint in those hazel-coloured eyes, behind the round shades, when he dropped them a fraction to peer at his daughter—she remembers that. And the man's confidence. Trista believed he'd live forever.

Not the case.

'Duke' Morgan.

Two simple bloody words: Duke / Morgan. One a moronic nickname.

Crossing to a small wooden desk next to the kitchen door, Trista opened the top drawer to take out a large, hardback edition of *The Golden Treasury of Myths and Legends*, illustrated by Martin and Alice Provensen.

A gift from Papa when she was three.

Opened the book at page 102, and stared for a while at the photograph tucked in there. A man kneeling on a street, about to be executed, gangland style.

The woman wondered why she thought of that now, of her dad and stupid Morgan and the life she'd lost. Her father's killer wasn't the problem this time—at least, there seemed no cause to believe so—and dead parents were the last things she needed to wallow over.

No, there were the far more recent murders of Daniels, Thomas and Béroul. Hence that equally thick folder over by the window, full of details about the crimes and the men.

She put this distraction away, again swivelled the vinyl.

All three men being Marcella's minions—far from vital ones, to be sure, but worrying enough once grouped together. Someone was apparently slapping out the

Cornwall family.

Still, there remained questions. What were Tommy and Berry doing together at the Caxton Building when they were killed? It wasn't their usual port-of-call.

Why was Daniels in the Holts' neck of the woods?

Trista had preliminary bets cast on 'Anguish' Holt, though she'd play things vague till the arrival of dead-set proof—Governal's preferred method.

Anyway, if he weren't a threat before, Holt would definitely be one now after the idiocy that took place after midnight, in apparent retaliation for Daniels' death.

Trista paused to inspect the paintwork on the middle finger of the right hand. Not bad.

She then blew out her cheeks.

Couldn't believe Marcella hadn't put the kibosh on the whole idea. Sure, in their meeting a couple of days before, Trista had suggested that the Holt family might be involved in the Cornwalls' latest drama, but she cautioned her boss to wait for evidence.

So what did Marcella's flying circus orchestrate?

A hit on Lou Holden.

Holden being 'Anguish' Holt's oldest friend. Three decades ago, they arrived on a boat together from the Emerald Isle, and Holden was most-trusted Holt family driver. Not such a brilliant career for the man—and stranger things had happened—but she decided she'd better ask Governal about it.

Holden. Out for a spin in his '74 Ford Torino—the same model, with the same red-and-white paint detailing, as the popular one from TV series *Starsky & Hutch*.

Making the thing easy pickings to spot from afar.

Trista further couldn't fathom how it was she first heard about the incident in a one a.m. newsflash on the radio. Governal got a call from Tintagel five minutes later, and when the woman opened the door to let him in, she could see he was equally appalled.

"One and all," the man muttered, one of Marcella's

favourite expressions, as he brushed past and went to the kitchen to pour a stiff drink for her and a Perrier for himself.

"What on earth is this din?" Governal commented, wagging his head at the turntable.

"Sorry, I don't have any Bing Crosby."

"Forget about him. Give me Tom Waits any day."

After switching records accordingly, they sat together and waited.

According to further word from Tintagel, Marcella's performing artist lieutenants organized everything—a trap whereby they positioned a dozen guns either side of Holden's residential street, and waited for—what? Revenge? Thoughts of Daniels, Thomas and Béroul?

She doubted this.

In ten seconds of disproportionate violence they had blown Holden's brains all over the leather upholstery of his shattered vehicle, outside his family home.

Trista could almost picture the scene; felt ill doing so.

Why the fuck didn't any of these people consider the wives widowed, the kids left behind? That was when she spilled nail polish, a streak of pillar-box-red, across her wrist.

"Bugger."

Went to the bathroom basin, used a cotton bud soaked in remover to clean up the mess. Turned on the tap and washed her hands and face, cupped water into her hair.

Stood back, standing before the large mirror, to comb that hair. When wet, it came down past her shoulders. Often, Trista felt like hacking it short—yet Governal insisted she should keep things long and in the way.

"Just another mask," he appraised. "People are bound to underestimate a girly blonde. That gives you an extra foot in the door I was never able to exploit."

Before Governal left, at around 4:00 a.m., Trista passed on additional instructions.

"I need you to do two things for me, Gov," she

announced as they approached the twice-bolted front door. "Is it possible for you to organize with the bureaucracy, or whoever, over in Ireland to get a copy of Isidor Holt's birth certificate?"

The man looked down at her. "Senior's, or Junior's?"

"Oh, gee. What d'you think?"

He broke into a grin. "Senior it is. Shouldn't be a problem—give me a week. I'd ask why, but no doubt you want it to be a surprise."

"Someone knows me far too well. You old bozo."

"Takes practice. And the other matter?"

"Check with your police department contacts. I want to know about a sergeant, name of Tusk."

"What's the slant there?"

Trista shrugged. "He seemed far too helpful the other night, when I was called in to Taylor Daniels' murder scene. And O'Dar acted uncomfortable."

Once her neighbour left, the woman had stripped, headed straight over to the window, and been there since—up until spilling nail polish, at any rate.

Wandering from the bathroom back to the living room and a stifling breeze of warm dawn air, Trista glanced with a smile at the collection of fellow blonde, 8.3-inch figurines on the mantelpiece. They were situated next to a battered, deep, four-drawer legal filing cabinet (in grey) on the right, and above a Coleman oil-burning heater that would not be used till next winter.

"Morning, ladies," she said.

These were a set of Japanese dolls, the first of which, positioned in the centre atop a small plastic pedestal, was a present Governal had brought back from a business trip to Osaka. Trista would've been ten at the time.

While the girl had initially supposed it was a souvenir, this plaything ended up being Governal's baptismal assignment—after she tore wrapping paper off, he said she'd need to find out everything possible concerning the contents, and then report back.

Never wanting to disappoint the man, his young charge set about her task. Eighteen months later, just after turning twelve, the report was finished—and she'd learned Japanese.

The early days of the 'mission', as she liked to call it, were far from satisfactory.

There was nothing in the school library, nary a morsel in the city one, to pass on a single clue. The only books she found were historical missives on the Edo and Meiji periods, the Pacific War, and much hoo-hah about Commodore Matthew Perry's bullying coercion to open Japan to trade in 1853.

She still remembered that initial research assignment by rote, and had continued updating it—one of her few hobbies—over the years.

Turned out, Licca-chan was the Japanese equivalent of Barbie, though far more popular over there than her American predecessor.

The doll was introduced to Japan in 1967 (when the only James Bond film set in that country, *You Only Live Twice*, hit cinema screens, almost a year before Trista received hers) courtesy of a toy company called Takara Co. Ltd., founded by Satoh Vinyl Industries, Ltd., in 1955.

The firm flouted a motto that, translated, read 'Playing is Culture'.

Takara also ended up being the weak-link.

She'd found their brand name on the packaging and searched for a local distributor or importer. There were none at the time. Therefore, Trista decided she needed to write Takara directly. After her first letter was lost or ignored, the girl realized it could be quite possible no one at Takara knew English—and, armed with this notion, was determined to learn at least rudimentary Japanese.

Trista found a teacher in one of the waitresses at the only Japanese restaurant in the city. A mission unto itself, since she'd had to convince Governal to take here there for lunch, and he played miser when it came to eating out.

She cornered the kitchen staff and employed her tutor while Gov was in the loo.

In order to pay for the lessons, Trista agreed to wash dishes at this restaurant two nights a week after school.

About a year later, the girl felt sufficiently able to word her correspondence with basic vocabulary written in hiragana and katakana, though the more she wrote, the better able she became to insert complicated kanji characters.

Someone at Takara sympathized with this avid overseas letter-writer, or entertained the notion that this could be a circuitous inroad into the Western market for their merchandise.

Either way, Trista became avid pen pals with a man named Eiichiro Tomiyama, although she never did discover Tomiyama-san's position at Takara—a drawback Governal criticized.

"Everything matters," he said. "Each detail. If you skip one single morsel, they end up biting you on the backside. For all you know, this Tomiyama character might be no authority at all. Maybe he or she's a toilet cleaner who took pity on a foreign kid?"

Still, the rest of the brief had the man's approval.

What she'd learned by then, and had updated over the decade since, was that Licca was created by Miyako Maki, wife of Leiji Matsumoto—who himself had conjured up well-known anime and manga titles like *Captain Harlock* and *Space Battleship Yamato*.

Maki was a manga artist too before she got married—yet renounced the career to become a traditional housewife.

Still, she retained the Licca legacy.

Over ensuing years, Licca, like Barbie, had figure and features, as much as her wardrobe refined to suit the faddish preferences of youth culture. In this case, our vinyl chloride resin heroine tended to be oriented toward Japanese sensibilities of height, looks, and fashion trends—so, in some respects, Licca made her American girls' forerunner look butch and chic-insensible.

The company, Takara, went to the extent of providing an extensive biography.

Family name? Kayama. She had a French father, a musician called Pierre. Her age was eleven, blood type O. She attended Shirakaba Gakuen Elementary School. The names of her best friends were Isamu and Izumi, Licca had an ex-boyfriend called Takeru and ongoing flame named Len-kun, and her twin siblings were Miki and Maki. Several other relatives joined the throng—including an older sister, Rie, a flight attendant mysteriously removed from the toy family line-up in 1974.

Trista had acquired one of those, for a small fortune, when she was eighteen.

Much of the information Trista learned from Tomiyama-san at the company over their six months of postal chitchat, and once ready, she sat Governal down in the kitchen, made him coffee just as he liked it (freshly brewed, strong, four sugars), and delivered her presentation.

Aside from the matter of Tomiyama-san's standing within the company, Governal had been impressed. He took her to a nearby ice cream shop to celebrate.

"See what you can do when you set your heart to it?" the man said, over his melting cone of cherry fudge chunk. "Knowledge is your armoury, Trista, and in the future a thorough understanding of people will be your best weapons."

Trista couldn't help smiling (again) at the memory—of both the notion of ice cream as a reward for a year-and-a-half's work, and the man's fatherly advice for a twelve-year-old.

Had it really been seven years since?

Stomach growling, she continued to the kitchenette.

Took a luke-warm TV dinner out from the oven: a bland combination of thinly sliced lamb with gravy, mashed potato that was grey-coloured and tasteless, and carrots that disintegrated when she touched them with a fork.

Washed the lot down with a bottle of Korev lager.

ISSY
[PRIVATE ROOMS, CHAPELIZOD HOUSE]

*I*ssy sat alone, zoning out with a late-night rerun of favourite show *CHiPs*.

While the television may have been relatively small for Issy's taste (a 23-inch screen), it was part of a remarkable piece of equipment that West German firm KUBA called a home entertainment system: the 289-pound, sailboat-shaped Komet, which additionallyboasted eight speakers, a Telefunken TW 501 phonograph, a magneto-phone wire recorder, and a tuner-radio.

The Komet ceased production in 1962, but Issy's dad picked up this unit for around $20,000 the previous year—a steal, considering what the collector's item usually fetched.

After ten months, however, Issy hardly saw the showboat piece of furniture for its worth, and stopped appreciating the lines two weeks into said investment. This objet d'art took up space (seven feet in width, almost six in height); it didn't match the rest of his furnishings, and was a hefty bastard to shift.

Think having a yacht in your sleeping quarters. This should've made Issy yearn for an admiral's cap. Instead—combined with the waterbed—he felt a trifle seasick.

Worse, still, the telly was a black-and-white.

So, as he relaxed atop the bed, head propped on two comfy cushions, watching his number one TV program, Issy remained dissatisfied.

Not considering much else, admittedly, except maybe the next drink—a martini, a Manhattan or a screwdriver?—when the black/white/grey Ponch and his police motorcycle wheels vanished off screen.

There was the news instead. And this update had slain him.

"—Scenes of ugly gangland violence today," a female newscaster rattled on. "Assassination... Mayhem... Horror..."

After recovering enough to think straight—one shot of icy vodka helped; he had a 50cl bottle of Krepkaya in the mini bar freezer by the bed—Issy tried to imagine his father's reaction.

And whether or not the man found out on the telly, too, or was informed by lackeys. Maybe a secretary piped up more safely via PBX?

Certainly someone would need balls to tell him.

'Anguish' might have to cancel his usual date with the angels: three beautiful, young triplets he kept on standby in a plush boudoir five minutes' drive away. Dubious, but still.

Rather, Issy pictured his dad screaming and shouting as he jabbed a menacing finger at anyone unfortunate enough to be close by.

At the very least, frothing at the corners of the mouth or sweeping out a pistol, raging, he'd be yelling something like "Kill those fuckers!"—very Pacino, de Niro, Sugawara, or Keitel.

Thing is, it was imagination. Issy didn't know how his dad'd react.

Hardly knew the man at all.

Isidor Holt, Sr., was as religious about keeping distance from others as some people once were of separating church and state.

God, Issy thought. *Poor bloody Lou.*

ALAINA
[ISSY'S PARENTS' QUARTERS, CHAPELIZOD HOUSE]

*T*he newsflash is on-air again, this time presented by a male announcer with a snapshot beside his head, a picture of a shattered Ford Torino. It plays across the big colour television beside a faux fireplace.

While reclining on a zebra-striped bathtub sofa in the middle of this spacious living room, Alaina Holt stares at the reflection cast by a window overlooking the night time bamboo garden. Sees a middle-aged brunette, holding onto a good figure, with an attractive (if hard, and markedly sagging) face, hair loosely tied in a bun.

Clad in a simple red dress, clutching a large glass of French cabernet sauvignon in one hand.

The woman murmurs, "Well," and lets out a sigh—more bored with her mirror image than aggrieved. "Lou is dead, or so they tell us in the reruns. What *are* you going to do about it, Isidor?"

Six feet from his wife, leaning forward in his simpler leather armchair, hands gripping the material as he stares at the screen, Isidor Holt, Sr., lets out a groan. The man had a silly little moustache that Alaina always despised, along with receding hair, his pate before that shiny to the point of reflecting light.

"Well?" Alaina repeats, to no further sound. "Look, why don't you go into the projector room, and do something productive like screening one of your silly yazuka films? That will cheer you up."

"Yakuza. I've told you a million times."

"It speaks!"

After a nasty snarl, Isidor complains, "Enough! I'm thinking."

"Oh, and isn't that just swell." Alaina takes a big mouthful of wine; fuck sipping, and then with the other hand lifts the phone. "While you attempt to do so, I'm going to get the Norwegian on the line."

Her husband, apparently not listening, has removed his spectacles, becomes preoccupied shoving face into hands, and whines, "Lou." Yes, the man had taken up sobbing.

Nonplussed, the woman gets an answer to her call. "Hello, Anders? Alaina. About Holden—*Mm-hmm*. Yes. Are you quite positive it was Queenie's goons involved?" She frowns. "I see. Well, I'm thinking confessions will go a long way. It is rather nice to have solid proof." Eyes narrowing, Alaina shifts in her position. "Well? Well. Sounds like you're evading the question. No? So, how is it I'm 'right on', as you say?" Has another swig of wine. "Exactly. Enough, then, to point fingers."

Having placed the phone back on its cradle with a loud bang, Alaina drains her glass.

"Isidor," she straight after announces, "Your men are idiots. They need long-absent leadership." The woman's look switches from the wine bottle on the coffee table to her spouse. "Cue: you. Now."

Isidor Holt, Sr., drops fingers from his head, and yet continues to lean forward, face screwed-up with obvious anguish—the epitome of his nickname. "But," says he, unseeing, "but... Lou—"

"Screw Lou!"

Isidor, having opened eyes, tears glistening atop his cheeks, behaves shocked. "That's harsh."

Topping up, the woman shrugs. "Just telling it like it is, baby." She sips now in controlled fashion. "So. What're we going to do?"

"Do?"

"Do."

"I don't know."

"Well, luckily for you—I'm here to fill that vacuum." Alaina's free hand falls back to the telephone, and she begins dialling. "Starting with your accountant."

"Why?"

"Because this is his responsibility too. Some of us care." Adjusting the receiver to the crook of her neck, Alaina makes herself comfy. "Joe? ...Alaina Holt."

"Mrs. Holt?" squeaks a tinny voice at the other end of the line.

Not for the first time, Alaina wonders why financial types were so damned pathetic, just like her better half. "Hello, Joe."

"Oh... um... hello! It's very late, ma'am."

Alaina smiles thinly. "Tell someone who cares."

"Right you are. How can I help you?"

"I have a quick question."

"Sure thing, ma'am. Shoot."

"When was the last time the Cornwall family coughed up our cut of business profits?"

Joe launches into his own coughing fit at the other end, before urgently whispering, "Uh... Is this a secure line?"

The woman smirks. "Sure," is the fib she offers.

"Well, um, since we don't keep books, I can't give you an accurate date per se."

"Humour me, then, with some kind of rough estimate."

"Approximately?"

"That *is* what I'm suggesting, Joe."

"Approximately?—Nothing within the past three years."

"Three? Did you just say three?"

"Give or take a quarter."

"And when was somebody going to tell us this?"

"Well... We were under the—*er*—impression that the Cornwalls were a special case."

Glancing at the man in the room with her, the one having a meltdown and still snivelling, Alaina turns away. "Who gave you that impression?"

There is silence for a few seconds, followed by: "May I speak frankly, ma'am?"

"Within reason."

"Well, now, um—ahh—Could I get a better idea," the

accountant says in a smaller voice, one she can barely hear, "of the perimeters you're setting?"

Alaina sits forward, patience shot. "Now listen here, Joe—I'm only going to say this once. I'll give you an impression from the back of my hand if you waste more time."

"Of course, ma'am." The threat seemed to have worked wonders. His volume certainly lifted a notch. "Mr. Holt did it, ma'am. Senior, I mean."

Having bit her tongue, Alaina settles for a quip instead. "I would hardly think my son has any say in these matters."

"Yes, yes, of course."

Then why say it, idiot?

"Mr. Holt, senior, told us the Cornwall businesses were to be allowed certain financial privileges that the other families know nothing about."

"I see. I'd say three years' scot-free has more than abused those rights. Wouldn't you?"

"Of course, ma'am. Shall we bill them?"

"And create that dangerous paperwork you try to avoid? No."

"Then—How...?"

"Don't worry your little mind, Joe."

Having placing her index finger on the switch hook to sever the connection, Alaina left it there. "Moron," she says, mulling over that just learned.

Isidor peers over from between fingertips in the steeple position. "How on earth do you function when you get this drunk?"

"Easy. Alcohol steels me to deal with dipsticks like Anders, Joe, and *you*."

With her free hand, the woman refills her glass almost to the top, finishing her second bottle in the process.

"Anyway, looks like that bitch Queenie did it." Having sipped the wine twice, she lets the liquid roll around her mouth, before swallowing. "Killed your precious Lou."

This proclamation triggers more tears from her husband.

"Uh-huh." Alaina has to sigh.

"What shall we do?" whimpers the man, who is staring at the floor.

"Only one thing for it—you know that. We need to summon our champion."

"Is that completely necessary?"

"Why else would I still have my finger on the phone?"

Isidor sits up, wipes under his eyes with a handkerchief, and the eventual verbal response is a reluctant one. "Yeah. All right."

"Beautiful." With that, Alaina dials through to Isidor's secretary, using her own extension to forewarn the lady.

Effie is quick at answering, more confident than Joe the accountant in the prior call. "Yes, ma'am?"

"Effie, get me Moore Holt." Phone receiver again positioned between right shoulder and right ear, Alaina lets down her drink to fire up a cigarette with a gold-plated Dunhill Rollagas lighter.

"What?" she mutters—inhaling, and then exhaling, in short order. "I haven't the faintest idea. Try the YMCA Turkish baths on Söze Avenue."

After more wasted seconds, several swigs of red that take the level precariously low, and a tamped-out cigarette, she finally has her brother on the line. Tells him what he needs to know, keeping matters simple.

"Wuzzat?" He says at last.

This makes Alaina wonder if she's going to have to repeat the lot. Decides she needs another drink, says, "Did you get anything at all that I just told you, Moore?"

"Sure."

"And?"

"Course I'm up for it, sis. I'll kick serious butt-action."

4

TRISTA

[NOW—12:30 A.M., ST. SAMSON'S BAR & GRILL]

*Y*eah, she acknowledges, so this looks bad.

Fact there's blood all over the floor, amidst other debris, gives the game away.

Shit.

TRISTA
[MIDDAY YESTERDAY — TINTAGEL APARTMENTS]

*"W*hy? Why do I need answer to you?"

Marcella was seated before a grand piano, back to her

63

niece. Hummed a few bars, and then sighed.

"Explain that."

"Because it's what I do," Trista said. She, in turn, wondered the need to explain at all.

Had her arms crossed, over an expensive linen frock (lesson learned last time), leaning against one of the few spaces of wall minus pictures.

A row of carved chairs with comfy velvet cushioning and tapestry backs were lined up before her in a row—intended for audiences, most likely—but Trista declined to sit. Their velvet was ruffled, new-looking. Didn't invite unwanted derrières flattening out the material.

She and her aunt were alone in this, the music room, on the ground floor.

Diffused, coloured light entered the space through a stained-glass window that seemed to tell some skewed story of a castle and knights jousting in merry olde England.

On the wall, above and behind the piano, hung faded portraits of composers like Chopin and Rachmaninov, plus others Trista failed to recognize.

After tinkering with keys on the piano in an attempt to play something by Wagner (at least according to sheet-notes Trista had spied), Marcella shook her head and grunted.

"You want to grill me? Me—The head of this family?"

The younger woman glanced at the ceiling. For strength? For something. "You did say to keep the bastards honest."

"So, Trista... Are you inferring I'm one of these bastards?" Still Marcella refused to share eye contact. "Well, my girl?"

"Okay, honestly?" Trista released arms to straighten her one-piece. "I just want to know why you authorized the hit on Holden."

"Why? *Why?* They were bleeding us. Good men died." The C-key was depressed, followed awkwardly by E, and then G twice.

Trista had to resist an impulse to push the elderly lady aside and demonstrate how to really treat a beautiful instrument such as this. It would be ironic, given that Marcella bankrolled her lessons.

Narrowing eyes, she focused again on her aunt. "More of them will die here on in."

Marcella hesitated above the next key. "Still."

"Still—what? Are you going to continue playing show-tunes, or talk to me?"

"Careful with the tongue, little girl."

Trista could now see Marcella's angry scowl in the mirror-like varnish of the piano proper. Decided on the spot to badger an ulterior slant.

"Who put you up to it, boss?"

"I told you not to call me that."

"What would you prefer? Auntie?"

The older woman hit several keys at once, making another discordant din. "Marcella will do fine. And I make my own decisions." Her voice rose above the fading piano. "I am not a puppet on a string."

Time to tread cautiously, Trista understood. "I know that." Still, what this woman required was a good shake. "Which is why I'm surprised you'd do something so stupid."

"How dare you?!" Sheet music tumbled to the parquetry, as Marcella swung round. The glare was sizzling. "Nobody speaks like that to Marcella Cornwall. You hear?"

Trista gazed straight back. "So sue me."

"Eh? By God, I have no idea why I put up with that lip."

Crossing arms again, the younger woman dared a smile and a quip—"You put up with it because you trust me."—that seemed to tame the beast.

Marcella sat back on the piano stool, looking her age.

"Agreed." The lady grimaced. "And now, the shit has hit the fan. What am I to do?" Rubbing fingers together, even the semi-paralyzed ones, she darted eyes about the room.

Trista wasn't sure she entirely believed the performance—there was so much about her aunt she'd never been able to fathom—but gave benefit of doubt its due.

"Which shit are you talking up?" she asked.

"Which? Can't you see it? The feculence pouring upon us from all quarters. All sides, do you understand? I need someone, Trista." It was Marcella's turn to wrap herself in arms, like she was chilled, or scared. "I need a champion to play the Harp against Moore Holt."

The Harp.

This cold was catching. Without moving a muscle, the younger woman felt her innards recoil. "Go on," she said.

"Trista, everyone—all I've got to offer—is running yellow."

Swivelling on the stool, and then standing to walk toward her niece with open arms, Marcella came across an oddball fusion of loving, fearful and proud.

"Anyway, you're the best of them. You're my girl. Aren't you?"

TRISTA
[TWO DAYS AGO — CEMETERIES EITHER SIDE OF THE MUIR ÈIREANN]

*T*rista crosses from one funeral to the other in the same morning. The first is a low-key Cornwall affair, the other a crowded Holt extravaganza.

Grieving widows and bawling children were a feature at both, as too're the mingling hoods with bulges beneath suit lapels.

Flowers offered a bonus extra, and Trista noted the different tastes. At Daniels' one there is an excess of *erica vagans*, while the Holden bash boasted far too many bunches of shamrocks.

Men and women milled about the two ceremonies, dressed predominantly in black. Dark glasses appeared to be an additional requirement regardless of gang affiliation.

Governal must've received the memo, as he advised her to dress in both.

Given the oppressive heat that time of morning, Trista chose a simple, short-sleeve cotton number (in black), had her hair held in check with a black headband, and wore a pair of Céline oversized sunglasses—better to hide behind.

Glad of these when she spotted 'Duke' Morgan scowling away in his wheelchair, surrounded by a gaggle of goons.

Otherwise, Trista had no intention of shedding tears, though the music brought her close—for the wrong reasons.

At the Daniels shindig, she suffered through a dribbling, off-key rendition of 'Sweet Nightingale'—all "Come along! Don't you hear the fond song, the sweet notes of the nightingale flow?" *et cetera, et cetera*—and the Holden party further depressed, when a quintet of uilleann pipes dropped a droning 'Molly Malone'.

Trista cottoned on early that the funerals shared the same hearse: a midnight-painted, low-riding 1960 Cadillac Superior Coachworks number with impressive fins either side at the back, the number-plates reading DED-666. First time Trista noticed that, she was gobsmacked. By the end of the morning? Blasé.

Governal, while putting in an appearance at Taylor Daniels' service, declined the trip across the river. "Too many people there know me, and anyone related to our Cornwalls will not be welcome," he assessed. "Better for you to go alone, scope out things. Hardly anyone will bat an eye. You're still a relative unknown."

"Did you just make a pun?" she'd asked.

"Never."

And hour later, Trista skirts the Holt affair, wondering

what exactly she was supposed to be scoping out—aside from a lot of people in pain, thanks to an unnecessary murder.

That's when she notices Isidor Holt, Jr., in a throng of mourners. She'd never met the man before. Dressed as he was in more conservative fashion than she had observed in photographs—a stylish black suit with stove-pipe trousers—Trista likes the ensemble far better than flashier outfits worn by the other men in this place.

Somewhat curious, she moseys on over.

The Holt heir-apparent had a cigarette in the corner of an annoyed mouth. Exceptionally handsome he might be, but harried all the same.

Trista decides it's better to keep on going. "I'm sorry for your loss," she says as she passes close by.

His eyes, darting down, catch hers, and in that moment she almost forgets to breathe. For a flash of a second, she does wonder if he's somehow placed her, so returns the look. His pupils were dilated—odd, given how bright it was that time of morning—and around them sparkled a rim of cobalt blue, more intense than she'd imagined possible.

Removing the ciggie, he inspects this well-wisher, and Trista understands then that he can't recall or decide who she might be—though covers well.

"Thanks," he says, with a quixotic smile, killing earlier irritation.

Having stopped beside him, trying to act natural as she remembered how to inhale, Trista plays for time. "Could I borrow a cigarette?"

The man's smile blooms. "So long as you return it." He offers her an opened packet of Royale. Selecting one with surprisingly steady fingers, she leans forward in order to receive also a light.

"Might be hard to do so," she says.

"You from out of town?"

"Different circles." She smiles in return. "Thank you."

Straight after, Trista waltzes off in the direction of the parked car—though glances over her shoulder and sees that he's watching. Doesn't know why on earth she feels this way, but is satisfied and a little thrilled.

This is madness.

Having ground half a cigarette underfoot on hallowed turf, Trista jumps into her Mustang, guns the engine more than necessary—startling a few nearby people—and speeds faster than she needs to away from the scene.

Drives to a dive of a pool joint the other side of the river, in safer terrain, where she proceeds to get very hammered and plays the game poorly, losing over a hundred dollars.

At some later point, Governal swings by to carry her home.

TRISTA
[6:30 A.M. YESTERDAY — THE BOWELS OF THE CHURCH OF ST. MICHAEL]

*E*arly every Saturday, from six o'clock through to ten, come high water or stifling, hellfire conditions—such as this day's—Trista assisted at a soup kitchen.

She ladled, scooped, passed out plastic plates and bowls, filled paper cups, made small talk, and then washed up and helped clean.

Working there was something she'd done going on two years, since these people—volunteers and destitute guests together—had aided her on the streets at a particularly dark time in the woman's life.

This kitchen was housed in a basement beneath the Church of St. Michael the Apostle—a vast, fortress-like Roman Catholic parish located at 8-10 Petroc Avenue. It was on the corner of East Pyran Street, in the Upper East Side, two blocks from Dumnonia Bridge, which spanned the muddy waters of the Muir Èireann.

The place doubled as a homeless shelter, the venue for local boxing matches, and an ad hoc rehearsal space for all-girl punk band the Rancid Raiments—through whom she'd met those running things.

While Trista didn't have time for your standard Christian zealots, Elton McMurphy and his aids could hardly be said to fit that mould. Rather, McMurphy ran the place like an open-minded carnival float, welcoming everyone regardless of faith, background, race, persuasion, or dress-sense.

They had surprising support from St. Michael's head priest Father Isaac, an elderly liege who found day-to-day operations bothersome, and only put in an appearance for the sermon on Sundays.

If he rolled up on your welcome mat, you might be hard-pressed to take Elton McMurphy seriously—and would consider shutting the door in his face.

This was a short, rotund man with a bushy black beard (it reached his belly) and receding hairline. His uniform consisted of a suede vest two sizes too small, over varying tie-dyed shirts, with a pair of incredibly flared slacks. He opted for having his shirt open to reveal a peace medallion that, at first glance, resembled a bath plug, hanging from a solid silver chain atop a purple haze of also-dyed chest hair.

"We couldn't have gotten away with half of what we do prior to Vatican II," Elton once admitted. "Like allowing people with lip piercings and upside-down crosses to practice music in these here hallowed halls. As for my wardrobe, Heaven forbid."

This particular morning, Trista almost called in sick.

She'd never before missed a day, but was suffering from the alcohol downed the night before over reckless games of pool. So she coerced herself to work harder, some kind of penance, hair held in check by a red paisley bandanna, its own contrition, and barely communicated with a soul.

Which seemed fine today, since everyone behaved so damned depressed.

Trista was dishing up yet another bowl of would-be minestrone, when she saw *him* stroll down the steps and enter the basement.

Possibly it was the suit alerted her—it looked like the one he'd worn to the funeral, though the tie was AWOL.

Straight away, she busied herself with people waiting in line; face downturned, hoping the man wouldn't catch on. Guessed she was in the right place for a spot of prayers. Didn't know why, but her chest tightened, and she felt a little faint—blamed the sensation on the stupid hangover.

Still, from the corner of her eye, she was able to espy Elton McMurphy approaching, a shaking of hands, thence retiring to his tiny school desk the other side of the basement. They shared a coffee. Chatted like old friends.

Meantime, Trista endeavoured to keep head down and steady her breathing.

At long last, some ten minutes later, their visitor exited the same way he'd arrived.

Trista had to finish serving before she could take a break. Rather than beat about pointless bushes, she went straight over to Elton.

"Feeling better now, Triss?" McMurphy asked from his stool. He appeared to be going over accounts.

She leaned against the desk, said, "Marginally."

"The assistance is always appreciated."

"Thanks."

"Pull up a chair." McMurphy motioned to the stool's brethren (Trista declined—it looked rickety, and she wasn't in the right state for a tumble), and then he leaned forward on elbows. "You look like you could use a yack."

"Actually, I have somewhere I need to be. Sorry."

"No fuss. I'm always here."

"So I noticed." They shared a smile.

"D'you mind if I ask you, Elton—What was that guy doing in here earlier, the one gift-wrapped in the nice suit?"

"What, you mean Mr. Holt?"

"That's his name?"

"Mm."

"Looked a little swanky for these parts."

"Issy's one of our more generous benefactors."

"You're kidding?"

"Not at all. Comes in every week, with a satchel full of cash." Elton placed a single finger to his lips. "Between you and me. Don't tell anyone."

"Sure. But this side of the river—in a Cornwall neighbourhood?"

McMurphy clicked his tongue. "You mean, him being a Holt, and all that nonsense?"

"Well, there are... rules."

"Pfft. There goes a decent fellow, Triss. You know what he told me?"

"No—What?"

"He told me that gangland boundaries don't matter to the homeless."

"Mighty big of him," Trista muttered, loud enough for her friend to hear.

Said Elton, "Ahh, try not to be so cynical!", and followed this with a resounding chuckle. "Issy is right on the mark. We were close to bankruptcy when he started making donations last year. You could say he's been a saviour."

Trista discovered herself wondering if this was ammunition she could use.

Didn't think it would be.

TRISTA
[AFTERNOON/EVENING, YESTERDAY — KAREOL HEIGHTS & LOCAL AREA]

Back at her place, post-hangover (medication helped), after the meeting with Marcella (which didn't), Trista now had to contend with Governal.

"You're going to die," he deadpans.

Glancing over from the mirror, where she was busy doing a trial-run with her make-up—wondered whether to play it minimal and boyish (and therefore more capable, in men's opinion), or go for a more sultry look with smoky eye-shadow—Trista takes time out to sigh.

"Gee, whiz. Ta for the vote of confidence."

"I'm serious, Triss."

"I know you are."

She doubts the man's listening, since he steamrolls on: "You might know how to shoot one of the things, but you've never used a gun on a person before."

"Me?" Trista angles her head to one side. "I'm hoping I won't have to."

Governal shakes his. "Why does that not surprise me?"

"How do you mean?"

"You always did play the over-optimism card." It was his turn to sigh. "To a degree. By the way, make-up wise? I'd go with glamour. Stun the bastards."

Once they'd worked an appropriate and effective 'look'—actually, Trista did the work; Governal merely criticized—she removed all trace of make-up using baby oil. Her mother would've baulked. The lady insisted on an expensive cold cream, but Trista found this better for her skin, not to mention more affordable.

"You look as shiny as one of your Licca toys," Governal comments from the bathroom doorway, having swapped an espresso for a daring glass of milk.

While she dabs her face with a towel in the looking

glass reflection, to remove most of the residual oil, Trista briefly pokes out her tongue. "One day, we're going to put *you* through the hoops cosmetics wise."

"What, and cover up this handsome demeanour?"

"Only in your dreams, darlin'."

The two headed out for minimal drinks with an early dinner, scrowled pilchards and miniature pasties at a family-owned place Trista loved. Between dishes, after sipping at his mineral water, Governal slid across a bunch of documents.

"You'll be playing tonight under an alias—Marcella doesn't want it known who you are."

Picking up a driver's license with a photo, Trista squinted to read the fine print. "So. 'Ludia Schnorr'. OK. Huh." Straight after, she polished off a single highball. For nerves, she'd told herself when ordering the drink.

"Notice the detailing?" Governal says.

One could detect an element of pride in the man's voice, if you bothered searching, so she looked closer at the documentation. "These look legit. They're really good."

"I had them done by Dutkiewicz."

Trista glances over the table. "The guy who takes a month of Sundays to get anything finished?"

"Man is an artist. You can't rush art."

"Then, how...?"

"I paid him extra—and stood right behind, cleaning my gun, while he worked."

"Ahh."

"And this, here," Governal taps one neatly-typed sheet on the table, "is the bio for the mutually agreed arbitrator."

Trista allowed eyes to run over the page. "We've met," she murmurs—which makes Governal look at her long and hard. "But he won't remember me. Don't worry."

"Don't worry, she says." The man breathes out in loud fashion. "All right. I also took the liberty of organizing a second nom-de-plume, this one for when you get out of there. Not even Marcella knows it."

"Why the secrecy?" asks Trista, after he handed her a social security card.

"Don't trust anybody. You know that."

She briefly compresses her lips. "Oh God. *Henrike Vogl.* These names get better and better."

"I try. Are we done here?"

"Sure. Your treat?"

"I swear I paid last time," the man grumbled.

After dinner, having put paperwork carefully away, the two took a stroll along the right bank of the Muir Éireann.

Trista briefly considers spilling what she'd learned in the morning about Isidor Holt, Jr., but feels this isn't the right occasion.

Their route takes them past summer food stalls and, at one point, close-by an itinerant amusement park that's crowded. Trista can make out whoops from the roller coaster.

Dusk had fallen half an hour before. Night reigns.

The water in the wide river beside them sits strangely calm, casting a perfect, upside-down reflection of the busier district the other side of the river—in Holt territory.

Governal is far from restful.

The man had been brooding since before supper, and barely touched his dish. He always played cards close to his chest—Trista kidded herself if she thought she were the exception to this rule of thumb—and she knows she will have to wait for him to unveil anything.

"Seriously... Yes, that word again," he eventually says while they walk, eyes looking ahead, "*don't do this.*"

"Governal." Trista takes his left hand in her right. "I don't have a choice. The die is cast, as they liked to chuck around in the dusty Shakespeare plays you used to drag me along to."

"I never took you to see any Theatre of Cruelty."

Trista smiles. It's a fragile attempt at one, she knows that, yet an accomplishment all the same. "Even so. Depends how you see old Willie."

That's the moment Governal ceases to walk and, still holding her hand, makes her stop and turn to face him.

When she was a child, she'd been in love with this forty-nine-year-old man. Guessed she still was, in many respects, despite the age difference. He knew her inside out, had kneaded the clay from age five.

"This is not your stage," he says.

"Maybe I have a hankering for footlights."

"I'm serious."

"You said already. Well, so am I."

"You know, in all likelihood, you'll have to break your vow?"

Trista flinches, resorts to quoting a nugget she heard from this same individual years before. "Sometimes, we don't have a choice."

If he gets the reference, Governal chooses to ignore it. "This isn't what we groomed you to be."

"A killer?"

"A throw-away reparation."

"Huh. That's why I thought I'd pull a Michael Corleone."

"Sweetheart," the man mutters, "*The Godfather* was a popular film."

"Your point?"

With a quick manoeuvre, Governal now held her hand in both of his. It was as possessive a gesture as it might be caring. If anyone else did this, she'd knee them in the groin. Thing being, Governal was the only member of the opposite sex she completely trusted.

Trista believed that he, in turn, judged her not by the length of skirt hem, but for instincts and skills he'd helped ingrain.

"Aside from the fact that this isn't a movie?" The man raises both brows. "In all likelihood, they caught a screening too."

"Ahh, but I'm not going to place a pistol in the cistern," Trista says, putting her free hand atop his. Wills it not to tremble. "I'm going to stick one between my legs."

TRISTA
[HER PLACE — AROUND 9:00 P.M.]

"*V*oilà: my .25 ACP Beretta 950 Jetfire."

Trista had laid out the Italian-made compact gun on the coffee table between them, next to two eight-round magazines and a closed switchblade.

"If I position it between my thighs, tucked close to the crotch, they shouldn't notice in your Joe-average pat-down—unless someone gets frisky." Trista tapped her left temple. "In that case, I wouldn't have much choice anyway."

Governal said nothing, just observed, meaning that Trista had started to babble.

"Small, light—it weighs in at little more than a family-sized block of Cadbury Fruit & Nut. Pretty nifty."

She'd picked that specific example since she knew how much Governal cherished his weekly chocolate stash.

The man lifted the firearm, checked balance, aligned it with his eye. Trista wasn't sure when she realized she'd been holding her breath while he did so.

Governal had no family, and she'd never once seen him in the company of another woman—aside from her aunt. While Trista still had said aunt and a mother, she was infinitely closer to this no-nonsense individual. What he said mattered, even as she pretended otherwise.

"The Jetfire's an older weapon, first manufactured in the '50s," he mused. "I'd say this is sourced from that initial production crop. Who sold it to you?"

The woman shrugged. Said nothing.

"It's a lady's gun, or you keep one up your sleeve as back-up for worst-case scenarios," Governal adjudged, "and I've met this particular piece before." His eyes left the weapon and went straight to Trista's. "Haven't I?"

Trista was about to shrug again, thought better. "I lifted it from Mum's bedside drawer."

"Mm. I remember now. About fourteen years ago, Morgan asked me get her something. For protection."

"What—from *him*?" The way Trista said the pronoun turned it into a sneer.

Governal frowned, but there was humour licking the edges of his mouth. "If Blanche genuinely needed that kind of protection, I would've passed on something more adequate."

He lifted the pistol again, looked like it offended him.

"Yeah. All right. Small, I'll give you that. But this baby's not as easy to shoot as it looks to be, and will barely poke holes through a sturdy leather jacket. It's a pop-gun."

Trista listened while she got changed in front of the man, putting on an elegant, black, raw silk dress with a leopard-print, fur-wrap collar (some indication she felt chilled to the bone), and a necklace of pearls that'd also belonged to her mother.

"I know," she said. "But I can't exactly smuggle in an Uzi under my arm."

"Exactly. So if you are going to do this, aim for the soft spots: the eyes, the throat. Empty the magazine and lay this bastard out."

Smoothing out stockings, the woman nodded, while ensuring they were fastened correctly at the thighs. Took the gun and strapped it higher up.

"Okay."

Governal aped dissatisfied. He poked her—hard—in the shoulder. "You hear me?"

"Sure." She stood before him and lit two cigarettes. "I'll be okay."

He took one of the fags, stared at it for a moment, and then inhaled deeply. "Good," he said straight after.

Of course they both lied.

TRISTA
[LAST NIGHT—ON THE WAY TO ST. SAMSON'S]

*T*rista stares through the car window, seeing, yet not really taking in, the other vehicles with their headlights driving alongside and from the opposite direction. There's a haze to the air, caused by humidity, and the smell of exhaust.

She couldn't tell Governal.

Couldn't admit that her palms were sweaty, throat scratchy, nerves shot full of lead. Didn't say she was petrified, or whine as he waved her off outside the apartment.

Their route takes them through a seedier part of Cornwall territory, cruising past male-crowded pornographic theatres with marquees that read 'Naked are the Cheaters', 'A Taste of Hot Lead', and 'Young Nymphos'—along with a playhouse that surprisingly advertised an amateur production of *West Side Story*.

Trista was going to die tonight. If nothing else made sense, that thought blinked and gyrated, just like the kitsch neon signage outside.

No chance.

The gaudy district slowly changed and cleaned itself up into one where big bookstores, restaurants, bars, and music shops dominated. They were close now to the neutral turf where they'd find St. Samson's.

Governal understood.

The fatal nature of said rendezvous.

Moore Holt's reputation touted the man as a virtuoso of the Harp in this town, since he had a record of eighteen wins, no losses. Trista never played an intra-city round, while her alias Ludia Schnorr was completely unheard of.

No wonder betting odds'd already been stacked in Moore's favour.

It's why Governal tried to call things off. But they—

neither of them—had a choice. That bugger of a die really was cast. In bronze, if you want to get finicky.

How soon till she got there?

A few minutes at best, worst, or whatever the case might be.

Trista glances at her wristwatch, yet has teared-up and can't see the thing. Steeling herself, or at least trying her best to, the woman squeezes lips together until they hurt.

Breathe, she thinks. Breathe. In/out. That's a girl.

Just like Gov always said.

She was thus preoccupied when the car came to a stop.

Despite its showboat moniker, St. Samson's Bar & Grill was more spit-and-sawdust, a stand-up bar with some old chairs and wooden pub tables.

On the walls were framed pictures of prize-fighters likely dead and buried, along with big match announcements yellowed by age, and hanging pairs of gloves that belonged to retired champions. A massive bay window offered the panoramic view of a narrow, ugly street with few passing cars and a shuttered redbrick factory opposite.

This venue had been recently bought out by a group of punks whose only attempts at additional furnishing were Sex Pistols 45s stuck on a pillar at eye-height next to the bar, a large banner that said 'Nazi Punks Fuck Off!', and a set of powerful second-hand speakers through which to crank bootleg recordings of live gigs by Blondie and Black Flag.

The bar proper featured most prominently—a curved, cedar structure, with a laminated bench top. Despite the run-down nature of the rest of the premises, it stocked José Cuervo Clásico tequila and Baron de Sigognac Bas-Armagnac in massive quantities, fancy signage for same safely behind safety-pinned bartenders.

The new landlords were the Destroys.

While usually moonlighting as a rough-as-guts punk band, its members were front-men for an anarchic 'concern' that ran amphetamine drug distribution in this part of the city and, on the side, dabbled with black-market groceries—undercutting government luxury taxes on imported food destined for fancy restaurants, things like truffles and Russian Beluga caviar.

They'd been granted permission from existing underworld fraternity types, so long as they paid a cut of profits—and were willing to oblige by traditions like the Harp.

When Trista arrived, she was met at the entrance by the group's vocalist Chris Destroys.

This was a sharp-faced man in his early thirties, with a recently-dyed, multi-coloured Mohawk, four silver sleepers in each ear as well as one in the right nostril, a set of distressed clothes, and a drawn Colt .32 belly gun in his mitt.

The man who would play the role tonight of neutral referee welcomed Trista with a thorough left-handed pat-down, pistol pointed at her all along, but precious little in the way of conversation.

"Miss Schnorr." He intentionally pronounced it 'snore'.

"Mr. Destroys."

When his fingers began their slow crawl between her thighs, Trista gave the man a proprietary look that stopped him in his tracks.

Though it was obvious he didn't know her from mud, she vividly recalled Destroys from two years before. Guy'd been her dealer, he'd once beaten up her best friend Felice, and she slept with him one time for a fix.

Content she wasn't carrying, the man lowered his weapon to usher her into the bar.

"The Holt party," he said curtly, "isn't here yet."

"Okay. By the way, you missed a spot."

"What?"

"A streak of natural brown, right there," Trista said, pointing to his hair.

That only made the punk scowl more, so she studied

her surroundings.

The minimal furniture, aside from one table, had been pushed to a rear wall, next to an exit sign, for this evening's event. That single table sat in the centre of the cleared room, with one chair placed either side—neither in a position benefitting from the superlative street-front view.

A red-and-white checked paper table-cloth covered the table, and in the middle were placed a carafe of chilled water, a large ceramic ashtray decorated by boxing motifs, two greasy-looking tumblers, and a square plastic Tupperware bowl of peanuts.

Trista stopped gawking once the front door opened with a clatter.

A pint-sized man entered, and then stood still to be checked for weapons.

This newcomer proved difficult to see properly, since he had on a ten-gallon hat, impenetrable sunglasses, and his lower face was tarted-up by a midnight cowboy handle-bar moustache.

Since he was also wearing a black, tassel-sleeved leather motorcycle jacket, with a white string-mesh top beneath and tight black vinyl pants, Trista wondered briefly whether a member of the Village People had stumbled into their lair.

But on closer inspection, there were giveaways aside from diminutive stature: pale, almost luminescent skin, a lot of dark freckles, and a mad grin far from jovial.

He may not have known her—they'd never officially met—but this man had already decided Trista's fate.

"Hullo, dollface," Moore Holt drawled, aviator shades turned in her direction, just as Destroys was concluding his cavity search. "All set to give up the ghost?"

THE RULES OF THE HARP

No one remembered, exactly, when it was that the Harp

became the de facto means to settle scores and iron out differences of opinion between various criminal factions in this city.

Your standard round was played at a designated time on neutral territory, bringing together two assigned 'champions' who were required to be weapons-searched by an armed, third-party adjudicator.

As with similar games like pinochle, binocle, and bezique, the Harp was a trick-taking card game. It also involved melds (think belote), in this case involving a limit of two players (the champions), using a 48-card deck.

In the accepted citywide version of the Harp, four cards were dealt to each player, four placed in the kitty.

The remainder of the deck was placed between the two.

If someone had three nines and no ace, the cards needed to be shuffled and dealt again.

Then, starting with the person not the dealer, players alternated, deciding whether they wanted the first card they drew or a second, as-yet-unseen card. Players both ended up with a thirteen-card hand.

The dealer began by bidding for the kitty. The eventual winner of this bid turned over the four kitty cards, moved them to his hand, and then placed four cards down in his 'capture' pile.

You melded and played—as is the custom in games like pinochle—with one caveat: if a player took all the tricks, they scored the full 25 for play, and the other player scored a zero and had their meld stricken.

There'd been, on occasion, a case where the player who did not take a trick had a capture pile, and that might contain counters, but it was considered unsportsmanlike to reward a perfect play in the Harp, taking it away in two-handed play because of a pre-stocked capture pile.

In an alternate version popular on the west side of the Muir Èireann, where the pastime was said to have originated, twenty cards were handed to each player, with four cards dealt between two piles.

Bidding ensued: the dealer had to bid, beginning at 300 points, and the game proceeded back and forth at a minimum of ten points, but skipping forty and ninety—believed to be unlucky numbers.

The winning bidder chose a pile of four cards and melded their hand as normal. His opposition also melded theirs.

The individual who won the bid was expected to bury four cards that were not used in the meld—and when they chose to bury, 'Triumph!' needed to be declared out loud.

After that, the players did normal trick playing until all the cards were gone. The person who got the last trick received ten bonus points.

You then counted the points between both parties to make sure the bidder made his/her bid.

The major issue with the western variant was that while it could be a laugh to have so many cards available for the meld, it was quite the handful at 20.

What made the citywide Harp fair?

Cheating was difficult, with the two-player system based more on luck than anything else—although a good player seemed always to find a way to beat the other, lesser individual.

Overall, the Harp could be a rip-roaring, fast game for the casual observer.

There was much back-and-forth in the scoring, and the nice thing was that with four extra cards to choose from, your hand could go from bust to brilliant very quickly... or the other way round.

The outcome was usually a winner-take-all affair, leading to an official apology or equally public reparation.

On the odd occasion—the case in tonight's affair—execution of the losing champion was the price to pay, as an example and all that.

As an aside, punters unrelated to affected parties could bet on the outcome of contests, with odds assessed by bookies around the traps. High rollers of all shapes and sizes did love their flutter.

Given such high all-round stakes, this game led occasionally to the odd dispute, using means other than the cards—a break from tradition that was generally frowned upon.

The Harp was supposed to prevent such ugliness.

TRISTA
[JUST AFTER MIDNIGHT—ST. SAMSON'S BAR & GRILL]

*M*oore Holt has thrown the table onto its side. There are cards over the linoleum floor, as well as two smashed glasses, a few lonely ice-cubes, an overturned ashtray, a hat, and uneaten peanuts.

"Cheat!" he screams. "Liar!"

It's straight after the accusations that Trista pulls her pistol—and all hell honestly does bust loose.

TRISTA
[NOW — 12:31 A.M., ST. SAMSON'S BAR & GRILL]

*F*uck, she thinks, vision blurring. This hurts so much.

Fuck.

5

ISSY

[TWO DAYS AGO - CHAPELIZOD HOUSE]

*T*ime was eight o'clock in the morning, obscenely early, yet Issy and Brangien were already late for their dizzy date.

He'd received a telegram the day before. It announced that Lou Holden's funeral service was set for Centerville Memorial Park, proceedings to commence at 11:00 a.m., "with appetizers thereafter"—whatever on earth the sender meant by these.

Issy had nothing in simple black and, suspecting Lou despised his fashion-sense, dressed down in one of the old man's mothballed business suits.

'Anguish' owned hundreds of the things, wrapped in plastic and tissue paper, hanging in his walk-in closet. Issy doubted he'd miss a single one.

This suit had a Saville Row label inside the jacket, it was

a squeeze compared with Issy's regular clothes, and the material smelled musty. He aired it out overnight—after a couple of sprays of Yatagan.

Asked Brangien to purchase him a new white shirt, and topped the lot with a (previously discarded) narrow, wine-coloured tie bearing a knight's head and sun motif. Lou had presented this to his master's son for his fourteenth birthday.

It seemed appropriate, if completely passé.

Sleeping through the alarm was something Issy hadn't quite counted on but should have expected; especially given the morbid, late-night toasts he'd made to the dead man, flying solo drinking Lou's preferred Knappogue Castle.

No surprise, then, that he was dazed and had a hangover.

"C'mon, Issy," Brangien called from a dejected side of the grey gravel driveway where his parents allowed the eyesore of a VW to be parked. "We're way behind schedule."

The man had just chugged down three glasses of water, along with aspirin and a raw egg (a preferred Lou Holden cure for the day after the night before), but sights and sounds still hurt.

"You kidding?" he objected, carefully locking the house's front door. "In that thing? We'll be late to our own funeral.

"Har-de-har."

"Can I walk?"

"Nope. Hop in, lover-boy."

There was a towel on the passenger seat—the Beetle's roof leaked on a regular basis—and its aircon gave up the ghost years before. Even this time of morning, the heat was getting oppressive, especially in this sorry excuse for a tin can. Issy pushed down the window (the winding knob was busted), regretting the tight fit of the suit as much as their choice of wheels.

After the engine sputtered, harrumphed, and then his driver crunched gears, they started to move—bouncing was a better word for it—in the direction of the main road.

Issy glanced at the speedometer. "I know bumper cars faster than this."

"You in a rush to get to Lou's send-off?"

"No. I hate cemeteries."

"You look a treat, by the way."

"Shut up and drive."

An hour was wasted scoffing down an over-fried, oil-soaked breakfast at a diner that had some gall to name itself Quality Street, and then Brangien fussed for thirty minutes more at a market florist's.

Said she was trying to choose the right bouquet.

"We are not—*not*—getting the man a humdrum bunch of Irish clovers. They're hardly flowers. They're plants."

Settling on white orchids, and needing another half-hour to get underway since Brangien flooded the car's engine, the two arrived just before ceremonies began. Once they parked somewhere discreet, Brangien opened the glovebox and handed Issy a small pewter flask with a screw-cap.

"What is it?" Issy asked.

"A hangover cure. Special recipe."

The dram tasted icky, like cough syrup mixed with drain cleaner. Not that Issy had tried drain cleaner, but this was what he imagined it'd smack of.

He pushed the flask back at the woman. "Use the rest to clean your toilet."

Brangien however, ignored him while she ogled herself in a compact mirror and reapplied glossy red lipstick. "You keep it. I'm busy."

Clicking his tongue, Issy tucked the small bottle away in his inside jacket pocket.

They did not bother locking the car.

Holt family priest, Father MacCumhaill, was an old hand at funeral services, and sounded it.

"The future does not belong to the fainthearted; it belongs to the brave," he warbled in a loud, dull voice that had to contest with screams and wails from Lou's widow and three daughters. Otherwise, this place was crowded with mostly unaffected Holt minions and their wives, collectively hamming mournful faces. Some went so far as to blow into their hankies.

"Bunch of hypocrites," Issy muttered.

"Shush."

Brangien hovered beside him, a protective hand holding on his left arm. She wore a big black bonnet on top of her copper curls. The two stood in the shade beneath a tree with blooming orange honeysuckles.

"At least they remember Lou's name. I only ever called him Simon."

"Huh."

Issy felt more scattered than before, and there were odd spots before his eyes.

He also had a curious sensation, like he was adrift from everything around. When he peered at Brangien, he hardly felt more secure—her face could not be clearly seen because of shadows cast by the hat's brim, which fashioned an inky blackness down past her nostrils. The resulting apparition came across morbid.

Looking at the dusty ground on which few blades of grass dared to grow—a majority trampled anyway—Issy chewed his lower lip.

"Most of these people didn't give a shit about Lou. You get that, don't you? They stepped all over him in their rush to Da's inner circle."

Brangien dropped her fingers and nudged him instead. "Look," she nodded covertly, indicating the other side of the closed casket above a large hole, "there's your mum, over with the priest, and your dad behind her. They seem genuinely sad."

Grudgingly, Issy looked over and stopped gnawing. "Good actors," he decided.

Without needing to check, he could feel Brangien glance back up at him, heard the blowing out of cheeks. "Don't be such a sourpuss."

"Whatever."

"All right, be one, then. I'm going for a walk— someone needs to console the merry widow, though I don't know why that responsibility falls to me."

The woman trudged away under her large hat, leaving Issy to scowl a trifle more and light a cigarette—no matter if it wasn't the done thing at a formal church service.

That was when he first laid eyes on *her*.

"I'm sorry for your loss," this newcomer said, stepping close.

Somehow remembering to remove the cigarette, he stared at the woman with a sensation akin to shock, heart hammering in his chest. Honestly? He'd never, ever laid eyes on anyone so dazzling.

God, he thought, she makes funereal attire look somehow magnificent.

"Thanks," he managed to say; hoping the hang-on attempt at a smile didn't come off foolish or awry.

Having paused before him, her long, golden blonde hair snaring morning sunlight in ingenious ways, coming across halo-like, the woman removed sunglasses and looked up. "Could I borrow a cigarette?"

The remarkable hazel eyes there, surrounded by pale skin, finished him.

"So long as you return it," he mumbled, offering an open packet before he had a clue what he was up to.

She selected one, and then leaned forward to receive a light. In accommodating, Issy inhaled a glorious, woody fragrance, jumbled with Moroccan rose, hazel, and a hint of sweat.

"Might be hard to do so," the girl said in blasé fashion, while a small flame licked round the cigarette.

That caused him to wonder. "You from out of town?"

"Different circles." She produced a smile. His heart

now hiccupped. "Thank you."

Straight after, without allowing opportunity for a snatch of further dialogue, the woman strolled off into the sunset—or at least in the direction of the parking lot.

Observing her departure, Issy wanted to call out something, any damned thing, but he couldn't think up a single clever line to holler.

Still, for one brief moment, she looked over her shoulder, their eyes again collided, and he breathed easier. The woman climbed into a classic highland green Ford Mustang—at the very same moment that someone pulled at his sleeve.

"The bitch was awful," griped Brangien, standing again at his side, her big bonnet running interference with Issy's vision. "I don't know why I bothered."

ISSY
[BEFORE 7:00 A.M. YESTERDAY—THE CHURCH OF ST. MICHAEL]

*T*here was actually good reason Issy laid aside thirty-three percent of his illicit financial gains from Disco Inferno.

Once a week, he paid a call on one Elton McMurphy, at a religious house over the river.

He took a cab there every time. This seemed a wiser thing to do than alert his family, their hangers-on, or other (dubiously, Issy believed) interested parties. Besides, he enjoyed the clandestine nature of these trips.

Being a day overdue this week—usually he dropped off the dosh on a Thursday or Friday afternoon—the man found himself up earlier than he had been in years.

While Issy often went to bed, after a night out, at this time, he had absolutely no recollection of rising and shining with Heavenly exuberance.

According to their xeroxed brochure, the church had a soup kitchen shindig from six o'clock every weekend. He'd found himself wide awake at five—mulling over Lou's funeral and that girl with the killer eyes—listening to the Derek and the Dominoes' *Layla and Other Assorted Love Songs*, his first independent music purchase at age thirteen. Not bad that he'd picked up on Eric Clapton before the man became completely famous.

After then watching fifteen minutes of a *Josie and the Pussycats* rerun, Issy went down to the household kitchen to make his own breakfast.

Another first.

Still, how hard was it to stick cornflakes, milk and sugar into a bowl?

After that, he strolled a mile away in half-light, and called a taxi from the payphone near a Golden Fleece service station. When it arrived, the cab driver was a pale-skinned fellow with thinning, white-blond hair. He could've passed for albino, but more likely was of Scandinavian descent. The AM radio, which was turned up loud, had a person sobbing on-air.

"Someone lose their dog?" Issy asked, stifling a yawn.

The driver sat up straight, continuing to look ahead. "You ain't heard the news?"

"No. What?"

"Pope kicked the bucket," said the driver.

Issy leaned forward, stunned. "No. Shit. How?"

"Heart attack. The blamed Micks're all goin' mad." Straight after he said the words, this man glanced into his rear-view mirror. "You're not a Catholic—are you, sir?"

Sitting back, Issy mulled the thought over before speaking. Doubted his parents would care—and he couldn't remember actually having any kind of faith. "Not much of anything."

The cabbie nodded. "You know there was two popes once?"

As a matter of fact, he did. He'd read up the previous year on the papal schism in the 14th and 15th centuries, when several men concurrently claimed to be the true pope. "Your point being?"

"Well, if there was two popes now, wouldn't need to be all this bellyaching over who'll fill the dead bod's boots."

"There is that," he agreed.

Since his watch still played dysfunctional, Issy had no idea what time it was till the taxi pulled up round the block from St. Michael's.

On a Georgian clock tower opposite, Issy was appalled to learn that seven a.m. was thirty-odd minutes away.

"Oh, God," he muttered, and then paid his fare and stepped out.

Thankfully, there were few people on the streets to see him dressed in the same suit he'd worn to the funeral service. Didn't know why, exactly, but he now felt attached to the thing and figured it might've had something to do with the girl.

He'd never heard of a lucky suit—was willing, however, to give it a whirl.

Issy had met this McMurphy character over a year before. The fat man woke him in the early hours of the morning, even so a later time than it was now. He was passed out in a drunken stupor on some street corner or other, Issy couldn't remember where.

Anyhow, McMurphy was kind enough to sit him up, fuss about, and wipe off some of the vomit with a tea towel decorated in Scottish tartans. Made amusing small talk, and then handed him a cup of steaming hot chocolate.

This was in late winter, after all. There was snow on the ground.

Issy was touched, once he was sensible enough to think. While the cocoa tasted awful, this Good Samaritan had possibly saved his life. What was that worn-out missive about the comfort of strangers?

Later, he found a written message tucked into his pocket, so next day, after recovering sufficiently, he telephoned the man to apologize and offer thanks.

And it ought to've ended there.

McMurphy's card, however, sat on Issy's dresser. Some kind of silly remembrance that there existed people worth a damn. The church's address details were also printed on it. After another week, he lost patience with himself and sent Lou over the bridge to look into things.

Via their driver, Issy had been informed of the good deeds that Elton McMurphy and his small band of followers did for the local community. Couldn't account for the feeling, but he was touched. A month on, after money started filtering in from his 'office' work at the club, he determined to set aside one third to help them.

Why one third? He was unsure. Hardly a grand cut, but not penny-pinching either.

Hence his presence here, at an unearthly hour, to deliver their pot of gold.

Issy briskly turned the corner, cut through an open gate in the shadow of this stark old building, and went straight to the side door leading to the basement. Took the stairs three at a time—thereby almost colliding with a hobo on his way out, carrying a cup of tea in his hands. Issy apologized, and took the rest of the steps more cautiously.

In the gloomy basement, which smelled of over-boiled cabbage and urine, his eyes took a moment to adjust. Once they did, however, he couldn't believe them.

About twenty feet away, beyond a horde of derelicts in desperate need of a tailor, the other side of a big table covered in a check-pattern paper cloth—behind large metal cooking pots and an assortment of crockery, cutlery and paper chalices—stood the girl.

The one from Lou's funeral was serving up gruel.

She might've traded dresses (for one green and functional), put on less make-up, and had her hair wrapped up in a gauche paisley number. Her face may have been downturned to the meals she handed out—yet despite all these impediments, Issy knew he'd recognise her anywhere.

TRISTA
[NOW — 12:32 A.M., ST. SAMSON'S BAR & GRILL]

*M*oore Holt ran away.

Well, the man didn't exactly run—he turned tail to jump through the plate-glass window fronting St. Samson's.

That was after she shot him in the forehead.

Only two feet away, and still the bullet didn't penetrate his thick skull.

But, having pulled the trigger once, Trista stopped shooting—giving Holt his moment to gut her. Used a blade as cleverly concealed as her pistol, and then he leapt out the window, shrieking, one more of her slugs striking the man's derrière.

Nobody else remained—Chris Destroys, the adjudicator, had fled at the first sign of trouble.

Which left Trista alone in that empty bar, with its prize-fighters on the wall and a deck of 48 cards spread willy-nilly across the floor—interspersed with cigarette butts, nuts, two bullet casings, a discarded cowboy hat, and spilled blood.

The bay window, smashed, bore a Village Person-sized gaping maw leading onto a deserted street, Nina Hagen cooed low-volume in German on the in-house system, and sounds of sirens drew closer.

Trista's lucky prize? A four-inch hole in her gut.

Already, vision was blurring, the world cascading away. She needed to drag these things back into workable sync, somehow.

Still fell to her knees, swayed, and then forced herself up. *Pull yourself together*. Not just the stomach. Her very wits.

And then confusion reigned.

How did she get to this point again?

There was something—something to do with a round

of trump.

Marcella hovered there, fragmentary, in front of Trista, next to, inside her head. "You're my girl," the matron's voice reverberated, "aren't you?"

Trista blinked rapidly, forcing herself to think as much as push Queenie aside. Cue: a shiv, briefly glinting before her, prior to a quick action of slicing and dicing.

The Harp.

The Harp was what they'd been playing. A contest. She'd shot someone—Moore Holt, it'd been Moore Holt—and she was stabbed in return. Not all her fault. In spite of his killer rep, she hadn't been able to take the arse as seriously as she ought to've.

Then glass, flying everywhere, refracting light, and howls in her ears. Thought it might be Holt's, but realized she was the one crying out.

Huh?

Must've passed out.

Breathing rapidly, shallowly, Trista forced herself back to her feet and tottered.

Upright, pressed against one wall. Tummy in agony, the room spinning. Couldn't fathom how much time had passed.

Sounds now of people other than herself—a crowd out there, beyond the broken window. Knew she needed to pull together, to move, and fast. The rear entrance.

Faster.

ISSY
[YESTERDAY EVENING/NIGHT]

*H*e decided to pop out with Brangien for dinner.

Nothing special about that.

They ran through the typical blather, skimming surfaces, undercutting home-truths. The only real thing Issy could think about was the girl he'd met for ten seconds at a funeral, and otherwise had seen dolloping out morsels to the poor.

Issy didn't know her name, and kicked himself for not thinking to ask McMurphy. Was the first to admit he was overwhelmed, perhaps intimidated, but at least he now knew where she could be found on Saturday mornings.

This untitled enigma remained in mind right through an otherwise superb entrée of colcannon that came with scallions, leeks, onions and chives, a side dish of Dublin Lawyer, and several tins of imported ale.

Most of what Brangien gushed about sped in one oblivious ear and fled the other. While she made partial inroad by repeatedly insisting he go with her to Disco Inferno—it was Saturday night, after all—he declined.

Saw off the woman before midnight, a farewell sealed with a peck to the lips, after which Issy ended up wandering streets. Couldn't say why, not exactly. He should've been exhausted after waking up so insanely early, and had never before turned down the opportunity to pick up at his father's club.

12:45 a.m. found him outside Holt jurisdiction, down the road from a certain place he knew. One of those new punk-rock joints, where they dressed shabbily and played poorly performed music far too loud.

Yet Issy liked the dissolute nature of St. Samson's, and they served a particularly good Celtic Crossing.

Him being restless and in the neighbourhood, the man decided to drop by for a couple of shots—a nightcap, and all that jazz.

ISSY
[NOW — 12:46 A.M., ST. SAMSON'S BAR & GRILL]

To be honest, he had no real clue what to make of the scene.

For starters, there's broken glass on the pavement in front of the bar, and splashes of red nearby that looked worryingly like blood.

To be sure, this could've been debris from your regular barroom brawl, he understood that. Hadn't been so sheltered he never witnessed one—his people were mostly Irish, remember?—but the number of police cars (eight, at a quick tot-up) hinted otherwise, at something pushing major.

The time? No idea. Busted-watch syndrome.

Paramedics from two squads had taken over parts of the street left unoccupied by visiting constabulary.

Christmas lights flashing, all reds and blues, with the usual associated presents, such as coppers in uniform—touting drawn revolvers.

Guessed he'd have to skip the drink.

Suddenly, from a dark alleyway close to Issy's right, an individual lurched straight at him. He had time to raise hands defensively, is also about to holler for assistance, but—no.

No.

This isn't not some random assailant. He's seen her face, desperately pale in the streetlight, a rotating red flashing across it and making her eyes sparkle.

It's the girl—the one from the cemetery.

Now so close to him that his arms automatically fold around her narrow frame. Someone he met once, saw from a distance another time. One moment he was alone, vexed, dissatisfied, thirsty. The next? Embracing, hugging for all that's worth—and more, besides.

At some stage, amidst sirens, that harsh illumination, and entwined smells of stale liquor and hazelnut, beyond her breath passing across his cheek, lips briefly touching his, the absolute perfection of the moment in spite of an obscene array of distractions, Issy understands the truth.

As obscure and ridiculous as it may seem? He loves her.

Next up?—He intuits that she's dying.

TRISTA
[NOW — 12:47 A.M., ST. SAMSON'S BAR & GRILL]

Not because she's decided to give up the ghost—no way.

She clutches onto this person for dear life. Needs to use him, whoever it might be. This stranger, a possible meal ticket out of the here and now.

Strong-arms herself to stay conscious. Leans in close and cosy.

Fact is she can barely stand. Over his shoulder Trista observes cops and bystanders all about. Her brain is muddled, woozy. The agony in her gut towers above everything.

Suffering, under that, through broken-record thoughts of Governal, of how he might feel were he to learn she slipped up and failed years of training.

Defective flashes of Marcey's Doc Bedier scattershot her brain, a hack with a maroon velvet bowtie, greasy hair slapped over the pate, and shifty eyes you'd never, ever trust—'less you had no choice. A doctor disbarred by the state for malpractice (surprise), but one indebted to her boss.

She manages to stay close by the taut flesh of the man's throat, mumbles, "Can you," in a voice that doesn't sound like her own, "take me—you know—to a doctor I know?"

This saving grace holds Trista's face with both hands, leaning in close. His words depth charge everything.

"Yes, yes, of course. But we'll do one better—I'll take you to my mam."

Which is precisely when it hits her, slices deeper that Moore Holt's blade, through pain and confusion and madness.

She recognizes the speaker and that chin wagging right

before her eyes. Comprehends whose arms she's stumbled into, that this 'stranger' is actually somebody she knows all about, and recently met.

Isidor Holt, Jr.

Son of this city's primo shithead, and nephew of the lout she placed a couple of caps into—promising (so earnestly) to take Trista to his mother, Alaina Holt. Wife of this town's #1 arsehole—and sister of the man she just shot.

Holy shit, crosses Trista's mind.

Somehow—Somehow—she remembers to thrust her purse his way, the one with the Henrike Vogl ID.

Swoons straight after.

6

ALAINA

Alaina Holt made sure of being present when the ambulance pulled up outside Emergency.

She paid scant attention, however, while three paramedics clambered out to wheel in their patient, intercepted inside sliding doors by the casualty staff. These people were excellently trained, and meet-and-greet appeared nowhere on her job description.

On the other hand, the presence of young Issy, walking behind the new arrivals, *was* her responsibility.

Wearing a black suit, with darker patches on his jacket likely caused by blood, he seemed frazzled and his face deathly pale—the spitting image of the boy's voice over the phone twenty-five minutes earlier.

He'd woken his mother, blathering down the line,

103

caused her to sit up in bed and tell the boy to calm himself. She could hear Isidor Senior snoring in the next room, kept her tone low.

Alaina then got dressed straight away, and had their new driver Mary whisk her over.

This woman prattled incessantly the entire trip into town, exhausting her passenger. Gulping down two strong espressos prior to the ambulance's arrival, Alaina was still trying to properly awake, not to mention shake off the effects of last night's merlot.

"You need to help," Issy said to her now, very earnestly, pushing anguish and plaintive eyes.

His mother nodded. "I'll do what I can."

"Please."

"Issy, sit down before you fall down."

"No. Not until I know she's going to be okay."

"That could be several hours. What's wrong with you? Anyone might think Queen Mab paid a visit. Sit."

Her son slumped onto the nearest orange plastic chair. He looked exhausted. "Can you do it?" came out of his mouth.

"I don't know. I have no idea. I'll need to see the patient's charts, assess her condition." She looked down at her son. "This *is* a woman, correct?"

"Uh-huh."

"Drugs?"

"No!"

Alaina glanced over a partition at a group of people surrounding the trolley—all speaking fast, checking ABC, inspecting the body, organizing medication, taking notes. "We need to stabilize and reduce the bleeding before treating the injury," someone wisely shouted.

Having returned gaze to her boy, Alaina frowned. "So who is she?"

"I don't know."

"I'm sorry?"

"I said, I don't know."

"Well, what happened?"

"I don't know."

Alaina felt like shaking this good-for-nothing, yet buried the impulse. "So what *do* you know?"

"There's so much blood."

"That much is apparent."

"I think she's dying, Mam."

"Enough nonsense, Isidor. Leave the verdicts to me. Does this girl at least have insurance? We're not a charity organization here."

Which was the moment the boy appeared to remember something worthwhile at last. He checked his jacket, first took out a tiny hipflask, pocketed it again, and then produced a purse, a beige pigskin number. "There's this."

The thing had bloody fingerprints.

With a measure of distaste, Alaina opened the purse up, straight after inspecting contents. "Henrike Vogl. She's a foreigner?"

"I have no idea."

"German? My, your father would throw a tantrum— you know how much he hates them."

"Mam. Please."

"Yes, yes. I'll see what the staff can ferret up concerning our Miss Vogl. Sounds German. In the meantime, I want you to stay right here. Do you understand? Issy—do you understand?"

"Yeah."

Sounding at wit's end like he did, the boy provoked a level of sympathy Alaina believed she'd moved beyond. Without second thought, she laid a hand atop his head. "Yes?"

"Yes."

Nine-and-a-half minutes later, Alaina had finished checking notes (a puncture wound produced by the stabbing motion of a knife or similar object, and subsequent penetrating abdominal trauma; evidence of significant intra-abdominal injury with probable vascular trauma), changed into a hospital gown, and was scrubbing up.

In another minute, a nurse she didn't know was placing surgical gloves over her fingers, even as she decided the best course of action (textbook stuff: performing emergency surgery to repair damaged tissue or organs, and remove objects that penetrated the skin), so as to salvage the life of a stranger her son had begged her to save.

Still, Alaina wondered if the patient had any medical insurance.

"We're checking for blood type and cross-match, Doctor Holt," said an elderly assistant she did recognize, but whose name she had forgotten.

"BUN and serum creatinine levels too?"

"Of course, Doctor. ABG, and the other usual laboratory testing."

Alaina nodded. "Very well. Let's proceed. And for fuck's sake, find out if an insurer's going to foot the bill."

ISSY
[2:37 A.M.—ST. MAIGNENN'S HOSPITAL]

Over an hour in a hard plastic chair, surrounded by night-shift staff who scuttled about doing their chores—and having re-read boring details on a patient services poster (held up by different coloured thumbtacks) far too many times to count—was enough.

Issy lurched up, stretched his back, swivelled hips, peered at the bright, white ceiling—and silently prayed. There was a first for everything, it seemed.

Henrike.

He'd been mulling over the name since first he learned it.

On the PA system, they had Tchaikovsky's '1812 Overture' on repeat, a sound track punctured by occasional announcements instead of cannon fire. Hearing the composition multiple times over, conjoined with the smell of the hospital, made Issy queasy.

A scattering of magazines on a nearby tabletop didn't help, since most were ancient, and he worried about bacteria invested in their pages.

Still, one of them, titled *Rock Superstars*, attracted attention since it had Pete Townsend on the cover and promised coverage of The Who's 1975 tour—Issy'd gone with Brangien to one of those performances while celebrating her eighteenth—but the frontispiece further listed an interview with Rod Stewart, and he recoiled.

When at last Issy inquired of one of the nurses—a woman with a white skirt far too short for long legs—whether Brangien might be about, she checked a duty-roster and said it was her colleague's night off.

Caused him to wonder where he'd parked his brain. He already knew that. Brangien had told him over dinner an eternity ago—was, by now, having a grand old time at the Disco Inferno.

Other ambulances came, parked, and left, ushering in people with broken bones, alcohol poisoning, and a man with a suspected appendicitis.

There was also one 'B&T', which an edgy young intern explained meant 'Bagged and Tagged'—a body ready for dispatch to the morgue.

ISSY
[8:14 A.M.—ST. MAIGNENN'S HOSPITAL]

That B&T ended up being his uncle Moore.

Issy found out later, didn't know what to feel.

Now, however, the news was ancient. Sunshine streams through a single window—one recently cleaned, given its clarity and sparkle—and pools beside the steel cot in which a girl lay.

She could be mistaken for sleeping, if not for the

ventilator stuck in her mouth and various drips and tubes crisscrossing the bed.

The sunlight's soft afterglow draws attention to gloriously pale skin and this girl's golden blonde hair, which conspired to partially obscure her closed eyes with their long lashes.

Issy cannot tear his away.

Helen of Sparta, he'd decided, had zero on Henrike Vogl—too beautiful as she was for the Spartan trappings of a modern hospital. And, yes, he straight after felt a ridiculous waking joke for thinking such things, but didn't give a flying toss.

Having adopted a seat between window and bed—a blue vinyl armchair far more welcoming than the orange one in Emergency—Issy now sat with hands clasped.

Over by the closed door to this private room stood his mother Alaina.

Arms crossed, she was back to civvies. Looked very tired, yet still bore a stethoscope round the neck.

Issy could tell the woman pined for a glass or more of vino—not that he was capable of paying his mam much attention, aside from having expressed gratitude.

"So," he says, leaning forward, trying to get closer to the patient without making it overly obvious, "will she live?"

Moments pass before Alaina responds. When she does, her voice is hollow.

"Issy."

"Yes?"

"You know her fingerprints were all over the gun that killed Moore?"

He frowns. "So?"

"So—this Vogl woman, the one you implored me to save, in all likelihood murdered your uncle last night."

"Did you?"

"What?"

"Save her, I mean?"

"Of course I did."

Issy's hands came up to rub his face. "Thank God," he mumbles, causing his mother to gawk at him.

Then he adds:

"You rescued her."

MARCELLA
[7:34 A.M.—TINTAGEL APARTMENTS]

"*W*e need to locate Trista."

"Governal," said Marcella, standing before French doors that overlooked the swimming pool and garden, her hand stroking a lace curtain, back to her visitor, "you overly worry. You saw this morning's papers. Moore Holt is dead."

"And where's our girl that did this favour?"

The woman turned only her head. Lines no doubt furrowing the brow, she consigned reasonably stern eyes upon the man in the doorway. "That's rich, coming from *you*."

Governal, as usual, unaccountably held Marcella's glare. "Meaning?"

"Well—you're her guardian. Not I."

There was not a noticeable shift in the man's expression. A minor narrowing of the eyes.

Still, Marcella shied away.

"Don't look at me like that," she complained. "You have no right." After letting the curtain go, she frowned. "I had Geoffrey check with all hospitals in the area. No one has been admitted under the name of Ludia Schnorr—alive or dead. So I'd say our girl's lying low, bless her."

The man's silence continued to be unnerving.

"All right then. How about that judge fellow?"

GOVERNAL
[7:35 A.M.—TINTAGEL APARTMENTS]

*"H*ow about that judge fellow?" Marcella says. "What was his name?"

She places gold-framed spectacles atop her nose, and turns to peer at a bound book on the desk that might be a diary.

"He would have witnessed everything. Here we go." The woman jabs a finger at one page. "Chris Destroys? What a ridiculous handle."

Governal almost allows a smile. No more ridiculous than 'Anguish' Holt, 'Duke' Morgan, or 'The Norwegian'. One reason he'd skipped out on a ridiculous nickname, unless you considered 'Gov' to be one—but he allowed only Trista and a single other person to call him that.

"No one seems able to locate the man," he answered easily. No point telling Marcella yet that Destroys' body was floating in the bay. Time for that later.

He'd already located Trista too, under her other alias Henrike Vogl—admitted to St. Maignenn's in the early hours. Understood that, while the overall condition remained serious, they expected her to recover.

But he couldn't go visit, known as he was in the west, and St. Maignenn's being Alaina Holt's own hospital. Had sent an associate instead to keep an eye on things, while he worked a hunch here.

Thing was, Governal hated hunches.

He needed to know, one way or another, the truth. And this hunch concerned Marcella Cornwall's behaviour of late.

Maybe she was a percentage point beneath the usual level of rage because of advancing years. Perhaps the woman was concerned about a family member. Maybe, just maybe, she'd lost a little of her nerve.

The maybes and perhapses irritated him, granting

something to focus on while Trista lay beyond a direct ability to help.

With Destroys out of the way, there was nobody alive to finger Henrike Vogl as the Ludia Schnorr who turned up to represent Marcella Cornwall, against the also-deceased Moore Holt, in a game of the Harp.

From his police sources, he'd learned that fingerprints were an issue, put out the fiction that Henrike was an illegal immigrant: an underpaid part-time cleaner at St. Samson's, who might have inadvertently handled the weapon involved in Holt's demise.

Governal already had the bureaucratic paperwork filed.

Meanwhile, what of Queenie?—Another ridiculous nickname.

BRANGIEN
[NOW—HER FLAT, ON ANGLESEY DRIVE]

She huddles in the centre of the double bed, atop a quilt that's decorated with conjoined yellow rainflowers and carnations.

Dressed in a tank top and shorts, muddy Converse sneakers—without socks—still on, Brangien has her face buried in her hands.

There's a box of Kleenex nearby, about a million scrunched-up tissues littering the bed and the floor, while an empty box of Moctezuma Chocolates lies pillaged beside her knee.

The blind is closed, the small room dark. It's difficult to make out the disco and pop star posters plastered over most available wall space, or the large shrine of photos of she and Issy that takes up a hefty remaining chunk above the dressing table.

For the first time in months, the stereo lies dormant.

The woman lowers hands, wipes mascara off cheeks, and then tugs on her lower lip a little violently. Allows it to

111

flip back at her teeth. Stares at the two fingers responsible, eventually rubbing them together to remove traces of red lipstick.

She had followed Issy the night before.

Couldn't say why, not exactly.

Maybe it was her best friend's distracted, distant behaviour over dinner? She'd like to infer that the key motivator was concern, but suspicion and distrust rang closer.

Hence, she'd tirelessly bird-dogged his long city stroll.

Had seen him embrace that other woman, and then carry her, unconscious, to the closest ambulance.

Witnessed, from across the street, the expression on his face.

7

TRISTA

*T*hings drift through. In dreams, she surmises—deluding herself.

Fragmentary, over-simplified moments, shades of Tristan Tzara splicing them together in his arthritic dotage, after one too many Luis Buñuel surrealist martinis—the duffer.

There's a drip-dripping sound, very regular, exceptionally annoying.

The world seems sticky and hot.

Bugger, she thinks, somewhere at the back of her mind.

Nothing else properly sinks in.

Sticky, sweltering—check. It also feels like it's raining and sunny at the same time, as if the middle of autumn. There's falling flora, a grey/blue sky, and a child looking

113

from mist that rears in the surroundings.

Eyes everywhere, taking place of tumbling leaves.

Years back. She does intuit that.

The evidence? A familiar/forgotten double-storey weatherboard house, built in Dutch Colonial Revival style. That broad gambrel roof with eaves flaring out over the long sides makes the house still resemble a barn; the sight causes an ache in her heart, along with a degree of apprehension. So, too, does the wrap-around verandah, a later addition built by Trista's papa.

A thousand-odd Licca-chan dolls dance around the edges, peripheral touches, climbing and marching and lingering—but when she focuses upon them they vanish.

Instead, leaves and eyes blow about this place in a stiff breeze.

None of Dalí's burning giraffes to speak of, but there are earthier garbage bags strewn across a lawn that has grass thirty inches tall, and an overgrown garden too. Dead milk cartons and plastic bags are snagged in that helter-skelter.

A Hills Hoist clothesline rotates at unnatural speed—fanned by wind catching in haggard, sun-bleached garments washed and hung six months ago on lines once taut, now sagging in forlorn ways.

Clothes put through a rinse-cycle six months before—the afternoon prior to Trista's father's death.

Closer to this house, the heart loses most pang. Reality, or this morphine-addled substitute, shifts and bends. Memories segue darker, mining depressed spaces, since the home, once Heaven, slipped into an abyss.

What did this mean? Living with a suicidal, inebriated, TV-addicted mother in a rundown shit heap that used to be their castle.

Stilted images stutter past, mimicking stop-motion camera work: Blanche in a stained pink terry-towelling robe, blonde hair tangled and knotted, lying atop a couch. Alternating between drunken hysterics, laughing until she cried, and real tears while howling at the ceiling.

A leaf—or was it another amputated eye?—flitters past Blanche's face as she settles upon vague stupor, a chipped mug of sherry ready at her lips. She's attempting to focus on the telly, alternating laughter and the occasional hiccup, watching *Steptoe and Son*.

Enter: a shade, a rearing god-man's, too fantastic to squeeze through the doorway from the hall, which anyway rested at a bizarre right angle.

"Blanche," booms this intruding spirit.

Our woman pauses mid-sup, hardly fearful, since her gaze is still fixed on the telly. "Oh," she mumbles. "Hello, DuBois."

Observing this awkward transaction is a girl of four, going on five.

Peeking down from her hiding place on the mezzanine, obscured by a white wooden balustrade. She cowers lower, terrified of what might be witnessed crossing their threshold.

When it enters, however, this house-calling bogeyman loses all vestige of mystery.

In fact, he's a bland, unimposing half-pint, one that sports a sharp nose and a terribly small chin.

His tan suit, the little girl decides, is the same colour as diarrhoea.

This man has two similarly brown paper bags (large, full ones) tucked beneath each arm.

"Dammit, Blanche," he grouses, voice reminiscent of a jockey's.

Her mother raises the fractured chalice in a quarter-hearted salute, eyes glued to Harry H. Corbett in monochrome on the screen.

"Just leave the groceries," she says. "I'm not feeling social." (There's a loud hiccup.)

The man's comeback is anaemic: a comical sigh, behaving like the weight of the known world lingers on those poo-tinted shoulders.

Just as the child Trista had to cover her mouth with both hands to smother laughter, she senses an authentic fellow beside her.

Turns quickly to find that this is, indeed, so.

He stands a few inches away, partially blending with shadows. Left hand on the railing, a telltale lit cigarette in his right one, while he watched the mundane soap opera of Blanche and DuBois.

"How you doing, Trista?" comes his voice in a low, gravelly tone. This man had been decanted into a dark suit with flecked-wool detailing, the white shirt bearing a skinny tie in a blue foulard pattern—making him resemble Rod Serling at the start of each episode of *The Twilight Zone*.

Trista liked to stay up to watch that on Friday nights with her mother, depending on whether the woman had passed out. Not for the first time, the child wonders how he got into position next to her without making a sound—there was something *Twilight Zone*-ish about that too, but it made her happy.

"Governal," she whispers, old and wise enough to know to keep her voice soft. "Did you bring me more books? More crayons?"

"Hm. 'Fraid not, love." He doesn't remove eyes from the unfolding spectacle downstairs. Takes a slow drag on his fag. A trail of smoke settles her way, but most is exhaled toward the ceiling. "You've gone through the others already?"

"Yeah!" The girl can't repress a giggle.

Anyway, her mum and DuBois were too busy bickering about something—the TV set had been switched off, so this is unsurprising.

DuBois says, in a hard-nosed whine, "Blanche."

"What?" shrieks Trista's mother, physically upright now, and cranky.

The child, beside Governal, automatically recoils—a recent habit.

"What, DuBois?" Blanche adds, more controlled, even if unaware they were being observed. "*What?*"

Turning away, Governal kneels on the carpet before Trista, like he's all set to propose. She thinks he has the most beautiful smile.

"Listen in. I have some questions for you, angel," he says, a blend of noble and reassuring—like the white knight in a cartoon she loved. "Hope you don't mind."

Trista responds somewhat bashfully. "That's okay."

"Good girl."

"Is there a prize?"

"Sure, I'll shout you ice cream."

"Chocolate?"

"Whatever you like."

"Okay."

"All set?"

"Mm."

"So—number one. Let's start easy. How tall is the man down there?"

"I'm sorry?"

"How tall is he?"

"Don't know—five-feet, eight inches... maybe?"

"How tall am I?"

"Kneeling?"

His smile broadens. "Standing."

"Oh, *um*, about six-one."

"When is Blanche's birthday?"

"April 21st."

"Your impression of DuBois?"

"Silly!"

Governal nods. "You have a canny gift for details."

"Was I right?"

"Close enough, kid."

"Not a kid anymore. I'm almost five."

"I stand, or squat, corrected."

"I'll let you marry me when I'm eight."

"Then I am a lucky man. Tell me, Trista, what age

would you say I might be?"

"I don't know. *Old*?"

A frown creases Governal's previous calm.

"Huh. Maybe I overestimated your finesse. I'm only thirty-four."

Straight after, he flicks his head toward the bedrooms on the upper floor.

"Now," he says, "why don't you go put some dresses and things together in your room. You'll find a suitcase there. It's yours now."

Thinking of her mother, Trista glances below.

DuBois has started to pace, hands clasped behind the back. With his posture and that beak, he resembled, in profile at least, a vulture striding across their living room floor.

"It's time," the vulture dictates to her mother, "to start figuring things out."

Trista pays no attention to Blanche's response. 'Time to start figuring things out' sounded peachy to her. Maybe DuBois wasn't so silly?

"Are we," she murmurs, "so, are we *going* somewhere?"

Governal leans back on haunches, looking her over with an honesty she'd remember to the grave.

"Sure, kid, sure. We're going on an adventure."

The flaky dream sequence closed itself up into blackness then.

TRISTA
[GOVERNAL'S PREVIOUS RESIDENCE, LION'S ESTATE — 15 YEARS AGO]

*S*he'd been almost five.

That special occasion came three weeks after moving in with her little suitcase.

Didn't celebrate her fifth in the presence of either her papa (murdered last summer) or mother—who had remarried a few days before (to Marshal 'DuBois' Rohault), and was still off in the Bahamas on her honeymoon.

Since Trista had no other family, aside from an auntie never met, she blew out candles with Governal for company.

Her one wish? That this saving grace would turn around and wed *her*.

While his home—now theirs—wasn't near so grand as her parents' in its hey-day, this was far cleaner and more welcoming than what Trista had got used to over the past months.

A single-storied brick dwelling, it had been painted off-white, in need of a recoat. There was a discreet little porch at the front, covered with climbing bright green ivy, and a brass nameplate next to the door, *Morrois Duff*, that had corroded a similar green.

The little girl loved it. Having the birthday bash there, with a single VIP guest, suited her just fine.

After finishing slices of a sponge cake overloaded with mock cream, Trista leaned on the kitchen table to watch her new mentor's party trick: taking apart a revolver and explaining how it worked.

"This is the firing pin," he said, focused on his task, "and this here, see? We call it the cylinder."

Observing Governal disassemble, and then resurrect, said firearm was like being privy to a magician who gradually revealed trade secrets.

Maybe, Trista later thought, he explained everything from the beginning because he suspected what could be in store.

That would answer why, five days after that birthday, he took her into the back yard to show how to aim and shoot a Colt .45 automatic.

Though Governal lived in the outer suburbs—his nearest neighbour's place was two hundred feet away—he'd thoughtfully screwed on a silencer.

And, since it was a bright day, they lingered in the

shade of a sixty-foot Cornish Red rhododendron.

"Stand with feet apart," he advised concisely, while she deliberated about biting her nails. "Arm straight." The man then raised the gun to demonstrate. "You might never need this, but better to know." He fired once, and a bottle exploded forty yards away.

Alternatively, Governal didn't have any clue what to do with a girl.

***

Either way, over the next seven years Trista's ad hoc father trained her as best he could, which was something.

Dedicated his life—and appeared to have shelved a career—to cultivate the child. Initially refused to let on why (that revelation came later), and never acted the self-sacrificial prima donna.

He taught her not only about shooters and shivs, but accounting, bookkeeping, history, art, classic novels, cooking, even science.

The science, admittedly, boiled down to weapons again.

Governal gave lessons on making explosives by combining gasoline with ammonium nitrate (the fertilizer used to feed his prized Mexican vanilla orchids), or vinegar with baking soda.

One Easter they spent hours, first making egg-shaped replicas of the World War II Russian RGD-5 anti-personnel fragmentation grenade, packed with black gunpowder, and after that painting them festive colours to place about the house.

When she was ten, Trista's yuletide present was one she had to earn.

Having taught all that year how to hot-wire different kinds of automobiles, Governal drove to a Ford showroom, jimmied the door, and pointed to her 'gift': a brand new, highland-green 1969 Mustang GT 390.

Trista was in love, thanked Santa, and had the vehicle

purring in seconds.

These things, of course, took place outside regular school hours—which Governal insisted she attend. He dropped Trista there and was waiting to pick her up after the bell rang. Extracurricular training started in the car journeys home.

Toward midnight, seven days a week, they'd indulge in a one-hour session of what Governal liked to call 'Rollick Time'.

This involved two or three rounds of cards over a bowl of ice cream in the kitchen.

The dessert was homemade, something the man delighted in creating. Most evenings, Governal would experiment with different flavours, using a variety of fruit, nuts, herbs, spices, seeds, even vegetables and meat fats.

The kitchen, Trista learned quickly, was his favourite room in the house.

There were six others hardly used, aside from functional activities like sleeping, toiletries, and storage, while the windowless hallway served as a thoroughfare from front door to the kitchen, which sat at the back of the house, beyond a brick archway.

They ate in that kitchen, listened to the radio there, talked, joked, and conjured up bombs.

It may not have been much—think rough, unpainted brick walls, with worn linoleum flooring—and looked like it belonged to someone's grandmother.

There was a vintage green-and-white Camelot-brand gas oven, one kitsch cuckoo clock that didn't work (his *Third Man* touch, Governal alleged), a wooden herb rack, a portable TV, various pots and pans (blackened from use) hanging from hooks, a small transistor radio in brown leather casing, and shelving that sagged because of age and the amount of books (plus other objects) placed atop.

These things coated in a layer of grease from cook-offs they had.

Similarly tainted, the curtains at two windows either

side, north and south, hung faded to the point you could no longer tell what kind of flowers were included in the design. Maybe sweet briars. Real ones sometimes bloomed in the planter directly outside the window to the south, adding an apple-like fragrance to the room.

Otherwise, the smell here was a miraculous combination of milk, chocolate, gun oil, paper, metals, vanilla, and coffee beans.

The only contemporary furnishings?

An annual Pan Am calendar—courtesy airline freebies, boasting glamorous stewardesses and pilots—and the sparkling coffee maker Governal always polished.

Trista did school homework at the large, rectangular kitchen table, a varnished Victorian antique sitting at the centre of the room. In the exact same position, she assembled and tore apart various guns and, one time, made gelignite.

On the other side of this table, Governal gave lectures, demonstrations, or otherwise cooked and crafted ice concoctions.

They would road test the results before midnight, in that kitchen, over cards—with the radio switched to a station spinning jazz tunes.

Their games included pinochle, twenty-one, gin rummy, truco, and one-eyed jack. When he was particularly happy with Trista's progress, Governal allowed old maid or snap.

From day one, life was never made easy for his young opponent—this man was excellent at all things cards-related, and played to win. Trista had no success with a single hand until age nine. She lost count of losses while they still numbered in the hundreds.

Once she turned eleven, after culling four cards from the deck, Governal introduced a new game he called the Harp.

Also primed-up his protégée on a social 'philosophy' to digest while they played.

"I don't get it," Trista said after, eyeing her cards.

"The game, or the idea?"

"Both?—But mostly the philosophy thing." She made her play, and immediately regretted it once the man effected his.

"What's not to get?" he murmured over a cigarette in the side of his mouth, as he nodded to the sounds of Cal Tjader.

"Well, you know."

"Pretend I don't."

"Um." The girl fiddled with cards, flexing one.

"Don't bend them," Governal warned. "Some people mistake that for cheating."

"Oops. Sorry." Trista placed her hand carefully on the table, face-side down, and looked across. "Gov... Shouldn't people still like me, even if I don't play this Harp game?"

"Sure, they should."

"But won't?"

"Look at it this way." He mimicked her gesture with the cards, and killed the fag. "They'll pretend to, because of your family connections. You must make people genuinely dig you, Triss. If people like you enough, they'll tell you anything."

"Is that important?"

"It will be."

Trista had placed her left elbow on the table, slouched forward, and placed her chin in the palm while listening.

"By the way," Governal added, giving her an extra scoop of pumpkin-and-caraway-seed ice cream, "you're tipping your mitt with that bad posture. A poor hand?"

"Awful."

"Bad as the ice cream?"

"Not your best." Trista toyed with orange gunk in a bowl.

"Yeah, I think the caraway seeds were pushing the envelope."

"Can I ask you something else?"

"Sure."

"Am I supposed to make *everyone* like me?"

"Hell, no, that's impossible. Only the ones you need."

"How do I know who I need?"

"Trust me—you will."

"And the rest?"

"We have to keep them on their toes, off-balance—wavering between knowledge and ignorance. Cause them to fret about where, precisely, you stand."

TRISTA
[LION'S ESTATE — 1972]

'*F*amily connections', that was what he threw out there, maybe without allowing adequate consideration—though with Governal, this was hard to believe.

Family. What a funny word.

By the age of twelve, Trista could count on the one hand how many times she'd seen her mum since Governal took the girl on seven years before.

Given her father was dead, and Blanche's sister too busy to give a niece the time of day since she was born, the only tangible family Trista had were Governal, his lectures, a shit-load of books in the kitchen, the man's ice cream recipes, assorted dolls he brought back from trips to Japan, and his guns.

In 1972, pushing fourteen, she had met her mother one time more. Otherwise, same life story.

That year, Governal took advantage of his connections with Boss Tanaka—the kumichō of a Nagasaki syndicate—and through them organized visas and a travel itinerary, so that he could whisk her away on the first vacation she'd had since a beach trip with the parents: two weeks in the Land of the Rising Sun, birthplace of Licca-chan, and a chance to flex her Japanese language skills.

They went to the opening of the Winter Olympics in

Sapporo, and then travelled down to Tokyo—first by ferry, after that bullet train—where she witnessed one thousand Liccas collected together at a doll museum in Yokohama.

In the evening the same day, at a new-fangled sushi train restaurant in Ginza, they met a trio of Governal's local acquaintances.

One of these being a beautiful woman, forty-odd but looking younger named Kohana. She walked with a cane ("Got myself recently stabbed," this lady said, nonplussed, in very good English). Another was an elderly thespian called Shimura-san (there with Kohana) who reminded Trista of a cuddly teddy bear, and then there was rambunctious thug Tanaka, up from Kyūshū—to whom even Governal played deferential.

The Japanese party consumed more saké than raw fish. Trista and Governal stuck to water. Still, she did get to talk with this Kohana lady, who remained completely sober and advised her, over a mesmerizing smile, that, "These men like to believe they run things, but really it's us doing so."

That night, the woman escorted Trista (alone— Governal feigned a headache) to see a traditional puppet theatre known as Bunraku.

Kohana had changed into a dark, elegant kimono decorated with rippling water, bamboo and birds. The performance was called *Sonezaki Shinjū*, which Kohana translated as 'The Love Suicides at Sonezaki'.

"It's by Chikamatsu," the woman whispered, prior to the show commencing. "The most popular of his domestic love tragedies, first performed in 1703."

These elaborately dressed puppets, each of which was usually manipulated by three people, were only part of the package. A sweating chanter, up on a swivelling podium to the right of stage, recited dialogue for all the characters— young and old, male or female, warriors and townspeople—and also seemed to be relating the spectacle of each scene and explaining the events taking place. Next to him, a blasé shamisen player twanged away, accompanying a drama Trista couldn't get her head around.

While hoping she covered well, that bewilderment must have been obvious.

"Worry not," Kohana said in a soft, clear voice beneath the ruckus. "Half the time, I don't understand—and, in this case, all sadly ends in a suicide pact."

Next day, a remarkably recovered Governal took her to Yasukuni Shrine.

On the train there, he said, "I love this country," and then paused. "Yet it's important for you to see the flipside of human nature—how here they can glorify war as well."

"What about Kohana?" Trista murmured. "Do you love her? I would."

Governal smiled wistfully. "We've had our moments."

***

Around this point in growing up, Trista experienced another kind of emotional flux.

Physically, she was getting tall, the crown of her head having reached Governal's shoulder. Her body had sprouted long, skinny legs, just as baby fat about the face started to diminish and an adult beauty slid through.

A nascent sense of pride matched these emergent looks, one fuelled by boys at school and on street corners who stared at her and looked needy. By older men, running eyes along her pins when she wore a short skirt, wolf whistling at safe distance.

It was ego that spilled over into something ungamely, a kind of arrogance.

Yet beneath the veneer continued to reside an individual with precious little faith in self, a fledgling woman who might've been filling out and extending in all the right places, but otherwise represented an emotional minefield.

These munitions being the anger Trista had pruned since age four, tea bagged by bitterness and resent. Still young, believed she was all grown up, could not hope to be in such circumstances, and more than a little wild.

A handful for Governal, Trista understood that later, but he battened down and put up with the lot.

Tried to do so by keeping her focused and grounded. To intuit, through the fog of frustration, that while being proud had vital moments, she needed to avoid becoming its slave. Better, he insisted, to nurture humility if she were to truly succeed.

"*Succeed at what?*" she demanded to know, this far more often.

Starting arguments, something that rarely happened when Trista was an enamoured, worshipful child, became the norm—making most ideas Governal posited fair game to be contested or more frequently ignored.

This teenager also began exploring her budding sexuality and the power she believed that granted. She therefore painted toenails while sitting in a languorous position, wearing hot pants. Took longer to clean the ice cream from lips with her tongue.

Governal, however, appeared immune.

He'd frown on the odd occasion, remain mum at others, threw out the stray opinion, but anyway hunker down to plough on with training.

TRISTA
[THE FARM — 1973]

*I*n the midst of these times—an era Governal once had the cheek to label their 'Blue Period', riffing less on Picasso than slang for a fight—he and Trista walked an uneven dirt path across a Cornwall property in the countryside.

This dilapidated oasis was called O'Roark's, or just The

Farm.

All round were rolling, dusty fields where not much survived aside from stunted stringy barks and mats of interwoven alligator grass that crept over the dry soil.

"It never surprises me," Governal had commented to Trista when they first drove up there. "This land ought to be more fertile, given the amount of interred corpses."

"You're kidding."

The man acted like he was—put on what, for him, was a goofy expression, one that instead annoyed his charge.

"Sure," he mugged.

Yet here they were, ring-in bone orchard or not.

Out of this desolate land sprouted a clapboard farmhouse, along with a barn close to collapse and an outdoor loo. The three structures had been arranged in a triangle and in close proximity, like their hack architect expected the place to be raided. Otherwise, the only man-made objects were tumble-down, O.K. Corral style fencing, a 19th century water pump, and one useless hitching post for mares that hadn't lived hereabouts for over a generation.

On the ground between these structures grew nothing, not even a hardy weed.

Rather, dead-letter tyre tracks made the only impression in the earth, mostly old ones worn down by rain and wind. Behind the house sat the skeletal remains of a T-Model Ford, rusted up, all worthwhile parts stripped.

The closest neighbour was three miles away, the nearest shop seven—a combination two-pump service station/general store built in the 1920s, where prices were inflated, all edible stock stale, and the man running the place looked to be one hundred not out.

Trista loathed The Farm and everything in its vicinity.

There was something morbid about the air, punctuated by regular gusts that carried loose, lifeless topsoil into your nostrils, your mouth, and your lungs.

The exceptionally basic amenities did not include a hi-fi, meaning Trista couldn't play her favourite Suzi Quatro and Status Quo records. In the kitchen there was, however, a hand-cranked iron coffee mill, old as Methuselah yet still functional, so Governal seemed happy.

The place shaped up as ideal for weapons training—an activity they undertook every day, regardless of weather, over the next three summers. While Governal claimed it was pursuit of this pastime that caused their relocation for a few weeks over school vacation, Trista suspected he more intended to get her away from boys she'd started seeing, to escape a contemporary musical path he wasn't into.

On this particular day, walking the track about a half mile from the farm buildings, Trista edged most memorable for too much make-up, straight blonde hair that fell to her waist, a tartan crop-top (little more than a bikini), and a pair of denim shorts cut off dangerously close to nether regions.

"You can usually tell if someone isn't honest by watching their eyes," Governal, focusing on a hazy middle-distance, instructed beside the girl. He wore no jacket—it was late summer, very hot—and he had hands clasped behind his back like an old soldier. "If they look upward, they're lying. Simple, really."

Trista placed a cigarette between vivid red lips. "Huh. If they know it's a tell, why do it in the first place?"

Governal had a droll, lopsided grin. "You're catching on. And the pros are an exception—they'll look straight back and won't finch a muscle." Then, once he glanced at her, the grin faded. "You're too young to smoke, Trista."

"Have I lit the thing?" she snapped, looking ahead.

"No. Good point. But I do think you should wear more clothes and less house-paint."

The girl stopped right there on the trail, Governal's pace taking him a few steps ahead before he also paused and turned.

"You're *not* my father."

In retrospect she could imagine it was hard to take her seriously—this little girl who thought she was now a woman. Judging by photos she later perused, the amount of mascara and blue eye shadow, so amateurishly applied, made her resemble less vamp than colour-blind panda.

Governal, hands now on his hips, sighed. "There's a shame."

GOVERNAL
[THE FARM — 1974]

*H*e awoke to gunfire.

Tumbled out of bed, clutching for a .45 on the bedside table. Stood instead with a naked Licca doll in his fingers—bent and twisted into the shape of a gun.

A Trista trick, he understood. Annoyed now, marginally less concerned, no matter the continued shots.

They came from outside, staggered, sometimes several seconds between. The fact there was no screaming or shouting gave additional relief.

He pulled on trousers and a t-shirt, quickly washed the old face, ran fingers through hair to neaten it, and strode out into the yard.

Trista, aged fifteen, stood just beyond the outhouse, legs apart, taking aim with that absent automatic. Fifty yards away sat a target with a photo on it, recognizable despite all the bullet holes: Marshal 'DuBois' Rohault.

An explosion, and Rohault's left eye disappeared.

Governal approached with caution, making small noises so as not to startle the girl. After several steps, he realized this was pointless—she was ignoring him. Once he closed in, Governal further noticed she'd absconded with his cigarettes.

An empty packet of Kent lay by her bare feet, alongside scattered stubs, and she had a lit fag between the fingers of her left hand. The gun now rested on her right hip.

"There are some," he said, circling to the front of the girl, "who would say that's unladylike."

Trista exhaled smoke instantly snatched by spiralling dust in the breeze. "What? The smoking? Or shooting my step-dad?"

He studied her face, checking details beyond a surly façade and too much foundation. "I suppose it depends which end you're on."

"Guess."

Their second summer here, a spot Trista obviously hated. That was part of the equation—helping her build barriers against persistent discomfort—as well as an opportunity to knuckle down into 'education'.

There was privacy here too, a sensation Governal appreciated since he didn't feel like people were watching, observing.

He'd put up with a kisser full of dirt any day to imagine that.

TRISTA
[THE FARM — 1975]

"Speaking of family," Governal said, "it's about time you got to know them."

Yes—that word. Again.

On the rough table before them, a heavy-duty wooden one covered in cuts and divots from decades of preparing meals and possibly improvising torture, Governal had spread a folder's worth of photographs and documents.

She and the man were in the large space that comprised the interior of the farm, aside from two, later-addition bedrooms. He'd switched on an overhead bulb to get some decent illumination, no matter that it was the middle of a particularly bright day outside.

Next to the paperwork was an ashtray with a smouldering cigarette (his), a mug of coffee (hers; he'd

finished one), a dead hand with a royal flush (Trista's—
she'd won, for a change), and the Colt .45 automatic—
there only for easy access in emergencies, Governal
insisted.

On the back of a flyer for an opera company called
Grand Opera Librettos' production of *Tristan und Isolde*, the
man had inscribed a string of tiny sentences in his overly
neat hand.

Otherwise, there were mug shots of Trista's father Al
Rivalen, her mother Blanche Rohault (née Rivalen, née
Cornwall), Marshal 'DuBois' Rohault, Marcella Cornwall,
and Isidor Holt, Sr.

A who's who of other personalities' photos had been
pushed to one side.

The top one there showcased an older man with a ring
of white hair. Each picture had the name typed in white on
black adhesive tape, using Governal's new pet Astro Label
Maker. The man with the white crown in the second pile
had only one word on his: *Geoffrey*.

"Why's that joker have just a single name?"

"We'll get to him. These are the key players to focus on
for now," Governal says, pushing Geoffrey's pile further
away, and taking a swift drag on his fag.

"What's the point?" Trista asks, hardly captivated.

"Well, if you listen in, I'll tell you."

"Why?"

"Because."

She doesn't pretend to hide a yawn. "Gee, that's
mature."

"Pot-kettle-black."

"But you're an old fart. You should know better."

Ignoring her, Governal rotates the pictures in order to
provide a better view. "Not that old," he mutters straight
after.

The photo of her mum, Trista notices, was a bridal
snapshot from when she'd married her dad. Blanche
looked so young. Isidor Holt's photo also looked ancient.

"Can't you invest in recent happy-snaps?" she says.

"That's not the point. This is a history lesson as well."

"Oh, hurrah."

"Trista, you have to know all of these people at least as well as you know me."

"Well, that's easy—*Do* I know you?"

"I believe so, yes."

"Huh. Could've fooled me."

"May we proceed?"

"Okay. I can cheat. I'm related to two of them, and number three is dead."

"You need to know more than that, kid. You'll have to understand the ways they tick, how they relate to each other—and therefore to you."

"What if I don't give a shit about a single one?"

"Never an option."

"Well, how about Isidor Holt? What's he doing here? Arsehole's not family."

"I'm including him because of his long relationship with Marcella."

"Don't you mean antagonism?"

"I know what I mean."

"Huh. Are you sure he didn't accidentally fall into the set, along with that opera flyer I am surprised to see?"

"Not mine, I swear. But I needed note paper at the time."

"Uh-huh."

"Returning to the subject of La Familia, allow me to be straight."

"By all means, you opera lover, you. Don't let me hold you back."

Governal nods—to himself, or to Trista, is unclear. "So. Your parents want to have you over for dinner to celebrate you turning sixteen next week."

Trista immediately recoils. "DuBois isn't my dad, either."

"Yeah, but he pays for all this." The man indicated the

room around them; meant more than that. "Pays me."

It hurt—every single time—Governal reminded her that she was a business arrangement.

"Whatever."

"It is what it is."

"Whatever."

"Trista."

"What?"

"Cheer up, Charlie," the man abruptly breezes, somehow shifting the mood of the room up a notch. "There'll be free booze."

The girl took her cue. "Thank God!" She even smiles.

"And you can practice your wiles on my boss." Governal arches his right eyebrow, something he always did well. "Ask him to introduce you to your Aunt Marcella."

Then he chuckles too, a genuine thing that disarmed Trista, no matter if she did not want to be undone.

"You might also have Blanche give you some make-up pointers. You could seriously do with them."

"Hey!"

That was the moment he switched back to serious on her. "Jokes aside, Triss—regarding your aunt, you need to remember. You're either an asset to Marcella, or a threat."

"Can I be neither?"

"What do you think?"

Trista senses she looks glum. Can't help the expression. "I know." She studies a fresh pack of Kent on the table. "Can I have a cigarette now?"

"When I'm around? In your dreams, kid."

***

This 'party' for her sixteenth was about as much fun as Trista expected. Sadly, no target practice involving DuBois Rohault's head, but a highlight did arise.

After dinner, during which few words were spoken,

Blanche disappeared into the latest episode of *McMillan & Wife*.

On the other side of the lounge room, DuBois regaled his guests with tales of his ho-hum week's derring-do.

So when her stepfather ordered that she make him a drink, Trista obediently acquiesced.

That set off a warning bell behind Governal's eyes, though she doubted he saw her spit into the glass straight after using a soda siphon.

"Here you are, daddy dearest," she said, as she passed the concoction to her lazy step-dad, who sat with feet up on the couch.

"Who needs servants?" DuBois chortled, before tossing back his drink.

TRISTA
[THE FARM — 1975]

*I*n two regards, Trista counted herself fortunate at O'Roark's—there was no TV set (they always reminded her now of Blanche), and she'd found a secret place to squirrel away.

Had manufactured a nest, of sorts, in the old barn loft, a hiding place up a ladder that had most rungs broken.

The area there was covered in damp, ancient straw, over which she tossed a couple of blankets. Trista stretched out most nights alongside a hamper of stale snacks and a cyclone lamp, its wick kept down low so as not to be spotted from the house. Kicked back and read books Governal didn't know about, overdue borrowings that were vapid, romantic, fantastical, whimsical, or a combination of the four—in other words, literature her mentor would shake his head over.

One evening, three weeks after her birthday party and their return to the The Farm, Trista had retired to her loft, nose buried in a hardback copy of *The Well of Loneliness*.

She must've fallen asleep and reawakened, because suddenly things were pitch black—the lamp was out, and the book lay across her chest.

There was also men's chatter below. Not a one of them sounded like Governal.

These people had flashlights; apparent when lit-up arcs swept this way and that in the barn. Very carefully, the girl placed her novel aside and peeped over the edge.

In the torchlight, she could only just make them out: one man had on a fedora that cast his features in further shadow, a Thompson submachine gun at his side. Another, with a gaunt face and dressed in a long coat over a diagonal-striped polyester body shirt, buttons unfastened almost to the navel—not so much revealing as showboating an incredibly hair chest—was blocking the doorway to the building.

A third fellow squatted on his knees in a singlet and underpants, hands bound behind the back, while a fourth paced the enclosure with a belly that pushed out over a straining belt.

That was the only man she recognized, due less to his Charlie Chan moustache than the prominent gut: Jimmie 'The Rat' Vermine. Governal had fingered this man in a slew of photos, during one of the Cornwall clan show-and-tell sessions.

"—Knows everything, Ed," Vermine was saying, all low, brutal baritone, as he addressed the individual kneeling on the dirt. "You're a fuckin' copper."

"I ain't no fink, Jimmie!" shouted the man on his knees, well past the edge of hysteria.

Vermine stopped pacing, spat, shook his head. "Shaddup, Ed."

"Please."

"You a dill? You reckon I'd bring you out to The Farm, if'n we didn't know it were you?"

"I don't know. You've got to believe me, you... Oh God, you gotta listen!"

"Don't gotta do nothin', chump. Save your pleas for the big fella upstairs."

Charlie Chan pulled a revolver then.

Trista resisted trying to identify the thing. It had bullets—that was enough.

She wanted to tear herself away from this tableau, to stare up at the ceiling, curl up in a ball, cover her ears—but instead lay transfixed and watched.

"Goodnight, moon," sneered Vermine, as he levelled the gun at their captive's left temple, and yanked back the trigger.

The noise hit first.

In all her play with firearms, their only targets were inanimate objects like bottles and cans, or the occasional portrait of DuBois. While Trista therefore expected the volume of this single report, nothing prepared for the slapping thud straight after—caused by brains and torn away flesh striking a wooden wall.

Smell assaulted her next: the familiar scent of cordite, mixed with singed hair and something fresh, sharp, metallic.

The mark, that man Vermine called Ed, hung in the air on his haunches a moment, and then collapsed on his back. Stared up at Trista with wide, frozen eyes, the upper left third of his head displaced.

She understood immediately she was bawling. In silence, at least. But this made it difficult to see or pay attention to events that happened next, starting with the man in the entrance—Vermine called him 'Billy Blob'— being ordered to fetch a watering can.

His going over to the pump, filling the container, and coming back to do a spot of spring-cleaning in the dead of night.

Vermine strolling in circles while he hummed the melody to 'Rocket Man', and the hatted statue with the Tommy Gun, as immobile as he had been from the start.

While Billy Blob scrubbed and Vermine hummed and

that other man stood stock-still, Trista pushed tears away and began to wonder where Governal could be. Why hadn't he stopped this? Didn't he hear the screams? The gunshot?

Which was when it dawned on her.

These were Marcella's men. So was Governal. He didn't lift a finger because the order to kill someone had been sourced from above—it came from Trista's aunt.

***

She hung back; hiding in that loft more than an hour after the men finished burying a body, and drove away.

Not yet dawn, but it had to be close.

Trista slowly climbed down from her cubbyhole, a place she'd never return to—no matter that she left behind that library book. She avoided the place where the corpse had so recently sprawled, looked in every direction once she cut loose from the barn, and finally crossed to the house, silently entered, went to her room.

It was dark inside, yet she sensed a presence—someone seated in an armchair over by the stand-alone closet. Looking harder as her eyes adjusted, Trista made out an outline in the pale moonlight filtering through closed net curtains.

Saw the dull glint of the .45 on his lap.

"Where have you been?" asked Governal's disembodied self, a hint of anxiety squeezed between words. "I was worried about you."

"Obviously."

"You saw—?"

"I saw." Trista shifted weight, one foot to the other. "What are you going to do? Shoot me for being a material witness?"

"Don't be childish."

"Hard not to be. I *am* a child."

"So you are." She could hear him sigh. It sounded

done-in. "I'm really very sorry you had to see that."

Trista chewed at her lip, tasted blood. "But?"

"But it's the nature of this business. An underlying one, at any rate. You were bound to come up against reality at some point."

"Consider me blessed, then." The lack of response made her stare harder at the shape of the man she thought she'd known. "They said he was police."

"Possibly." (Short pause). "More likely, an informer."

"That makes murder acceptable?"

"No. Nothing does."

Governal stood then, and shuffled past her toward the open door, where he paused.

"Get some sleep, if you can. We need an early start—we'll be leaving here today. I'll wake you at seven, so you can get packed. Don't forget anything—we won't be back."

TRISTA
[LION'S ESTATE — LATE 1975]

Seven months after her sixteenth birthday, more than eleven and a half years after Trista had joined Governal in this suburban refuge, the man took her to a brand new location for today's tête-à-tête—the first one they had in the musty-smelling, if spotless, living room.

Likely, he did not want the subject matter tarnishing their kitchen's ambience.

That morning, they'd belatedly collected her driver's licence, since she was officially old enough to get behind the wheel.

Now, however, having made Trista kick back on a hard, lumpy sofa-chair, Governal stood before her, phantom-warming buttocks in front of a false fireplace with gas logs that hadn't been lit in an eternity.

"So—time for our penultimate lesson," came his

announcement.

Trista couldn't be sure, but the man looked constipated. His eyes neglected to meet hers.

"The notion that revenge is sweet," he added.

He threw a 5" x 7" photograph onto the table, which landed upside down. Trista noted the Kodak branding on the back, the year '1963' written in biro, before flipping it over.

Glossy, black-and-white, a little blurry.

She grumbled, "Another photographic accomplishment."

Leaning forward to better anyway see details, the girl took in an urban street, shop-fronts with broken glass, a few bodies (of men) lying about, and other ones—also fellows—on their feet with guns drawn.

There was a veil, like smoke, yet nothing could hope to obscure the sight in the centre of this road, to the right of the photo.

She saw a man there, on his knees, with black liquid (blood?) splashed across his face, held down by another who was preparing to shoot him in the head.

Our individual kneeling happened to be Trista's papa, Al 'Tennyson' Rivalen.

The triggerman she also knew, thanks to previous slide shows: 'Duke' Morgan.

Trista blinked several times, mouth open, yet forgot to breathe. Having come round the table, Governal patted her shoulder.

"What you do with this knowledge—how you act—is up to you."

How Trista acted was (first) by running into the kitchen to seize keys off their windowsill hook, secondly grabbing Governal's little beige book of names and addresses, and third rushing out into the cold evening.

She jumped into the driver's seat of Governal's Chrysler Newport convertible, legally for the first time, and started it up. Sweating, swearing and crying all at once.

Yes, Governal had given the girl countless lessons, yet still she crunched gears before sending the car flying.

Pulled over a few miles down the road, beneath a convenient streetlight, to scour Governal's book in hands that shook violently. Found what she was looking for listed under 'M'.

Drove directly to a small mansion Morgan owned down on the south side of the city. She could make out its Italianesque façade and ugly white statues of deities and nymphs, no matter how dark it might be.

The time was just after eleven.

Trista didn't bother checking mirrors or blind spots for obstacles, but otherwise religiously followed Governal's driving instructions.

Put the clutch all the way in, changed into reverse gear with the clutch still depressed, let it out until she felt bite, pressed against the clutch slightly and held it to avoid stalling or bunny-hopping—then gave more accelerator and released the rest of the clutch.

Took out, first of all, a two-headed representation of Roman god Janus, followed by Cupid, with its bow and arrow, in a loud crunching of plaster, chicken wire and stick-frames.

A man—Morgan, she realized—fell out the front door in silk pyjamas, cursing and shouting. He had a gun in his right hand that looked like a replica of the one from the photo. Blinded as he was by the Chrysler's headlights, the 'Duke' had no idea who then drove straight over him.

Trista felt the back wheels bounce over his body.

Headed home, swerving a bit and sideswiping bushes, but Governal was nowhere to be found. She did discover, however, two thirds of a Monkey Shoulder Scotch Whisky in one of the kitchen cupboards, and drank it all directly from the bottle before passing out—her head on the table.

***

Sometime late morning, Trista woke in the same position, beside a small pool of saliva.

Her head ached, neck hurt like buggery, her legs screamed pins-and-needles. Having downed several glasses of water, the girl felt more nauseous than revived, horror coasting through with the fluid. She wobbled along the empty passage and out the front door, past ivy no longer sitting pretty.

Governal crouched there on the front lawn, washing his convertible with a sponge and hose.

He straightened up when he saw her. "You all right, kid?"

"I ran him down," Trista said. "Morgan."

"I noticed." He nodded at the car.

"Killed him."

"We don't know that yet."

"I do. I drove over him." Trista covered her mouth with the back of her hand. "Oh, God, I'm going to be sick."

"We don't know that yet," said Governal again. "I'll find out—finish the job, if you want me to."

Trista now stared at him, feeling more desperately ill than before. "Who *are* you?"

"It's what I do." Governal blinked—a languid thing, yet the only time she'd seen him betray any kind of tic that might be deemed nervous. "What I did," he corrected, beginning to roll up the hose very neatly. "Fix things."

"Like killing somebody?"

"If the situation calls for it. I prefer not to."

"So this is the answer."

"To what?"

"Why you've spent all that time haranguing me."

The man's lack of response was enough.

"No," she said. "No."

He looked at her. "No—what?"

"No."

With that, Trista walked away down the street, along the middle of the road, taking care to step only on white-painted lines.

Left behind all possessions, did not look back, and wouldn't see this man again for a year and a half.

***

She'd sense him, of course.

Through all the stupid things, times and events she later tried to put behind her, Trista felt a protective presence that interfered only when she got too deep or fell overly far.

And far she did tumble.

TRISTA
[SOMEWHERE IN THE CITY — NEW YEAR'S DAY 1977]

She walks beneath flickering streetlights in sore need of repair. Still able to see (and hear) children screaming from hunger, an aged, bent-up lady in rags pushing a crippled shopping cart, two individuals sleeping on the footpath under piled newspapers and folded cardboard, men prowling past in cars on the look-out for bargain-basement sex or a quick fix.

Wonders why it came to this—couldn't there be anything other to life than hardship and starvation, lust and grifts?

No, there was more.

Such as working for criminal cartels like the Holts and the Cornwalls, closeted away behind velvet curtains, living off ill-gotten riches. Horrible deeds done by vicious people.

Or filling a vacancy with a police force more inclined to

harass and arrest the people around her than tackle the real crime and corruption above.

Trista lingers at a busy intersection where women pranced past in miniskirts, afros, and platform boots. It was bitterly cold—the ladies seemed oblivious—and she zips up her jacket, shivers anyway.

It was never—ever—quiet here.

The noise salvos about, each individual sound undercutting/overlapping, most of all the mundane: automobile engines that rev or purr, the blast of different horns, rock and roll tumbling down a street from one club and colliding with the country and western of another. A staccato buzz of overhead neons that switched on and off, or cycled through the different pastel shades of faded radiant.

The click-clack of defective air conditioners.

There is constant chatter from people roaming these streets, loud and blusterous ones granting better comfort than the soft and seditious. Homeless people, bums, dead-enders, the deranged—they caw out to nobody or everybody. Analogous seem the shrieks of horror and joy.

By comparison, the city sights underwhelm, and not always because of familiarity.

Obsolete saloons boasted cracked glass behind the bars in their window frames. There was broken signage and metal shutters on bygone pool parlours, which were smeared with unintelligible graffiti. Torn, fluttering flyers—sticky-taped one on top of the other—blanketed electricity poles.

Single-night hawkers in the shadows hocked hot merchandise—clothing and watches, lighters and cassettes—at portable stalls made from stolen milk crates.

Hell-mouth-dark alleyways reeked of garbage and excretion, the only vegetation being lost-cause weeds scrabbling for survival in cracks between buildings and the pavement.

Similarly parched gang members hung out in gloomy

alcoves, on top of their respective territorial worlds—parked as they were at the summit of puny flights of stairs.

The ground is this place at its worst, capped with the discarded: garbage, regurgitation, blood (new and old), broken glass, motor oil, used condoms, semen, human shit, clumps of hair, preowned tampons, rifled wallets, teeth lacking ownership, and empty syringes cast aside.

Fear, despair and disillusionment were distilled here aplenty. Poverty, muggings, beatings, shootings, prostitution and amphetamine trade simply part of the accepted woodwork.

She feels incredibly hungry, desperately lonely.

Takes out a super-short pencil to write, another hobby aside from collecting dolls—something she barely remembers. This is one nobody else knows. Helps her forget being famished. She has a battered blue folder in her shoulder bag; full of unfinished vignettes of local lives—etched onto scraps of paper and used serviettes fished from rubbish bins.

This time, she writes about Felice, a year younger friend who OD'd the week before.

Jots down the girl's hopes and dreams that had somehow survived life on these very streets for twelve months—which amounted to nothing, anyway, when she stuck a final needle in the arm.

Doesn't realize she's sobbing, until a woman sidles up in a boob tube and mini combo, to place a gentle hand on her arm. "You all right, honey?"

Trying to clear her vision, Trista first glimpses fingers with elongated, Chinese red plastic nails, and then looks up into a pretty face prematurely aged.

"I need to go home," she says, wiping her nose on a filthy sleeve.

"That's right, honey—you do."

***

Evening prevailed when she arrived, and Trista was soaked through.

Had been walking in the rain for hours, since she had no coinage to cover bus fares.

Stood outside on the road, staring at an off-white house and the Chrysler parked in the driveway. Aware of how absurdly hushed it seemed to be here, how shiny and new things appeared as they sparkled in a more restrained, docile artificial light.

Finally, made the call.

Once he unbolted and opened the front door, the man was silhouetted by more light from inside the house, and she couldn't decipher a single feature.

Stupidly, she knew this; the first thing to cross her mind was she ought to have cleaned up and dried off before arriving this way. Next, she realized she had no certainty—aside from the car outside—that this was actually him.

"Governal?"

Without a single word, this man stepped forward, placed an arm around her, escorted the dripping girl inside, and shut the door.

***

"You need to understand—and I pray you've learned—that revenge is not the answer, no matter how attractive it might seem at the time. It fixes nothing. Only increases one's pain."

The two were back in that kitchen, the one she'd grown up with.

It smelled the same and appeared exactly as before—aside from a replacement Pan Am calendar and a Lalo Schifrin film score on a new cassette player—but things themselves, she appraised, never could be.

Trista had submitted to the scalding bath Governal insisted on, and after sat in a loose-fitting robe (his), with a towel binding wet hair.

The man opposite looked aged, more than fifteen months ought to have accrued. Made her wonder how much the experience had done to her own looks—not that these mattered any longer.

Governal took a newspaper clipping from inside his wallet. Brown and yellow, covered with scotch tape holding it together, it was stained by leakage from the adhesive in that tape.

Very carefully, one could say almost reverently, he unfolded the paper and spread it on the table top.

"Here. This may explain better."

Turning it her way, Trista saw a date—March, 1953—and a minor headline that stated: *Woman Killed in Hit-and-Run.* The article would've totted up to twenty-five words at max. She didn't count. No photos, nothing to make the piece stand out on a broadsheet.

"I don't get it," she said.

"My wife Sophie," responded Governal from his side of the table, hands placed one atop the other in a casual gesture, "was the most beautiful lady you ever did meet."

Trista momentarily closed eyes. "You were married."

"Yes."

"How have you never told me this before?"

"You didn't ask."

"You didn't tell me."

"I'm sorry."

"Did she live here?"

"No. We had a place in the city. This house belonged to my mother."

He looked down for a moment, and when he raised his head once more there was a nostalgic, rather crooked half-smile.

"I remember trivial things. Crystal clear to the point

that, you know, the clarity kills me. They aren't important, not really—like the way her hips swayed when I watched her walk from behind. Sophie sizzled. The glee she expressed after tasting a dish cooked, realizing it was just right: 'Ooh la la,' she'd shout, like a goddamned French sous chef."

Governal's face compressed, and he wiped something foreign from his eye.

"Sheer radiance. Absolute joy. All those—jewels—gone. A barren thing left, not worth the living. That was me."

"Isn't that a bit melodramatic?" Trista asked, not unkindly.

"Well, I am old." The man sighed. "Yeah, I know we hear about this sort of... incident all the time, in TV shows, on the news. But it's different when it happens to you. And me? Well, I was somebody then with the resources to find out who did this arsehole deed, to locate the culprit. Yes, I sought out revenge. Found the driver who'd murdered her. For a while I let the prick plead for his life. He sobbed and screamed, and in between all that nonsense I understood he'd been stone drunk when he ran over Sophie. The term he used was 'headless'. An office shindig killed her, or that's what he wanted me to believe. So when I took his life, like he'd taken mine, I really did render him headless."

Trista stared. "You—?"

"Yes?"

"—Cut off his head?"

"Yes."

"Jeez. I thought running someone over in their front yard was pretty messed up."

Governal shrugged. "Different horses."

"Guess. Did that... Could that make you feel any better?"

"No, of course not—I think you understand now. Do you?"

Trista glanced away. "Maybe."

"Well, it didn't correct anything. Me? I learned I made a widow of a blameless woman, left two toddlers orphaned. So I hit the bottle hard, screwed up at work. No one in this business is irreplaceable. Marcella dropped me from her inner cadre to go leaning on people for DuBois, a demotion if ever you saw one, and I'd succumbed to the same evil responsible for Sophie's death. Lesson learned. I haven't touched a drop of alcohol since 1955."

"Then what about the Monkey Shoulder under the sink?"

"That? A reminder of those times. The last liquor I indulged in."

"You mean—I drank from a bottle opened twenty years ago?"

Having raised his left eyebrow, Governal said nothing.

"Shit. I think I'm going to be sick."

"After a year and a half, I'd say you're safely beyond any bacterial threat. Plus, that's a bonus pointer—don't go drinking other people's hooch without first asking. Now go get some sleep. You look done in. The bed's already made."

***

Her bedroom was just the same, dolls gathered together on a sideboard, right where she'd displayed them nineteen months before. Trista could see they'd been recently dusted.

She stopped in front of the wardrobe mirror. Dropped her towel and borrowed dressing gown to the floor.

Hadn't viewed herself in any kind of looking glass for an eternity.

The stranger peering back stood skinnier than she remembered, face emaciated and pale. Her hair, dyed pillar-box red, damp still, had no order to it and the ends were split, haggard.

149

When she turned her face slightly to the right, there was the checkerboard pattern Felice had shaved into the scalp above her left ear.

One last memento from a dead friend.

8

TRISTA

*A*fter another bath and a breakfast of unqualified champions—Canadian bacon with scrambled eggs on toast, along with leftover pecan and avocado ice cream—Trista could broach a topic (one aside from food) that'd been on her mind for a long time.

"So, who took the photo?"

"The one of your father?"

"Mm."

Governal was in the process of making a pot of aromatic coffee, but looked over. Understood precisely.

"A reporter I knew, with a tabloid over on Broadway."

Pushing around stray bread crumbs with her fork, Trista was interrupted by Governal's vaguely stern, "Don't play with your food," followed by an apologetic, "Sorry,

151

Andrez Bergen

"It's okay," the girl said. "Tell me more about this reporter."

"All right. I was late finding him—he'd already been tipped off to keep it out of the press."

Two fine china cups, decorated with starfish, appeared upon the counter. Trista sure she'd never laid eyes on them before.

"When I say 'tipped off', I don't mean paid money. The man had been recently worked over, fairly obvious given the black eye and a shaky demeanour. Anyway, he owed me a favour and I can be a wee bit intimidating myself when I choose to, so I walked away with the single remaining image. A test one. That accounts for why it's out of focus."

Having handed her a strong brew in one of the cups, Governal remained standing by the sink, his resting in the palm of the left hand.

Trista sipped. "Nice," she said. It was the best coffee she'd had since 1975.

"Service with a smile. I missed these moments."

"I know. I'm sorry—hope you get that."

"Water under the bridge."

"So they tell us." The girl sighed, briefly gnawed at her lip, and then put down the cup. "Hallmark expressions aside—who worked over your friend?"

"Wouldn't say. But when I tossed a few names his way, he visibly recoiled at mention of DuBois."

That made Trista start chewing again. "So, you think he—?"

"I prefer not to work with presumptions. But, no, I don't. Think. DuBois is a go-between, a pawn, hardly the decision-maker you'd need." Governal stopped talking, and looked worried—unusual for him.

"Go on."

"Someone else would've been pulling the strings."

"Who, then?"

152

"I don't know. I have little of the pull I once managed. Still, I'd say we're talking an individual or group of same higher up the food-chain."

"Like Morgan."

"Nah, too middling. The 'Duke' has a bunch of bullyboys and an agenda, you know this already. He's always been muscle, available to any bidder in this city that offers the right sum of money—and a morsel to step up a rung."

"Deals on wheels?" Trista muttered.

"Cute, but hardly hysterical."

"Has he worked out yet who put him into that chair?"

"No." Governal offered one of his faint, lopsided grins. "Some things worked out in our favour. Anyway, he might've been the trigger—someone else, as I say, loaded the pistol."

"Who?" asked Trista again.

"You want the same answer, or a different one?"

The girl finished her coffee, gratefully accepted a refill, and then leaned back. "Surprise me."

"All right. I'm not sure."

"Well, that's no fun."

"Sorry. If we look at your father, he was in with Marcey—"

"Being married to her sister, you mean."

Governal sat down opposite with his cup. "Actually, I don't. Family carries little weight in our line. But he was reliable, loyal; a member of the fold, and Marcella liked him. Those things, plus she got a clock-work percentage from the man."

"Isidor Holt, then, sticking it to the competition."

"Possibly. That's guesswork."

"Who else could it be? No one in their right mind would dare a hit on Marcella's interests—only Holt is a bigger fish, and mad enough to take the punt."

"So what I taught you has sunk in." Governal smiled again. "All true—yet still conjecture. You need to rein in that tendency. And Holt isn't insane, Triss. There's reason behind every one of his moves. We need a motive as much as proof—and likely they're interconnected. I've never been able to ascertain either. If he organized this."

"Then that's what needs to be found. A connection."

"If there is one."

"Enough with the ifs." Trista shrugged. "Anyway, if that is the case—you and your ifs—we'll look elsewhere."

"Sounds to me like you're in again like Flynn."

"Keep the clichés flying, you old bozo."

"Getting there." The man reached forward, placing his right hand over her left on the table. "So. We're a team once more?"

"*If* you'll have me back."

"Never a question."

"One condition."

"Shoot."

With a wan smile on her lips, Trista abruptly burped. "Oops—sorry. But exactly that, the shooting thing. I won't kill anybody."

Governal nodded, his answer belying the gesture. "Sometimes, we don't have a choice."

***

Once Trista had put on decent weight, about ten days later Governal home-delivered the news. Maybe he decided she was solid enough. Did so at the kitchen table, while testing out a new ice cream recipe of his own invention that involved juniper berries and Guaiwei seasoning.

Trista, scouring a tabloid opposite, was annoyed anyway.

"In case you've forgotten—it's your eighteenth in two months."

The girl barely registered. "Oh, yeah."

"Marcella is organizing the celebration."

That snagged her attention. She looked over. "What?"

"A party."

"Yeah—I heard you. Another one?"

"Yep."

"And this aunt I've never met says she'll be there? Hah."

"She should be. The festivities are going to be held at Tintagel this time. A coming-out. It's quite the honour."

"Coming out of where?"

The man shrugged while scanning handwritten ingredients. "Imprisonment?"

"No need to put yourself down."

"I don't know—I think I'd look debonair in a correctional officer's uniform."

"One word: yuck." Trista closed the newspaper. "Why this sudden interest from a woman who hasn't previously concerned herself?"

"Eighteen years of age is a milestone, in some people's books."

"So is a baptism. Marcella didn't show up for that. Or my dad's funeral."

"There were security concerns there."

Shifting in her chair, Trista narrowed eyes. "Does she channel money through DuBois in order for you to defend her as well?"

"Figured that out, huh?"

"You trained me."

"Then there's hope yet."

"Quite possibly. Can I tactfully decline this dumb soirée?"

"That would not be wise."

"No choice?"

"There's always an option—but some things remain healthier than others. Besides, you'll receive plenty of presents."

"So? Gov, I'm not a child anymore."

"I know, I know." Governal paused mid-stir over his bright yellow plastic bowl. "Anyway, we have nearly eight weeks. Should give you a chance to grow out your hair and redo it a half-decent colour."

He pulled closer a set of scales; grinned as he did so.

"Oh, and I think it might be best to desist with any shenanigans involving saliva this time round."

GOVERNAL
[EN ROUTE TO TINTAGEL — EARLY 1977]

*E*ven as he applied most focus on driving—important, since other people's lives were at stake—Governal spared a portion for his young charge in the passenger seat.

Behind overlarge sunglasses, beneath that scarf placed over her hair to protect the new 'do in the wind (despite the fact he'd put the roof up), he can tell she's nervy.

Kid covered well, but the stress snuck out in weird ways, like clenched fingers and a tendency to babble.

While she might've looked a million bucks (wearing a salmon pink, Cristóbal Balenciaga-designed silk slip of a dress) and more mature than her age (eighteen today), this was still a kid he delivered like a Christmas package to Marcella's insane menagerie.

More than merely guilty, Governal felt apprehensive and, yes, also stressed.

The traffic was thankfully light, and an hour into the trip their car passed by a post reading 'Tintagel: 2 miles'.

"My God," Trista remarks. "She's got a house with signs pointing to it."

"Not all she has." He glances in the rear view mirror, and then ahead again. "I can arrange permits with the local council to have markers pointing to ours, if you'd like."

"D'you really have that kind of pull?"

"Supposedly."

Glancing sideways at him, Trista laughs. "Are you serious?"

"Depends if you are."

"Good call." The bonhomie sadly subsides, replaced by a sigh as Trista also looks ahead. "Signage is not really something I aspire to."

Silence prevailed thereafter, until pinnacled turrets reared into a grey sky at the top of a hill they rapidly ascended. The sight causes the girl beside him to click her tongue.

"Tintagel?"

"Tintagel."

"I see Marcella likes to play it low-key."

He swivels his head to look momentarily at her. "All right, enough with the prattle. This is serious."

"I know, I know."

"Remember—if you don't want to be stuck with Blanche and DuBois, then you need to impress this lady."

"Can't I just be stuck with you?"

"Not an option."

"Huh. You once told me there's always an option."

"These people pay the bills."

"That, again? Gee, ta."

"You're welcome."

Trista momentarily twists her mouth to one side, an annoyed pout, and then says, "You need to work on your sarcasm."

TRISTA
[ARRIVAL @ TINTAGEL, EARLY 1977]

A deeply tanned gentleman with a ring of white hair, dressed in a tuxedo, intercepted them at the beginning of a long driveway. He had a hefty firearm tucked beneath one arm, and raised the other.

"ID?" Governal said, barely moving lips.

"Geoffrey," Trista replied under her breath. "Surname unknown. Age unknown—looks old to me. Older than you."

"There's a blessing. Go on."

"Marcey's go-to gopher for pretty much everything. I'm not a hundred percent, but that shotgun he's flaunting looks like an Ithaca Mag-10, gas-operated, semi-automatic chambered in 10-gauge."

"Good girl."

"Don't be patronizing."

"Sorry."

Governal wound down his window.

"Just me, Geoffrey, plus one—expected by Marcella."

The ring-in butler lowered his weapon. "Right you are."

"When did you get back from Rhodesia?"

"Last week, actually. Charming place—particularly the hunting. Anyhow, we'll chat later. Go straight through to the ballroom."

As they started moving again, toward several rows of vehicles parked next to a grand manor house, Trista leaned close. "Hang on. It's *my* eighteenth birthday party... and I'm the plus one?"

Governal behaved like he hadn't heard, concentration fixed on an appropriate place to pull in. "Names come when you earn them," he said a few seconds later.

"Did you just think that up?"

"No, it was in the instruction manual." He switched off the engine.

"*How to Deal with Unruly Teenagers?*"

"Something of the sort." Having placed keys in his breast pocket and handing her a salmon pink leather purse, Governal looked sharply over. "I said I need you to be serious. Can you accomplish that?"

"Sure."

"Every bit of your performance—how you behave between these walls, in fact as soon as we step out of the car—will be reported to Marcella."

Trista nodded as she held his eyes. "I know. Trust me."

"I do. I just find it difficult trusting them."

"We can do this."

"There's my girl."

Trista guffawed. "I'll let you get away with that one. C'mon. I have a shit-load of prezzies from utter strangers to unwrap."

***

Trista had never visited Tintagel Apartments before, though she understood her father virtually lived there before his death. Despite Blanche and Marcella being sisters, there was a ten-year age difference (Marcella the eldest), and they'd had a falling out at some point— meaning the two were estranged before Trista was born.

Tintagel was bigger than she'd guessed, going only by photos seen in research, and it exuded grandness best expressed in the pillars, the stained glass, and the height of the ceilings. But there also slid through a feeling of decay, of an over-large hovel well beyond its prime.

Sure, the grand chandelier in the ballroom—dangling from industrial-strength chains—was designed to overwhelm and impress, but Trista fretted those chains might snap.

Marcella's 'court' comprised about three-dozen people: regulars, plus special guests for today, all grouped together. A fair few were dressed in shocking hip attire that hurt Trista's eyes. Worse, the majority wore paper party hats. She had to fight not to turn away; was grateful when nobody offered her one.

These revellers, mostly men aged from nineteen to ninety, stared like they were trying to pigeonhole this teenage intruder—figure who or what she might be to Marcella. So much for this being her special gig.

Trista thanked lucky stars for Governal.

He scrutinized them in better ways, a kind of repressed snarl on his face that she cherished.

But the girl started at a loud proclamation—"Miss Cornwall will see you now."—that hushed the crowd.

"Relax, kid. Breathe," Governal said, having already slid a hand to her lower back as he gently propelled her forward.

The announcement had arisen from a short, slight-looking young woman standing at the foot of the grand staircase. An Asian chick with plum eye shadow and a huge black afro, meaning she seemed taller and no birthday-hat would fit.

"Recognize her?" Governal murmured.

"Sakura."

According to Governal's brief, this wasn't just some hired domestic help, but a bodyguard exceptionally gifted with knives and deathblows. Her eyes hardly registered the two guests she met, who then followed up steps, past giant tapestries and oil-painted portraits of dead people in gilt frames.

Further they went, across a plush blood-red carpet on the second floor, into a drawing room that was in fact two spaces conjoined: one well-lit, with more of the romantic pictures on the walls, and a second space, through a narrow doorway, that had curtains drawn and was inky.

Without uttering a single syllable, this Sakura person parked them in the small room with lights, and then performed a slow motion runner.

Hands stuck in his pants pockets, Governal looked at the empty doorway. Trista peered closer at paintings, losing herself in details of courtly love.

The voice, when it eventually came, originated from that other, darkened room.

"Hello, Governal. Always a pleasure," it said—a strong tone, edging masculine (but not quite there), tempered with age.

"Marcella," Governal nodded to nothing seen.

Trista stared toward the ill-lit doorway, irritated by these theatrics, yet trying not to show it. As her eyes adjusted, she began to make out a human-shaped silhouette in the other room. It could have been anybody.

She knew it was her aunt.

"This young lady would be Trista Rohault."

Trista immediately corrected, "Rivalen," which made Governal clear his throat. "Manners," she could hear him elucidate, though he said nothing.

There was, however, a faint chuckle from next door. "Rivalen. Of course."

"Be nice to properly meet you, Aunt Marcella," Trista went on, approaching the doorway. "That is—if you could get your shade to pass on the message. You might need coinage for Charon."

"Really?" the voice remarked. "Feisty thing, isn't she?"

Trista wasn't clear if the narrative approved, or this was a put-down. Governal's taking a step forward surprised her.

"Remind you of anyone?" he said.

"Mmm. Though I was never rude."

Governal casually turned a circle, and in the brief moment he faced Trista, his back to the doorway, he grinned and winked. Said: "Everyone forgets, once they get old."

"Cheeky," decided the voice.

That was the cue for Marcella to parade through the doorway into light, thereby revealing a hardly intimidating, elderly lady with short, well-manicured grey hair. She was dressed in a black woollen poncho and matching scarf. Having stopped before Trista, she took up the girl's hands in both her aged ones.

"I'd like to speak to my pretty niece. That will be all, Governal."

"Yes, ma'am."

Hands clutched, Trista made to casually observe Governal's exit, and watched the door close. Leaving her with this old duck that clearly liked to play power-games.

"So. Trista *Rivalen*," Marcella mused, squeezing her fingers, "I see your father in your eyes. Please do tell me all about yourself."

Straight after, the woman released her niece, strode over to a sofa chair, turned, and sat propped on the edge. Arms now crossed, Marcella Cornwall had an expectant look.

Flip, as she was a minute before—with Governal right here—Trista felt blood crystallizing in her veins. Said absolutely nothing.

Marcella narrowed her eyes. "I don't see any cat hereabouts. Do you?"

Under this lady's frigid gaze, struck speechless, Trista struggled to recall a single slice of her mentor's training, let alone advice for today.

One piece did stick, though: "Smile," he'd instructed, "and make it genuine—not a smarmy, half-baked thing."

So—she smiled.

Marcella apparently approved—"Yes, charming," she appraised—at least for the time being. "We'll help you rediscover your tongue later. Now, do you play the Harp?"

Following downstairs in oddly docile form, Trista's mind, in fact, reeled.

She'd attempted to engage Gov's lessons, tried reading her aunt's face. But Marcella refused to cooperate. Trista might have sensed a history of violence lacquered beneath the primer, but otherwise met a blank canvas.

No idea why, given these clues, she wanted (quite desperately) to impress the lady.

An easier way in which to accomplish this was by taking apart the hapless players Marcella matched her up against in a round-robin tourney of the Harp.

Through most of this competition, which took place over several hungry hours, Trista felt Marcella's eyes on her.

Wondered what had happened to Governal's.

In a patient manner that felt like its own lie, the older woman roved this ballroom, passing between or around several tables set up for concurrent games between pairs. Sometimes Marcella carried a flute of champagne in one hand, at others a cheroot.

Trista's aunt observed as every single player lost to the dumb blonde plus one, who'd gate-crashed court to attend her own birthday party.

***

"Trista, you play the Harp wonderfully."

Tournament over, Marcella had escorted her niece into a bright sunroom beside the garden. The two of them were alone, surrounded by a horde of houseplants. Back in the ballroom, the rest of the Cornwall entourage went about packing cards, tables, egos and tears.

Trista said, "Thank you." Still fretted over Governal's whereabouts, yet let on nothing of the sort. "Is there a prize?"

"Perhaps." Marcella parted a fragile silk drape to peer outside. "You knew that DuBois was cheating, yet said nothing. I find I need to ask—did you remain mum because he's your father?"

"*That man is not my dad.*"

She hadn't intended to load the sentence with baggage of such venom; it slipped out that way.

Marcella, however, did not flinch. "Go on."

The girl speedily calculated how to change the subject to something less personal; more (hopefully) what her aunt wanted to hear.

"Well," she mused, "they'd gawked and been on edge from the moment I arrived."

Turning her head just a fraction, Marcella looked over. "Who?"

"Your people in there, pretty much all of them. Seemed easier to keep the peace if I said nothing about the cheating, since it wasn't only DuBois."

Marcella sat back, her face revealing a disgruntled appraisal. "My people don't cheat."

"Maybe not right in front of you."

The older woman now made a loud, exhaling sound. It was in no manner intended to be pretty. "You do have a mouth on you, Trista Rivalen."

"Governal taught me to be honest."

"I'm sure. And yet—despite the cheating—you won anyway." Marcella squinted. "You're not practicing another kind of sleight of hand?"

"No." Trista shrugged. "I was lucky."

MARCELLA
[TRISTA'S BIRTHDAY PARTY, TINTAGEL, EARLY 1977]

A cake was unveiled, one that could stop a runaway stallion. Eighteen candles extinguished in one breath, before a hurrahing audience of aggrieved losers.

This girl had destroyed all, pros and amateurs both.

Later still, in the expansive kitchen—a place she often thought big enough to house a basketball match—while several members of staff scrubbed, cleaned, whispered and cooked, Marcella sat Trista at a counter table in a discreet bay window alcove away from the mayhem.

Giving the two women time to study one another.

"You have a posture to kill for," Marcella decided.

Trista raised her shoulders, an athletic shrug. "Blame years of ballet."

"Oh, a hobby?"

"You'd know. You paid for it."

The older woman clicked fingers at one of the kitchen staff. "Bring me a slice of that cake, would you? Plenty of cream." Then she slouched back, eyes washing over this young relative. "What did you wish for? ...You can tell me, since I don't believe the keeping of a secret avails anyone."

"That's a tiny bit sad, Auntie."

Marcella suspected a degree of sarcasm in Trista's use of the word 'auntie'. "No need to call me that. Marcella will do."

"And you still really want to know about my hush-hush wish?"

"Don't play the donkey, young lady—why else would I ask?"

"Sure. Okay."

"Out with it."

"All right. Donkey or not, I'd like to work for you."

"Indeed?"

"Indeed."

For some time, Marcella poked at whipped cream on the piece of birthday cake before her, until finally placing a dollop in her mouth. "You do have your shirty moments," she said, after savouring, and then swallowing. "Which is not a criticism. I appreciate frankness—it's something I've been deprived of since Governal had his fall from grace."

"I can imagine."

Marcella sizzled. "No. You can't."

"So take me on. Show me."

"You're a trifle young."

This girl lifted her chin, acted older. "Giving me a job means I don't have to sponge off Governal anymore—or DuBois. I'd actually earn what you funnel through."

So, Marcella pursed lips, thinking. "Trista," she eventually said, "There is no love lost 'twixt Blanche and myself."

"That's between you and her."

"Still."

"Still—Who cares?"

"Fair enough." Now she came to her real point. "Whatever is between you and DuBois—and, believe me, I suspect what it is—cannot be allowed to interfere with business."

The younger woman nodded, no hesitation at all. "I know."

"I won't warn you twice."

"You don't need to."

TRISTA
[BIRTHDAY PARTY @ TINTAGEL, EARLY 1977]

*T*he Cornwall family matriarch seemed preoccupied with cream atop her slice of cake, but not the thing itself. Her silver fork stabbed and twisted, scooped and patted. Very little made it into the woman's waiting maw.

"It's something I've been deprived of since Governal had his fall from grace," Marcella mused.

Aside from cutlery, Trista had been carefully observing the woman's eyes. While they did not avert or wander when she said this last sentence, there was something, a glint Trista could not put a finger on, that rang false.

"I can imagine," she said instead—which appeared to annoy the lady.

Dialogue continued, Trista inserting titbits Governal had drummed into her. With feeling, like he emphasized, without getting overly emotional.

Truth being, Trista felt stressed out, and prayed she didn't reveal this. Had in mind the packet of Knight's Honour cigarettes she remembered Governal left on the back seat of his car.

Trista bobbed when appropriate, agreed aloud at other points—in ways that didn't interrupt her aunt. More small talk followed, mostly about relocating to the inner city, to be close. On-call, when Marcella needed an opinion and confidante.

Then, two small glasses of Cock o' the North whisky liqueur were delivered to their table, clicked, the contents drained in one go—a deal apparently sealed.

***

By 5:00 p.m., she'd been dismissed from Marcella's

company.

Sakura escorted her through an increasingly drunk and raucous entourage in the ballroom, and out the front door—then the hired assassin conjured up another vanishing trick.

Taking in the quiet exterior of Tintagel, Trista spotted Governal down the driveway, talking to that one-named butler fellow Geoffrey—they were talking next to his Chrysler. At Trista's approach, Geoffrey affects a lame kind of bow and heads indoors.

Since she has one of one of Marcella's cheroots smouldering in her right hand, Trista takes a quick drag and exhales into a cold breeze.

Hands still in the pockets of his suit—it was definitely chilly out here—Governal looked at her with a degree of expectation.

"So, don't keep me in the dark. How'd it go, kid? And are you celebrating, or ought we to lament?"

***

During the drive home, roof down, herself at the wheel and hair free to revel in the wind, Trista glanced at her partner. The man was gazing at the horizon, all calm, like he had not a care in the world.

She decided she needed to interrupt that. "How come you don't know that guy's last name?" she said.

"Whose? Geoffrey's?"

"Yeah."

"He's not your usual suspect."

"That so, Gov? I thought you were good at this kind of thing."

"Well, it's not always easy. Some minor details are trickier to glean than others," Governal said, repressing a grin, while he scratched his chin.

"You think it's minor?" She kept the speedometer at around sixty. "Or funny?"

He dispensed with the mirth. "Good call. I don't. And this doesn't mean we stop trying to learn that which we don't know—right?"

Trista focused ahead at traffic. "Right."

"Anything else?"

"Mm. I think Marcella was holding something back."

"What?"

The girl again looked sideways at her passenger. "About you and your 'fall from grace', as she oh-so-eloquently put it."

9

ISSY

[TRISTA'S ROOM — ST. MAIGNENN'S HOSPITAL]

*H*e hadn't budged from the bedside chair in eight hours.

Well, actually, that was a bald-faced lie—there were two quick trips to the bathroom, the first of these only after he couldn't locate a chamber pot. Issy felt shy about using one anyway, private room or not, in the presence of this girl.

His right hand is numb—it'd been clasping her left one for over an hour. He studies her face, sees the occasional twitch of eyelids. What did they call it? REM sleep. She was apparently dreaming—one precious indication, aside from the assurances of doctors and nurses, that Henrike still lived.

Her face, so goddamned beautiful.

Innocent, like a child's in slumber, but the adult features reminded Issy of one of three girls in diaphanous white that stole his attention upon viewing Botticelli's painting 'Primavera' at the Uffizi in Florence.

It pains him to see her like this, yet he wouldn't give up the moment for the world.

When the ivory-coloured telephone suddenly rings on a dresser next to him, he almost jumps through the ceiling.

Has to carefully detach from Henrike in order to snatch up the receiver. Prays the sound won't interfere with her rest.

He says, "Hello?", and the word comes out too soft.

After listening to the individual at the other end, Issy frowns.

"What, right now?" More chatter. "All right. All right. See you in five." There's a phrase he doesn't catch, and hardly cares. "I won't be long," he concludes, before gently placing the receiver home.

Looks at the sleeping girl on the bed, touches the fingers of the right hand, which are slightly curled next to her cheek.

"Won't be long," Issy promises.

BRANGIEN
[CAFETERIA — ST. MAIGNENN'S HOSPITAL]

*T*he boy hadn't said anything from the other side of the table in five minutes. Well, actually, that was a lie—her watch indicated it might be closer to six.

Issy behaved edgy, eyes wandering the cafeteria without seeing a soul, his collar was loose, and he'd neglected to shave. Who was this imposter?

Having aggressively sucked at a red wax straw leading

into her milkshake, Brangien placed down the large, serially dented metal cup. "Haven't seen you in, like, forever," she remarked.

"What?"

"I haven't seen you in forever."

"Only been a couple of days."

"Like I say."

"I've been busy," her best friend murmured, and the way he did so made him sound, aside from vague, like he was being deceptive. Not straight out lying, but hardly speaking from the heart either. His gaze briefly met hers; as if to check she was appeased, and then switched to some middling distance over her shoulder.

Picking up the shake again, Brangien did more sucking, but did not taste. The drink level went down an inch before she ceased. Then this cup returned to the table. She stared at pink froth that had started to retreat.

Eventually breathed, "Oh."

Reached over, lifted a shaker, and added salt to her drink—to see if this might, at the very least, grab some kind of attention.

If he saw the manoeuvre, Issy hardly registered.

He blinked quickly (for the shortest of spans), and his lacklustre reaction revealed nothing there for Brangien.

ALAINA
[EARLY HOURS THIS MORNING — PRIVATE OFFICE, ST. MAIGNENN'S HOSPITAL]

*"I*sidor? Me. Moore's been shot. Dead. Now, don't get all excited. Shush. I need you to come and identify the body. Yes. No. Because I'm busy. Hmm...? *Yes, right now.*"

Placing the telephone back in its cradle, Alaina thinks about her brother and the child he once was; always would be.

Her back pressed against the wall, she slides down to the carpet, to cry for the first time in twenty-one years.

ISIDOR
[MORTUARY — ST. MAIGNENN'S HOSPITAL]

"*C*ause of death? Single ballistic trauma. Point of entry being the piriformis muscle in the gluteal region—thereafter severing the superior gluteal artery. This resulted in hypovolemic shock, with inadequate delivery of oxygen to vital organs. As is the norm in gunshot cases such as this, the traumatic hypovolemic shock, or failure of adequate oxygen delivery, was due to blood loss."

In other words, Moore Holt died because he was shot in the arse.

Isidor half listened to the rest of an often waffling appraisal from Dr. Almore. This man was the hospital's chief pathologist, and he filled out in great flourish a list of cuts and abrasions, a secondary (non-fatal) ballistic trauma to the head, and pre-existing genital herpes.

The other fifty percent of Isidor's mind attempted to ignore the smell of formaldehyde. Something he was used to, but in this windowless space it had been combined with another nauseating aroma that was familiar.

After the medico's speech ended, leaving Isidor to study the contents of a large glass cabinet while Almore filled in paperwork at his desk, remembrance came.

Monsieur Rochas Extra Strength for Men.

Alaina bought Isidor a bottle several Christmases before, likely because she knew he detested the stuff.

In this case, he assumed the source to be the good doctor. Moore had preferred his own delightfully au naturel scent—one reason the boy took a proper bath only once every few months.

Those squalid Turkish ones didn't count.

Yes, Isidor had come to ID a corpse. Took his time getting here—had breakfast, and then a rambling liquid lunch on the lawn.

Feeling ill wasn't supposed to be part of the deal, not that seeing Moore Holt slapped on a slab moved Isidor.

No, he despised the fool.

"Such a tragic loss, Mr. Holt," Almore commented at his desk, having paused in writing.

Isidor nodded a fraction, the right thing to do. "Yes. Quite."

"Did they catch him yet?"

In the process of running a finger across the smooth surface of a stainless steel dissection table, Isidor paused. "Who?"

"Why, the perpetrator of course, sir. Moore Holt's killer."

"Oh. Oh, yes, I do believe so." He had no idea.

After receiving a large beige envelope filled with official carbon copies of required documents, Isidor took one final look at the body.

Good riddance, you cretin.

ISIDOR
[THIRTY YEARS AGO]

*H*e had hovered on the doorstep of this Joe-average suburban home for minutes now, wondering whether to proceed with the plan he and Lou concocted.

The house's owner Solomon Brodsky had run rackets back in the day, but retired into obscurity over a decade before. There was nothing to fear here—the man was a relic of a bygone era.

So, without further dawdling, he bangs the bronze knocker, one shaped like a lion.

When, seconds later, the door behind the fly wire

screen opens, the man inclines his head while readying pretence.

"Mrs. Brodsky? I'm Isidor Holt."

Being a particularly bright morning, it was difficult to make out this householder in the dark interior, aside from a rather spectacular silhouette and entrancing perfume.

"You're the one Sol spoke of. He mentioned you would come," the woman says. There's a pause, she sighs, and then remarks: "So young. I was hoping you would be more handsome."

She dropped all of her h's—so textbook French, you could stick her façade on the Statue of Liberty, and no one would know the difference.

Since he was also beginning to see her better behind the screen, Isidor understood he needed to deal with a fading beauty with a Eurocentric ego. He made out an elegant blonde, perhaps in her forties. He'd had practice with fading or disappearing Europeans over the years.

"Sorry to disappoint—so I am. May I see him?"

"I suppose it is possible, but do not expect miracles, M'sieur... ah..."

She'd already forgotten, or is pretending. Either way, he decided to make things easier. "Issy." Threw in a bonus French accent of his own, pronouncing it as *eesie*.

Likely, she cottoned on to the undercurrent of insolence.

"My husband usually does not see anyone," comes her tart response. "Why should he see you?"

Isidor leans against the doorframe, tired of this welcome-mat conversation. "Look. I promise to be gentle."

That got things roiling.

"Excuse-moi?" Mrs. Brodsky pushed open the screen-door, the fingers of her right hand clenched, like she was about to strike him. "My husband is the greatest business man this city has ever seen!"

Crossing arms over his chest, Isidor otherwise had not

moved from a relaxed, leaning position. "Course he is, Mrs. Brodsky. That's why I'm here."

Seeing this visitor's lack of fear appears to undermine the lady's revolve.

She reaches a right hand to her forehead and rubs it, eyes lowered.

"That was... rude. I'm sorry. It's just I've had to keep so many bothersome types from him, you know?"

Isidor nods, now consoling and diplomatic, going so far as to erect a sorrowful expression.

"I completely understand, Mrs. Brodsky." He stands straight with an unthreatening posture, hands open. "My proposal will keep those rats away from him. Your husband is a hero—period."

The ruse appears to work. She grants a shy smile, something that would have been stunning a decade before.

"I hope so, M'sieur Holt," she says, remarkably remembering his name and using the h, while standing to one side in order that he might pass.

They walked single-file down a gloomy passageway—everything covered in a layer of dust. The house could have done with a several weeks' airing.

At a closed door toward the rear, Brigit stops and gently knocks.

"Sol? Is me. You have the visitor." After fifteen seconds, the woman reaches down to the handle, turns it, and very carefully pushes the door inward. "Sol?"

Isidor hovers close behind to peer over her shoulder.

There the legend was, in this mostly dark and musty room—slumped in an antique wheelchair of wicker and cane, crippled and forgotten.

Sol Brodsky: notorious gangland leader, number one in this city in his time, and legitimately applauded for his work in the fur trade. Washed up years ago—yet still in possession of controlling interests of the furrier business, as well as a print company.

Mind racing, Isidor awaits an introduction.

These things Brodsky had hung onto—the fur stores and the printing mill—would be preliminary building blocks Isidor and Lou needed, if they were to succeed in this new metropolis.

Another?

Wooing bright, beautiful young medical student Alaina Ohn—daughter of union racketeer John Edgar 'Fats' Ohn.

A work-in-progress, one made tricky by an existing romantic entanglement.

This also meant possibly inheriting Alaina's younger brother Moore, who, at age six, dressed as a cowboy and already wore a gun belt with bona fide six-shooters.

Isidor needed to focus on the moment.

After a few whispered words, Mrs. Brodsky retired to a window, leaving the gentlemen to talk business—but it was clear her husband remained deferential. His eyes often glanced over, whereupon she nodded or shook her head.

Either way, twenty minutes into the meeting, Brodsky began to sit up straighter, and the woman had a vague smile.

When she escorted him out, she tells Isidor that she had not seen her husband so alive in years.

There is reason for this: a deck Lou Holden brought with him from County Cork.

These cards had a fancy Irish harp on the back.

Within six months, the two men—using Brodsky's printing works, canny marketing, and 'Fats' Ohn's societal influence—produced 10,000 packs bearing that same icon from the Emerald Isle.

All sold out.

A million more would be manufactured by the following year.

And a game of cards that Isidor and Lou conjured up over whisky, taking the piss out of traditional French fare binocle—light entertainment supposed to help pass weeks stuck third-class in a passenger liner from Europe—was going to make them very rich.

Marrying Alaina Ohn three years later, after she graduated top of her class—that was supposed to be the glaze.

ISIDOR
[OUTSIDE ST. MAIGNENN'S HOSPITAL, NOW]

After signing the relevant forms, Isidor decided he had no illusions of visiting Alaina in an attempt to console his wife in her grief.

Instead, he circumvented waiting men, and left the hospital building via a discreet rear entrance. Outside, dusk was settling in, and Isidor felt strangely at a loss.

He further chose not to head to the Mercedes—even if having a German car at his beck and call was a point of irony Isidor usually relished. No, the replacement chauffeur babbled too much, made him get sentimental about Lou—and, more than anything, Isidor craved to break free from shackles that held him fast for years.

Heading out of these manicured grounds on foot, the man passed through an outer gate, and entered the real-deal, authentic world beyond.

Alone, no bodyguards, zero obligation—nothing.

He took a right, to proceed along a tree-lined footpath in the direction of the river.

Lou's death, and the demise of Moore Holt, affected Isidor in a manner he had not expected. Remembrances swam before his eyes, making it difficult to see the thriving city surrounding him.

He was Isidor Holt—and, in actual fact, a phony.

His real name he hadn't uttered to any one person for over thirty years: Ossi Stojka.

Until December, 1942, Ossi lived with three brothers and two sisters in Holt, a destitute village in Bacău county, northeastern Romania. Once he turned fifteen, Nazis arrived. The villagers they did not murder on sight were sent to a concentration camp, Auschwitz-Birkenau. While these refugees were not Jews, they were the next best things: Roma. Gypsies.

Members of a different race.

The camp authorities called this new place of abode the 'Gypsy Family Camp', where entertainment was provided by dint of gas chambers, prison guard beatings, rape, and medical experiments conducted by SS Captain, Dr. Josef Mengele, with assorted cronies. Typhus, smallpox, dysentery and starvation were their constant companions. Later official estimates held that 19,000 of the 23,000 Roma sent to Auschwitz died there.

When the Russians rolled up in 1945, the remaining Roma were too far gone to raise arms and celebrate, but Ossi found strength enough to tear off his brown triangle.

Parents, friends, his entire family were dead. His town destroyed.

And yet.

And yet, despite all this, he lived.

After recovering his health, in 1948 Ossi set out for the New World.

Also aboard the ancient liner *Moshulu* was a nineteen-year-old Irish émigré named Lou Holden. After sharing drinks on deck, lying on their backs side by side, hands held, to gaze up at the stars rather than the endless ocean before them and behind, the two became fast friends.

Made plans for an equally starry future.

It was at Lou's urging that Ossi aspired to imitate an Irish brogue, and then Anglicized his name—in the process taking on the title of a lost Romanian village as fit reminder of the horrors of war and the insane nature of men.

The insane nature of men. And women too.

Walking these streets, passing through midnight shadows and deep wells of streetlight, encouraged Isidor to further reflect.

Lou's idea it also was to start fresh in this brave new world, renouncing the violence of the past in their climb—together—to fame and fortune.

There stood a narrow bridge ahead, one that spanned the Muir Èireann. Isidor could have sworn he'd never laid eyes on it before but, judging by the brickwork, this structure had been there well over a century. He decided he needed to cross new terrain.

Where? Where had it all gone astray?

And why couldn't he see Alaina for the woman she truly was, beneath the glamorous veneer? As mad as her brother?

Isidor hadn't done this—the simple act of promenading his adoptive city—in far too long. Had placed memories and feelings on hold for an eternity.

Over the bridge, Isidor stared a while at a faded, ancient handbill pasted to bricks, one advertising a match between Jake La Motta and Tommy Bell. He listened to an old ballad by Johnny Fontane that came from a radio inside the shop behind the wall.

After some hesitation, the man went so far as to call in on this grocery.

Intended to purchase a pack of Camel, but further indulged in small talk with the proprietor there, mostly about the man's basket of beautiful looking oranges placed on the counter.

Ended up buying two, one of which he started to peel while crossing the street, just as a car turned the corner and slowed to a crawl. There were three individuals, difficult to make out because of the nighttime darkness, inside this vehicle. One of them, in the back passenger seat, wound-down a window as the car passed Isidor.

"Oi!" this man yelled, unnecessarily loud. "Get a haircut, you old coot!"

Instead of irritating him, the ridiculous nature of the war-cry made Isidor smile—right before he pitched the half-peeled orange at the back of the automobile, and it took off with squealing tyres and raucous laughter.

He pocketed the other fruit and smoked instead while walking. Stupid kids.

Thinking a little more, yes, but mostly remembering.

Half an hour later, having tackled a particularly steep hill, he wasn't certain exactly how he ended up at Tintagel—in Marcey's welcoming arms.

"You've come from hospital?" she whispered in his ear, after attacking the lobe.

"Yes."

"Moore Holt is really dead?"

He kissed her mouth. "Yes."

"Isidor, what about the police? Do they know?"

Having drawn back in order to better see the woman's familiar face, he took to rubbing his chin. "Not yet," he said.

10

ALAINA

[HOME ALONE — CHAPELIZOD HOUSE]

*"M*rs. Holt?"

She'd been reclining on the couch, the TV loud with an inane comedy boasting a laugh track—*The Love Boat*—that she hasn't bothered to watch. Was staring into space, listening instead to heavy rain falling on the bamboo garden outside the window, aware it was unseasonably cool.

With this intrusion, however, Alaina drew herself up and looked toward the open door, where a man hovered. One of hers, inherited from her father 'Fats' Ohn, rather than an Isidor henchman.

"You found him? You located my husband? Was he with her?"

The way this intruder shifted his weight from foot to foot and scratched his neck, below the chin, gives Alaina answer before he gets up the nerve to speak.

"Yes, ma'am. To both questions."

Three, idiot, she thinks. "Well, now." Having placed bare feet upon a cold slate floor, Alaina leans forward. Takes out a cigarette paper, rolls in Drum tobacco, and then licks the brown sugar flavoured adhesive gum, muttering, "I could kill him sometimes," as she searched for a lighter in her purse.

Finds the revolver there, caresses its grip, while her man lingers in the doorway, awaiting further instructions.

Didn't know why she hadn't already—killed Isidor.

"Do you have a match?" she asks.

"No, ma'am. Sorry."

"Never mind. Send in the Norwegian."

BRANGIEN
[ON BETHA AVENUE, OUTSIDE ST. MAIGNENN'S HOSPITAL]

*B*rangien stood beneath a torrential late-summer squall, soaked right through. Didn't feel it. Hardly cared. Paid little heed to a fresh, earthy smell that had settled over the city after a long summer.

She stared toward the La Tavola Ritonda Wing, up five floors, to a certain window.

Knew Issy was in there now, behind the glass, with that girl.

Bowed her head and cried, waterworks washed away by rain.

ISSY
[12 MINUTES AGO — TRISTA'S ROOM, ST. MAIGNENN'S HOSPITAL]

*H*e could not eat.

Hadn't been able to stomach much of anything over

the past forty-eight hours. Nor was it possible to sleep. So he tried to read—from an original, leather-bound 1717 edition of *The Works of Mr. Alexander Pope*, a particular page of verse epistle titled 'Eloisa to Abelard'.

He'd acquired the book for a university essay intended to be completed over summer vacation, but got stuck on the same words. Took not a single one in. This was like attacking a foreign language. He had also attempted Japanese writer Ryūnosuke Akutagawa's short story 'Rashōmon' earlier, albeit translated, but that felt equal dead-end.

Meaning the exercise shaped up worse than attempting to eat.

Still on the same sentence, hadn't turned a page in an hour, and he had no idea what it was about. Certainly didn't care. Instead, he kept wondering when she would wake.

The girl next to him in the hospital bed—well on the mend now.

This girl whose side he had been incapable of leaving. The stranger he was absolutely, insanely in love with. Putting the book down on his lap, opened at its incomprehensible verse, he turned gaze once again to her.

Wake up, he yearned. *Please.*

Unlike the literary attempt, at least this wishful thinking had some alchemic effect. Within seconds, the girl's eyelashes trembled; they fluttered, and then parted. Dilated pupils flicked about; she blinked, sat up, and eventually glanced sideways at him.

"Good morning," the girl managed, in a low, croaky voice.

Later, he didn't recall exactly what happened next.

How, within two minutes, she'd raised herself further from the dead, to be suddenly in his arms, and he was kissing her all over. The way in which she'd tumbled out of bed, ravenous, and pushed him against closed blinds by the window, making rowdy clatter, her dry tongue in his mouth.

He better remembered what transpired thereafter.

Kicking back on her cot, heads together, half-dressed, half not, as they lit two of the girl's cigarettes rescued from a ruined jacket that hung in the wardrobe. Then staring at the ceiling, faces an inch or so apart.

"That was incredible, Henrike, absolute madness," mused Issy, between drags.

"Uh-huh," she said. Her hand fell across his naked chest, toyed with hairs and nipples there. "Which hospital am I in?"

"St. Maignenn's." When he turned his head her way, she had a smile, albeit a wintry example of one.

"Isidor—"

"Issy. Isidor's my da."

"Issy, then. I have a confession."

"Go on."

"It's complicated."

"They're usually the best kind."

"Mm. Look, 'Henrike Vogl'—that, well, it isn't my real name."

He squinted. "Serious?"

The girl's fingers slid down over his stomach to the crotch and hovered there. "Sadly? Dead serious."

"I see." His squint segued into a frown. "I think I do. So, um... Who are you?—I mean, aside from the girl I met at a funeral, saw working a food kitchen, and then found stabbed outside some gangland spree?"

The girl lifted her head, honesty crossing the face. "My name is Trista Rivalen."

"And that's supposed to mean something to me because...?"

"Because I'm Marcella Cornwall's niece."

"Oh." Glancing at her, he added, without room for hesitation, "Then we need to get you out of here," which made her sit up, engulfed in a certain measure of gloom.

"Yes."

Straight after, she was on top of him, kissing him again. Paused to gaze into his eyes, the dejected moment replaced by a pout.

"Can you help me, Issy?"

"I'm not sure how."

"Please?"

He thought some, said, "All right. Yes, of course. I do believe so," and in fact there was a plan formulating inside his head. But he'd need help getting Henrike—*Trista*, he amended—out of this hospital. The place swarmed with Holt family busybodies. His scheme, however, required getting dressed and leaving her, something he was reluctant to do.

"Right now?" he fussed.

Trista examined him from the mattress with big, beautiful eyes. "I'm not safe here. You know that."

No choice, then.

So he steeled himself. Grabbed one last hug for the road and held on for dear life.

Then broke free, called home on the phone, and had their limousine come to pick him up outside. He kissed Trista on the lips.

"Wait. It might take me a few hours."

"I'll be here," she smiled again—a warmer variant, this one.

The subsequent car ride took a month of Sundays, and it didn't help that new driver Mary was a talkative pain. She rambled on about the change in weather and other things hardly useful for the full twenty-minute trip.

Trying to ignore her, without appearing rude, made it tricky for Issy to clearly think the options through.

One thing he understood he had to do was get over the feeling of this Cornwall girl—push the thing to arm's length from inside his skull. Her kissing him, between his legs, the smell of the girl's sweat and a sensation of her breath on his neck. *Move on, Junior*, he told himself. Time enough for nonsense later. Right now, she needed his assumption of the mantle of white knight.

Meaning he had to pull weight previously sidestepped an entire lifetime—in order to save hers.

They stopped by first at Disco Inferno.

Given the time, he deduced this'd be a best bet. Jumped the queue as usual, chatted as briefly as possible with the door-staff, pushed through a flailing crowd, and found her standing alone beneath the upstairs balcony's mirror ball.

On booming speakers blared one of those orgasms Donna Summer simulated in the seventeen-minute version of 'Love to Love You Baby'. Issy approached the woman from behind to put arms around.

"Brangien."

She turned slowly, had an expression of surprising gravity. "Issy."

"We need to talk."

"We do."

"Your place?"

"Mm-hmm."

After another trip in the loud-mouthed limo, he told Brangien everything over a 5:00 a.m. breakfast at her flat. Felt good to get it off his chest.

"So you're in love with her?" she said, while pouring another orange juice and swaying a little while listening to 'How Deep is Your Love' from the record player in the next room.

"Desperately." Issy leaned back in the sofa, right arm supporting his head. "Who would've figured I had it in me, eh?"

Slightly nodding, Brangien checked water boiling on the stove. "Yes. Who would've figured."

Issy realized he had to be in love—somehow he later resisted Brangien's bedtime come-hither routine, even though she was wearing his favourite skimpy negligee. The poor kid fell asleep around 6:30. Too much partying and fun, from the looks of things.

Before he left Brangien's place shortly after, Issy contemplated how lucky he was to have a friend like her.

Then he set off home—in search of one more piece of the plan.

BRANGIEN
[HER APARTMENT, STRAIGHT AFTER]

*O*nce the front door closed, she cut pretending.

Opened eyes, sat up, and started to smash dishes.

When that refused to help, she looked across at the telephone. Picked her way through ceramic rubble, located the address book, found a number, and dialed.

Had only to wait a few seconds.

"Hello? Can I speak to the Norwegian?"

After a brief conversation, Brangien placed down the receiver. Lit a cigarette. Fixed hair in the mirror and wiped off make up.

Smiled.

And then watched a single tear roll down her cheek.

She straight after struck the looking glass, but it didn't break. Held aloft her hand, inspecting fingers for any damage. Satisfied nothing was broken, she flipped records to put on 10CC's 'I'm Not in Love'.

Thought about what she'd this night learned.

Issy said he met this femme diabolique at the funeral for Lou Holden. That made pieces click into place.

Two weeks before, Brangien had been to see another man.

St. Maignenn's Hospital chemist (and aspiring pharmacologist) Alex Shulgin was a tall, rangy fellow who got about in a white lab-coat and black beret. He chomped at his pipe most hours in amidst shelves of prescription drugs.

Aged in his mid-thirties, Shulgin had prematurely grey

hair and eyebrows, yet his Stalinesque moustache was ink-black, like that was the only thing he thought to dye.

The man was a long-time would-be flame of Brangien's, constantly squeezing her arse when she stepped close. Even so, every now and then she took pains to fan the embers in order to obtain certain medication. Shulgin was a whiz at chemical cocktails, and recently had been synthesizing MDMA for resident psychotherapist Mit Leary—a different kettle of fish, since Brangien couldn't bend that prude anywhere near a little finger.

Easier, then, to go back to the source.

Two weeks ago, Shulgin had been jubilant.

"I've been trying different recipes," he announced in his Louisiana bayou drawl, indifferent as to anyone overhearing, "pharmacological 'arousal' reactions in the brain resulting from selective inhibition of PChE preferentially to TChE."

Meanwhile Brangien had coerced the man, his ridiculously loud voice, and self-gratified mien into the stock room, and quickly closed the door.

"Keep it a few decibels lower, would you?" she whispered.

"But why, cherie," said he, arms circling her waist, already sliding down, "with me straddling success?"

Brangien took hold of his wrists and held them away from her. "Oh, for goodness' sake, not right now. I'm supposed to be working."

That made the man act like he was sucking his thumb. The habit caused her to get more annoyed, but she needed a favour—hoped to get a little something for another night out with Issy.

Small talk and some body contact was part and parcel of the deal.

"So tell me about this success you've been riding."

He brightened at this invitation, lost the mental thumb, took the pipe out of his coat pocket, and held it in reverse as a kind of pointer.

"I *do* know what I'd like to ride right now," he said.

"Down, boy, down. Back to the success thing."

"More's the pity. Well, now, I took the synthesized MDMA I manufactured in bulk last month—you remember that, don't you?"

Did she ever. "Uh-huh." Brangien kept one eye on the empty office outside the door. Hopefully, it'd stay that way.

"Last week I decanted it with related compounds such as 3,4-methylenedioxyamphetamine, otherwise known as MDA, as well as 3-methoxy-4,5-methylenedioxyamphe-tamine—MMDA—and 3,4 methylenedioxyethylamphe-tamine, or MDE. A little bit for the brew, a little bit for the chef. I get an ahnvee, you know?"

"So?"

Shulgin bit down on his unlit pipe, and then released it. "Well, it was hard—trying different amounts of each to get things balanced and just right. But then... then I realized the missing ingredients. So simple, I could kick myself." He trailed off, staring at nothing in particular.

"Go on," Brangien urged.

The chemist blinked several times, very fast, and then glanced at his visitor. "What?"

"The recipe."

"Oh, oh yes! Well, simple, really. You take the different components of methylenedioxyamphetamine, shaken but not stirred, my dear, and add a miniscule amount of lysergic acid diethylamide—about fifty micrograms will do it—along with a cap-full of isopropyl alcohol, and a top-up of Drāno. Not too much, mind you. That stuff is dynamite."

"Drāno? What on earth made you think of adding Drāno?"

"A better question is why didn't I think of it before?"

"I guess."

"Right? So, anyway, you could say that what we have here," he went on in a sing-song croon, while reaching behind a row of outdated 1950s medical encyclopedias, "is Em-Dee-Em-Ay-Em-Dee-Ay-Em-Em-Dee-Ay-Em-Dee-E with the hint of lye, salt, aluminum and rubbing alcohol, and a sprinkling of the LSD!"

He chortled, causing saliva to run down his chin. Oblivious, the man held up a bottle of brownish liquid he'd got from its hiding place.

"My pièce de résistance, the fruit of all labours, la, la, and la again."

Brangien had tried to resist, but anyway now rolled eyes. "What exactly *are* you on about, Alex?"

"Well, is simple, isn't it?"

"Pretend it's not."

"This, cherie, is liquid love."

"How do you know it works?"

"By having tried half of one teaspoon last week—and I think I'm now enamoured with my neighbour's Chihuahua."

"That's normal. They're cute."

"Brangien—up until recently, I loathed this noisy pest. Hated the thing. Once was the time I used to fantasize about throttling it. Last night? I awoke blissful, dreaming of the little man licking my balls instead of his own."

"Ew." The woman looked again at the cloudy brown elixir. "Stronger than MDMA?"

"Stronger? Boo, this relegates MDMA to the caveman era. Once the compound is stabilized, reproduced and adequately tested, I'm going to market it as the *Love and Harmony Groove Pill*—make an absolute bugger of a fortune."

Which is why she'd acquired a small portion in a hipflask, ready to test it out on Issy and see if he finally feel head over tail for her.

Passed it to him in the car on the way to Lou Holden's requiem.

Seemed the dram worked just fine—just with the wrong girl.

TRISTA
[YESTERDAY EVENING — ST. MAIGNENN'S HOSPITAL]

*T*rista cautiously, carefully opens eyelids, and squints at the rush of bright light. Makes out the darker blotch of a person seated beside her, to the right. Governal?

No. As the shape swiftly becomes defined, she makes out a younger fellow, one she barely knows but is horrified to discover.

Isidor Holt, Jr.

Bugger.

Okay, Trista, she tells herself. Deal. Sham. You know the drill. But what to say?

Having risen to a sitting position, she almost throws up, and feels excruciating pain from the abdominal region. Trista groans, hair in disarray before her eyes. Can feel that man scrutinizing every damned move. She wants to die, crawl back into a hole, anything to avoid facing the here, the bizarre idea of now. But Holt is here, he is now, and likely he expects her to talk. A confession?

Decides the best way to act is like she has no idea.

Says, "Good morning."

"So, you are alive," he answers, handing her a glass of water.

"Seems... that way." After drinking half the glass, the woman submerges a finger, and then dabs either side of both eyes. "Dry as all hell," she says, looking straight at him. "Surprised to see you, Mr. Holt."

"Issy."

"Issy, then."

The man shifts in his chair, crossing legs. "Been here two days, actually."

Two days? Trista comes diabolically close to panic.

This isn't how Governal trained her, so she blames the medication they've had her hopped up on. She has to focus to repress the urge to scream.

"Wow. I was out that long?" Putting the tumbler down, she stretches arms, trying to get circulation happening while acting blasé.

"Morphine—since you were knifed."

"Oh. Yeah. Beautiful morning."

"Evening, Henrike." He nods at the window. "It's dark outside."

Trista stops her arms in mid-air at mention of the name. "And you know who I am."

"I do." Isidor Holt, the younger, places aside a book that had been on his lap. "They also say you might've been involved in the murder of my uncle the other night."

"Your uncle."

"Mm-hm. Moore Holt."

"He died."

"Yeah."

Trista's mind, still slow off the mark, wonders where Governal might be. Would he organize something? An escape? Could he? Or was she alone?

"Always look at the worst-case scenario and plan around it," she remembered him lecture several times.

So that's when she looks straight at this man. The enemy. Wasn't 'Issy' a girl's name? And why on earth was he really here? Not that any of this matters. Trista knows he's her ticket out. Governal mightn't approve of the tactics—but he was curiously absent, and she worked his methodology all the same.

Trista takes another sip of water, swirling it in her mouth to help banish some likely bad breath after two days knocked out cold. Drinks more to wash that done.

She leans over, covering the small distance between them, lays hands on his shoulders, and kisses his mouth. Gently at first, but seconds later, when he hasn't reacted, she gets more assertive. Pushes harder, rubs her chest against his, fingers rummaging through hair. Swallows disgust even as she accidentally swallows some of his saliva.

The man tumbles for it before long.

Soon after, lying on the cot together, mostly undressed, having (unintentionally) admitted to this man her real name, Trista poses the important question, the reason behind all of this.

"Can you help me, Issy?"

GOVERNAL
[YESTERDAY MORNING, BEFORE DAWN — OUTSIDE TINTAGEL]

*H*e lurked by a fifty-metre swimming pool, one obviously disused a long time, since it was covered with dead leaves.

Yesterday evening, he had intended to bust out Trista from the hospital, in spite of better judgment, but found her unconscious still and Isidor Holt, Jr., snoozing in a chair beside the bed.

Had no idea what to make of that.

Thus, Governal hesitated. Backed away to reconsider options, and therefore spotted Isidor Holt, Sr., out in the corridor. The way in which 'Anguish' acted—distracted, muttering to himself as he passed by—made Governal realize something was off.

He ended up following the father instead from St. Maignenn's, on foot, across town. It was odd for Holt to have shaken off bodyguards to go walkabout in this city— dangerous, even, for a man in his position.

Yes, he'd acted odd, but Governal was still in no way prepared for their final destination—Tintagel Apartments—or what occurred after they arrived.

That which he witnessed caused our man to understand, much as he preferred to believe contrary, that he really had no clue.

Having seen Marcella necking with Isidor Holt, Sr., on the dimly lit porch—that had undone him.

The leaders of two families constantly at loggerheads and bumping one another off? They'd been seated together there in a love-chair for hours, laughing and kissing over a couple of bottles of champagne.

What the fuck was that?

So stunned still that he relaxed his usual caution. Should've been paying attention elsewhere, especially behind, which is where the next words came from.

"Hullo, Governal."

He stiffened, and then turned, very slowly.

Looked at the fellow with his shock of uneven white hair, over the other side of the pool—dressed only in black, having dispensed with the usual dress-shirt. Instead, a Walther PPK, silencer attached, sat in his right hand.

Governal breathed out, part of a self-calming routine, and responded with, "Ah. Geoffrey. Good to see you."

The other man inclined his head, just a fraction, without moving his eyes. "You too, old boy. Though I always said snooping would be the death of you. "

Nodding toward the distant verandah, Governal said, "Meaning that?"

"I mean that. "

"Old news, or new?"

"Not that one needs to worry any longer. But ancient."

"Well." Governal blew out cheeks, looked away from the gun—knew he'd never reach his in time—and focused on a particular leaf on the surface of the dirty pool.

The thing was difficult to make out in this poor light, but trying to helped steady his nerves.

"Looks like you were prescient," he remarked to Geoffrey, right before the man's pistol spat twice.

At the time, thinking, *Trista—I'm so sor—*

11

TRISTA

[CHURCHYARD OF ST. ENDOC'S PARISH — NOW]

Yet another funeral, Gov, she thinks.

Yours.

Seemed like only yesterday that she lingered on death's doormat, dreaming of him and their past together, one in which the man got played by a young Patrick McGoohan.

Blame the narcotics.

Go on, then.

No need for vivid descriptions of atmosphere or terrain. It's a churchyard; the sky has little fluffy clouds, but otherwise is gloriously blue. There's a slight scent of manure in the warm air.

That'll do.

Trista closes her eyes a moment, searching out the

strength to do what really is necessary. Opens those eyes again to examine the people around—mourners, relatives, clergy, gravediggers—without truly seeing a single one of them. Scolds herself for being inept, and then looks again.

Deeper.

The gravediggers, a trio, are hungry. They're discussing a liquid lunch in low voices. Someone sobs nearby, but it's fake-and-bake. Several members of the crowd smack of impatience and irritability.

The priest reads funeral rites in the same tone that he announced marriage vows the evening before (she hadn't paid attention to the words then, and was determined not to listen now).

Did Marcella look appropriately upset? Trista peers at the woman in black, standing alongside a typically over-dressed entourage.

Maybe.

The standard refrain, "Ash to ashes, dust to dust," drifts across into earshot.

Trista tries desperately to keep feelings in check, like Gov would've preferred, playing it impassive and god-hopefully-nonchalant. Better not to feel. Glances down at the dirt surrounding her heels, and then back up to the mob.

People conspire to stand out, no matter that they might prefer not to—Trista's mother and stepfather, for instance, looking solemn, while Geoffrey hovered by himself and was impossible to read. Stenton 'Spider' Jones and his estranged glam-rock son David at opposite ends of the service. Taylor Daniels' cheap thug offspring, bearing nowhere near the class of his dad, towing along a harried mum and younger brother.

Honest cop McG, bent one O'Dar, plus ambiguous sidekick Sergeant Tusk.

Public Enemy #1 on Trista's guest-list is Anders Sánchez—a.k.a. the Norwegian—who stands to the periphery, in the shade of a sycamore. He smokes a pipe and is accompanied by a pretty copper-blonde in dark glasses, with a sourpuss mouth, someone Trista didn't recognize.

Since Anders had dispensed with his hat, she could pick the prick more easily. Tall, about six-four—that should've been the giveaway at the hospital—this man had fine, sandy hair above Nordic features and a Mediterranean complexion.

Wondered if she could borrow a gun (surely there would be plenty available) and shoot the bastard over Governal's grave. That'd be fitting.

"We have to stop meeting in places like this."

Trista actually produces a smile at the sound of that voice beside her. No, she wasn't alone here, either. Wasn't sure Governal would appreciate the irony, but she had a Holt as escort.

The guy that saved her life.

"Bet you say that to all the mourners."

"Only the ones wearing a dress."

Issy had his suit jacket—the black number still, cleaned up now—draped over his left arm, and as he leaned closer, the hand beneath took the fingers of her right. She felt the wedding band there.

He said in a low tone, "You all right?"

"Surprisingly?" Trista muses, looking up into intense blue eyes. "Yes. Thanks to you." Her hand gently squeezes his.

The clincher? She meant it.

When did that change?

ISSY
[THE HOSPITAL — YESTERDAY, 7:42 A.M.]

The limo pulled into a parking space, causing Issy to lean forward and interrupt his driver's scatterbrained flow of conversation.

Andrez Bergen

"I'll get out here, Mary. Take the rest of the day off."

More chatter bird-dogged him out. Having nodded without listening, Issy shut the door, threw on a pair of Wayfarers, and sauntered casually as he could across to the venerable entrance of St. Maignenn's. Took note of various individuals along the way: Holt family thugs he identified, some dressed as doctors.

At reception, he pretended for several minutes to read a tabloid, checking out other imposters over news that a new pope had been chosen. No schisms this year.

Placing aside the paper, he took an elevator to the fifth floor. Strolled past a new, revolutionary computer-doohickey annex, in which noisy dot matrix printers competed with a ward full of screaming babies next room up.

He came to a door, knocked softly, opened it, and closed the thing behind him.

Trista sat on her bed, dressed in a black silk one-piece with a leopard-print collar and a sizeable rip in the midriff.

"You came back," was all she said.

"You're surprised."

"A little."

"You look ready. Are you?"

"Mm."

Issy allowed himself to grin. "There should be a car waiting in the rear alley." Having said that, he took off his coat—it was warm again, even in this place—and a hipflask fell to the linoleum floor, clanging noisily.

Trista said, "Hello," and reached over first. Judging by her face, which had lit up, this girl wasn't the type to refuse a drink—had already unscrewed the cap and had the chalice at her lips.

"Uh-uh," warned her visitor, "I wouldn't, if I were you."

She swigged anyway—and swallowed in a hurry.

"What the hell is that? Paint stripper?"

"I did warn you."

Grimacing, Trista grabbed water and downed a quick glass. "Urgh. Where'd you get the despicable drop?" she asked, at the same time hastily dabbing lips with a tissue.

"A friend."

"Some friend."

"Same one who's going to help us now." Issy took the flask from her to toss into a nearby trashcan. "If you've stopped mixing drinks, maybe we can get out of here."

Having stood, Trista smoothed out her mutilated dress. "Lead on Macduff."

"Lay on, indeed."

"What?"

"Sorry. I've got to stop correcting people's Shakespeare. C'mon." Departing the room, the duo played up the part of happy young couple, an arm apiece around each other. Issy leaned in close, whispered, "We'll go via the back stairs. Nobody should pay any heed."

Trista rested her head on his left shoulder. "Yeah, okay—it's not like hospital patients don't regularly use the fire-escape."

This caused Issy to blow out in loud fashion. "Look, if you'd prefer to chance our Holt family men in the lobby, be my guest."

"I'm not sure how I should respond to that."

"No abrasive wisecracks?" He looked both ways down the corridor, and then pushed through the door to a set of dark stairs. "Hallelujah."

"Who are you?" Trista asked, following him through. "And what'd you do with the love-sick wallflower I met yesterday?"

"Figured the honeymoon period was over."

"Thank God."

They passed the fourth floor; as expected, there was nary a soul to be found.

"I also cottoned on," continued Isidor, Jr., "that you were using me to do a runner."

"So you've had a change of heart?"

"Revelations are one thing, Trista, but I'm a man of my word."

"That sounds terrible profound."

"It is what it is."

After descending three more flights and reaching ground-floor level, Issy paused at two large exit doors for the woman to catch up. She was holding her stomach and looked pale.

"You all right?"

"Will be, once I escape the lion's den."

"Right." He put on sunglasses again, shoved down the metal locking bar, and swung the right door open. Sudden daytime glare blinded him, in spite of the Ray-Bans, as they took a few tentative steps outside.

There wasn't a car waiting. There were several of them.

Men—some in hats, all with plenty of guns—were draped around these.

"Trista Rivalen?" announced a very tall individual at the centre of this vehicular circumference, a man in a brown fedora and long, camel-coloured trench coat.

Blinking to better see, Trista appeared to appraise their situation in seconds. "Issy," she mumbled, "when you said an automobile'd be waiting, did you mean the ones full of gats pointed at us?"

TRISTA
[HOSPITAL REAR-ENTRANCE — YESTERDAY, 7:59 A.M.]

Shit, crap, bollocks, bullshit—these were just some of the words conjured up in Trista's brain, on the fly, once she realized the predicament they were in.

The guy in the hat and trench coat, impossible to recognize right away, reached under his lapel to produce a firearm she believed she could better peg—also given time. Something she was fairly certain they'd run out of.

That's when her companion surprised her.

"I've got this, Trista," he announces, having unbuttoned his jacket again, and bringing forth a Colt .38. She'd no idea he was even packing.

Without wasting a moment, Issy raised his gun into the air and wasted two shots firing at a birdless sky.

"None of you twitch!" he yells. "Consider those warning shots!"

Staring at him, Trista managed to utter, "Oh, bugger, mate, now you've really started something—", before all hell really did bust loose, and everybody was shooting at once. No silly comic book sound effects, but an unearthly din as guns erupted in unison, causing bricks to shatter and fence posts to splinter.

"Move!" the woman shouts, grabbing the material of Issy's coat shoulder and tugging him after her. She broke into a sprint down the alley, yelled at him all the way, while mentally tossing desperate prayers that a zigzag through rubbish skips would catch some of the bullets raging in pursuit.

Above ricochets and explosions that pounded her hearing, Trista made out Junior's ragged breathing or occasional terrified yelp, and she had no idea how they somehow (somehow) reached a parked Stallion.

"Get in," Trista ordered, above the chaos, "and take the wheel."

"Er—No key," the boy responds, all panicky.

"Fuck the key. It's open. I'll get it started. Move!"

Some arsehole had begun using a shotgun, evidenced when a rear passenger window was blown out right beside Trista just as she leaned in, to rip aside wiring under the dash, and tried to get the engine going.

"Jeez, that was close," she hears her hanger-on appraise.

Says, irritably, "Had closer," as she fiddles more with the wires.

"When?"

"With your stupid uncle." The explosion of the right exterior mirror punctuates the sentence.

Issy had already placed himself behind the steering column and sat in surprisingly composed fashion, given bullets riddling the bonnet.

"Anytime you're ready, Trista."

"Not helping," is her answer. Goddamn you, she further tells the car, work. She'd done this a million times under Governal's watchful eye.

"Will you pull your finger out?" the would-be driver complains, as something whistled by her ear.

"Listen, Junior," she rails back, distracted, "this is all your fault!"

"That's right—let's play the blame game."

"You're the one who got us into this."

"You're the one who killed my uncle."

Trista laughs then. Has no idea why—likely it's the insanity of the moment and the certainty that they're both going to die in a poor man's take on Bonnie and Clyde. She grabs the man's face and kisses his mouth hard. Having pulled back, he looks dazed.

"Go," she says.

"Look, I'm not sure how many more hundreds of bullets we can duck."

"Time to do your part and start driving—the engine's running."

He leans close, gazing into her eyes, announces, "Hah!", swings the wheel—and kicked down on the accelerator. At the same moment, the back window shattered and the car's AM radio erupted into ear-splitting life.

Trista buries ears beneath her palms, catching only something about never being able to say goodbye.

"What's this hideous sound?"

"Don't blaspheme Gloria Gaynor. Best singer in the biz." Lazing back, Issy looks surprising chipper for a man recently on the receiving end of a million and one slugs, while currently sitting on a hundred m.p.h.

Having cranked down volume, Trista swings her head to survey what was happening behind. "No one in pursuit," she decides. "Well, I hope not. Who knows?"

Mouth open, Issy glances in the rear vision mirror, again looking worried. "I thought you were a pro at this sort of thing."

"You kidding? I'd never been shot at till today. Being stabbed is my specialty."

"We're going to die," the man whines.

"Hush up." Trista turns her attention ahead. "Take the next left, and then the next right. We're sticking to small streets. And, for fuck's sake, slow down."

Wasn't sure if nerves were the ones actually shot, but Trista has spots dancing before her eyes; puts it down to the after-effects of morphine.

"You hit?" she asks her driver.

"What?"

"Did they hit you?"

"No, they were using fucking guns."

Rubbing her eyes, trying to clear them, she mutters, "Are you a moron?"

"No—No, I'm fine," he breezes, a stupid smile stuck on his mush when he peers her way. Man was love-sick again, and just in time remembers to look ahead as he turns another corner for good measure—then slows to fifty.

Trista had to admit, he did this process with accidental finesse. Wonders if he might be delirious, so rephrases her previous question.

"Were you shot, Isidor?"

"Issy." He smirks, apparently more excited than scared.

This makes Trista give up asking. She looks him up and down. He seemed okay—a couple of tears in his pants, and a lot of dust on the jacket, no obvious blood.

"Slow down to forty," she suggests.

Speed wouldn't matter anyway, not with the car being

riddled with shells. This was any police officer's dream.

Still, there was one thing in the plus-column: allergic to knives she might've been, but not a single bullet struck her or the boy in the next seat, the one with the beam that now seemed less idiotic, more endearing. He'd held it together—got her away from his own father's hatchet men.

While munitions had been flying, she'd ransacked the mental filing cabinet that Governal forced her to construct. The process could be diabolical, not just because of raised levels of adrenalin and a car full of shrapnel that promised to break down any moment.

No, driving to the sounds now of the Bay City Rollers song 'I Only Wanna Be With You'? Sweet Jesus.

"We need to change rides," she abruptly decides.

Issy nods knowingly. "You think we're too obvious in this lovely crate."

"That, and I'd like to switch to one with better radio."

In a back-street warehouse district downtown, close by the river, the two exchanged their sedan for a classy little red, 1950s Alfa Romeo Disco Volante. Listened instead to Roberta Flack singing 'The First Time Ever I saw Your Face'.

"Well, I think it's safe to say we got away," says Issy, the passenger.

"For now." Trista, behind the wheel, chewed for a short time at her lower lip—then thinks better and glances at this man. "Thanks to you. Kind of. But where'd you learn to shoot a gun?"

Issy laughs. "Where did you learn to hot-wire cars?"

Raising one brow, Trista nods her head. "Touché." She then places that head on Issy's shoulder, and feels surprisingly happy there—but needs to focus.

"Where now?" he asks on her behalf, looking around as they pass over a bridge.

"I need to get to Tintagel—Speak to Marcella."

"Is that a good idea?"

"She needs to know what's happening." While they spoke, Trista mulled the memory of that gun, the one Trench-coat Man had produced. There was a photo Governal once showed her, of this rare 1968 Carl Gustafs GF 9mm pistol—owned by a notorious Holt family gunsel known as the Norwegian. It was his favourite piece.

The Norwegian: a bogeyman gangsters told bedtime stories about to scare one another.

They dumped the Alfa Romeo five hundred yards downhill from Tintagel and went the rest of the way on foot. Time? Around midday. Neither said a word, but they stayed close and their shoulders occasionally rubbed.

Issy breaks this silence.

"We did it."

To which, Trista laughs softly. "We did."

At the entrance to the manor house, there's surprisingly no security, and no one meets them on the path heading up toward the front entrance of the mansion.

This makes Trista slow down.

"What's up?" Issy asks.

Trista stopped on the lawn to take up listening. "I don't know."

Voices sounded from within, some kind of mournful dirge that people sang badly. Trista would've sworn it was a party.

"If this is a Cornwall family tradition," Issy murmurs, also tuning in, "then I have to say I'm a little concerned."

"Live a little," responds Trista, and then she sighs. Reaches up on her toes to kiss his cheek, says, "Issy—I want you to wait out here while I talk to Marcey. Holts aren't popular in these parts."

12

TRISTA

*"H*ey—don't leave me out here too long." That was Issy speaking, having squeezed in the plea between long kisses on steps leading to the verandah.

"Why?" she murmured in return, touching his lips. "Frightened?"

"Nah. Just need to use your bathroom."

Trista broke into a smile then, her heart skipping about in ridiculous fashion. "One thing I don't have to worry about. Think I wet myself during the gunfight."

Rolling his eyes, Issy said, "I'm not sure you'd call what we did fighting."

"Oh? Then what was it?"

"Running?"

Trista clicked her tongue. "Hah."

207

"Hey, you won't find me complaining—a tail between the legs suits me just fine."

"All right, all right. I'll be back, Rin Tin Tin."

She went straight up to the entrance, sneaked a look over her shoulder at the dazzling man below on the path, turned, and rang the bell. The door opened straight after, revealing Geoffrey, solemn like a mortician. If the man was surprised to see her, he did not display an inkling.

"Trista," said he, at his Basil Rathbone best, "you've come at a most unfortunate time."

"Why? What's happened now?"

"I'll summon Marcella—I am certain she will wish to explain herself."

With that, the man swiveled on his heel and headed back into the dark interior, leaving behind the bad taste of a worrying, unexplained mystery.

Trista waved at Issy and shut the door, lingering in the foyer. Felt it dingy after the glorious sunlight without.

While waiting, she stared at framed photographs on a wall. One was of Marcella, from her youth, when she raced cars and men and generally broke all the respectable barriers women were supposed to abide by. It was the war, after all, and most men were away fighting. The picture showed this dark-haired, twenty-something beauty perched on the door of a Ferrari, dressed in a leather driver's cap and jacket.

She already looked like she owned the world.

Next to this hung a photo of Trista's mother, here a girl in early teens. Contrasting Marcella's look, she had long blonde hair with a fringe, was holding a netball, and looked a bit like Alice from Wonderland. Had none of the confidence or nonchalance of her sibling—Blanche came across kind of creepy.

"Trista?"

Marcella's voice interrupted her, coming from the top of the staircase, and the elderly woman began to descend.

"My God. Is that you—?" She was wearing a black

crepe dress and shoes, had her gold-rimmed reading glasses on, and shuffled quickly down. "You're alive!"

Trista dared a minor smile, still unsure of the circumstances Geoffrey had hinted at. "I like to think so," she said.

In the process of looking her niece over, Marcella abruptly stopped, turned away, and acted pensive. "I have... something to tell you."

"What is it?"

"Terrible news."

Trista further dared reach out, took hold of her aunt's hands, and coerced her to look back. "You can tell me."

"Governal, he—"

"What about him?"

"Well." The usually icy eyes looked broken. "Well—"

"Well—What?" Trista knew her tone edged hysterical, but right then didn't give a toss.

"I don't know how to tell you this."

"Try."

"Yes. Geoffrey. He found Governal early this morning. Here." She looked over Trista's shoulder, struggling with something. "In the pool," was all she could say.

"In the pool," Trista echoed.

"In the swimming pool."

This was sufficient. Trista understood straight off. Governal hated swimming—couldn't manage a stroke at all. In spite of his meticulous nature, it was battle enough getting the man to bathe on a regular basis.

"He," the young woman swallowed, and then cleared her throat, "He drowned?"

"No."

Trista took a step back, found it difficult to breathe. Memories of Governal flooded through the airways. She had to force in a stopper, recalibrate the here, the now. Later, an inner voice railed. Scream to high heaven in your own home—even better at Lion's Estate—but not in this awful place.

So she pushed back into the role Governal groomed her to fill.

Trista couldn't tell whether the expression on her aunt's face was a close cousin of elation to see her alive, shock about Gov's death, or something else entirely. The older woman still held onto Trista's hands, and there was a glimmer of moisture beneath her right eye.

Trista said, "How?", to which Marcella aped befuddled. "How did he die?" she insisted.

"Does that matter?"

"Yes."

"Why—?"

"Humour me."

"Very well." Marcella clenched her fingers, hurting Trista a little with those pointy, manicured nails. "He was shot. Twice. It was dreadful."

"You saw it?"

"No. Nobody did, my dear. I told you—Geoffrey found his body this morning."

"So it happened overnight?"

"Appears that way."

"No witnesses."

"None."

"What was he doing here?"

"I have no idea."

A fresh kind of rage surged through Trista, caused her to see stars and lust after the nearest firearm. Only years of tutelage from Governal—whose murder triggered the fit— could smother the thing. She heard his voice beneath the din, coercing her to breathe, think, show nothing of a world gone to pieces.

Trista wet her lips, focused. "So who did this?"

"Who? We don't know."

"Then—what calibre?"

Her aunt dropped her mitts, wrung them, and uttered, "Eh?"

"The gun, Marcey. The casings. Have they sussed out

yet the calibre?"

"Why on earth would that matter right now?"

"It matters to me."

"But—But we're still holding the poor man's wake, and—"

"Bullets. Calibre. Please."

"All right." Pursing wrinkled lips, Marcella composed herself. "Doc Ambrosius said he fished out 9mm slugs."

"Was he certain?"

"Well, of course we need to have additional tests— Captain O'Dar is handling that."

"Was the doc certain?" Trista insisted, her voice surprisingly high.

"Yes."

Trista breathed in, short and quick. "The fucking Norwegian." Then she breathed out.

"Eh?"

"Anders Sánchez."

"Good God, girl, I know who the Norwegian is," Marcella snapped, edging angry. "But we can't be certain."

"I can. He uses the same calibre."

"Trista, there are so many guns that would equally fit the bill."

Shaking her head, Trista looked directly at her aunt. "Trust me on this. No one else could get the drop on the old man."

Marcella's reaction now came across marginally peeved. "You make Governal sound like more than a mere retainer."

"He was."

"But hardly Superman." When Trista didn't reply, Marcella added, "Or your father."

With a cigarette held between two fingers that she'd just set fire to, Trista breathed, exhaled at a distant decorative ceiling, and then stared into space. "Governal was the next best thing to me."

"I understand, dear."

"Do you?"

"Trista." Marcella came close again, this time with a firm, tight look shaping her kisser. "I've lived a long time, girl—had my fair share of tragedies and, yes, heartbreak. I do understand."

This brought the other woman closer to tears. "I loved him so much, auntie."

"I know."

"What will I do without him?"

"There, there. You will cope, as we always do. Our stock is strong. And while there's a time to mourn the past, we also need to plan for the future."

Having recovered wits and placed her cigarette in her mouth, Trista punched the palm of her left hand. "Agreed." The Norwegian was already in a set of imaginary crosshairs. "So, what're you thinking?"

"That there's only one course left to save us."

Trista eagerly nodded. "Uh-huh."

"Only one move we can make."

"Yes. Retribution."

Marcella's next words, however, decked her niece. "Seriously? I gave you credit for more intelligence. And I thought you didn't believe in revenge."

Trista raised her head and puffed more smoke. "Things change."

"That they do—but not in the way you think."

Less searching about for an ashtray than trying to restore that semblance of calm, Trista forgot to answer.

"Look at me," demanded Marcella. "I said, look at me."

So the younger woman did, holding her butt vertical to slow the burn reaching the filter. "I need something for this."

"Oh, for fuck's sake, use the cactus there." Her aunt nodded curtly at a small, bulbous houseplant on a shelf beneath the framed photographs.

"Thank you," Trista said, burying the thing. Pricked herself in the process, yet appreciated this different kind of localized pain.

"Now," announced Marcella behind her, "may I please have your attention?"

Trista steeled herself, finger in her mouth, tasting blood. "Sure."

"Then stop sucking your thumb and look at me."

The younger woman dropped her hand as she turned. "I'm looking."

Any dithering, empathetic lapse on Marcella's part was a morsel of the distant past.

"Swell. Now, I want you to continue to listen—and listen good. We're calling the peace here, Trista. We would never survive all-out war with the Holts. It's time to cut losses and build bridges."

"Build bridges."

"Exactly."

"I think you need to tell me—What kind of pontoons are you proposing?"

"Well. A wedding, for a start."

Trista came close to dropping any remaining thread of composure. "Yeah?" she squeezed out.

"With young Isidor Holt, Jr."

For a second (actually, more like half of one) Trista imagined her aunt was talking up a union between the heirs of both families, causing her stomach to begin to knot, as the side of her mouth started to shift into a smile. But taking in Marcella standing there, Trista witnessed the smug, self-satisfied countenance—and hope got snuffed.

"Huh," she quickly covered, at a loss for further words.

Marcella's eyes sparkled. "So—aren't you going to congratulate me?"

"You. And him."

If her heart had jumped into her mouth, that mouth tactfully said nothing. Trista nodded instead, a refrigerated sensation creeping through, making her pine for a dose of antifreeze. She needed to rediscover some sense of decorum.

Stalled with: "I thought you swore you'd never wed."

"Things change."

Whether this comment was a mockery of her earlier declaration or simply coincidental, Trista realized didn't matter. Those stupid dice had been cast.

"Well," she said. "You're in luck. I brought him with me—Issy Holt, I mean. He's waiting just outside this door."

Abruptly chuckling, like she had no care now in this world (which she likely didn't), Marcella put a hand on her niece's shoulder. "Heavens. Do you have intuition skills I was not privy to? How did you know to organize this?"

"Trade secret." Trista shoveled up a grin. "Wait here. I'll go get your present."

She wasn't about to lie to herself—as she walked calmly to the entrance, her head reeled, as she unbolted the door, her fingers threatened to shake and, having set foot again out into strong sunshine, Trista felt frozen to the bone.

She took one step at a time, almost in tears.

Once she reached the path, obscured from the main house by a tall hedge, Issy ambled up with a smile, placed arms around her, and mussed up her hair.

"Here you are," he said.

Eyes closed, she breathed softly, "Issy."

"I ended up going behind a tree."

Trista's eyes snapped back open. "Issy." She smacked fingers away. "Stop it." Broke free from his embrace.

"What is it?"

She shook her head, and then granted a grand smile. "Congratulations are in order."

"How do you mean?"

The smile was a short-lived one. Wrapping herself in her arms, Trista walked a slow circle round the man, keeping a couple of yards' safe distance. "You're going to be married."

Issy frowned, and then laughed. "What? You're proposing already?"

The woman stopped to gaze at his face. Could see the mirth slowly evaporate as he took in her own expression. "Not me," she finally managed to say.

The boy looked dazed—said "Huh?"—right before Marcella paraded out onto the verandah above, wrapped in a fox fur stole.

Trista heard her aunt's steps, mumbled, "I'm sorry," linked her arm in the man's, and coerced him forward into view from the porch.

Grand dame that she liked to play, Marcella stood at the head of the stairs, hands on hips, and beamed at her catch below.

"Ahh, there you are, Isidor. Ready to say your vows?"

TRISTA
[TINTAGEL — EVENING, YESTERDAY]

Guessed she had to hand it to Marcella Cornwall.

The ad hoc wake for Governal wasn't over, yet the woman managed to turn this event on its ear and rearrange things into a wedding ceremony before the sun had its chance to set—in the process bringing together dangerously volatile egos from both families, about fifty all up, including the enemy, Isidor Holt, Sr.

A working class banquet miraculously appeared in the ballroom: miniature Cornish pasties with Ballymaloe Relish, stargazy pie, and king crisp sandwiches (white bread, butter, and potato chips), alongside Spingo beer, cider, and Irish whiskey.

It was also a riddle where they'd dredged up the string quartet at short notice.

Half an hour after sundown saw Issy forced to pose with a blushing bride (the liberal amounts of rouge helped there), before a cake higher than the tallest person in sight, and flashes popped. The pale groom dressed in the same black suit he'd worn since Trista met him, though Marcella had a local drycleaner's give it a tart-up, and he bore a new white shirt with a narrow green tie of his consort's choosing.

The bride wore white—a gown that would've better suited someone forty years younger.

Through this all, Trista couldn't take her eyes off Marcella's fledgling husband, who also looked stiff and anxious and drank too much. His glowing wife didn't notice, since she was busy ogling Issy's father.

The only consolation being that Trista hadn't been asked to play bridesmaid.

Guests bounced between apologizing to Trista for her loss (meaning Governal, not the other), and congratulating Marcella and 'Anguish' Holt for their gain.

Issy they mostly ignored.

Post-matrimony revelries were bookended by Geoffrey, officiating on Marcella's behalf, and Isidor Senior, representing the Holt family. Both men behaved reserved and charming, a trait Trista was used to from Geoffrey, but she'd expected Issy's dad to be a mad tyrant.

The man even made time for small talk at one point, approaching the fringe where she stood swaying, thoughts most definitely elsewhere, to an interpretation of 'Trelawney'. He offered champagne.

"Let me pour some of this for you, missy," he said. His moustache jiggled when he spoke, and the way he pronounced 'pour' made it sound like 'purr'. "I gather you're the one that knocked off Moore Holt."

Trista remained mum. Felt like she'd throw up.

"I wanted to offer my gratitude." He held out a hand and, before she knew what was happening, they shook.

The whereabouts of Issy's mother—Moore Holt's sister as well as the surgeon who'd saved Trista's life—remained an unspoken mystery till Trista stole into an anteroom to escape this ceremonial depravity, and happened to switch on the TV there.

"...A police dragnet for Alaina Holt, the doctor wife of

city benefactor Isidor Holt," a male announcer was wrapping up, an unflattering photo of the woman over his right shoulder.

Apparently, the hospital assault had resulted in unintended other casualties and one death, with Alaina fingered as the architect of the whole shebang. Trista wasn't sure if anyone bothered to tell her son—and wondered why Isidor Senior appeared so damned unfussed.

To hell with them, Trista decided.

While other people who ought to've known better danced (badly) in the ballroom to Earth, Wind & Fire, Trista absconded with a bottle of Marcey's best rye.

Went to the dark, empty room at the back of the palace, where an open coffin lay in ignored state. Wanted to say a proper, private farewell to a man she loved more than family.

Trista placed a tumbler of mineral water with a slice of lemon on a small, round table beside the box, as well as an unlit cigarette.

Gazed at the body for a while, took in the waxy skin, before straightening his tie and leaning over to kiss a cold, rigid mouth.

Hours later, Issy entered and found the woman huddled in a corner close by the casket. She'd lost her clothes, burned a hand, and was insanely drunk—crying as she blurted out 'You Are My Lucky Star', Governal's favourite song from his favourite film.

For the second time since she met the man, Issy carried her to a better place.

TRISTA
[TINTAGEL — AROUND 3 A.M.]

Couldn't sleep. Had sobered up a lot, felt like misery, and was busy toying with Governal's gun, when Issy came back to her guest-room.

Says nothing, but looks so damned concerned.

She should've kicked him straight back out—but shagged the man instead.

BRANGIEN
[TODAY — AFTER GOVERNAL'S FUNERAL]

*T*he woman lies on the roof of her VW, parked to one desolate side of the churchyard, where no others cars could be found.

Trying to soak up sun, yet failed to warm anything.

The world had gone to shit, and she thought it sucked already. That arsehole the Norwegian was never supposed to take potshots at Issy—only in the direction of the awful bitch that he obsessed over. And now? Now, he'd gone and married ancient crone Marcella Cornwall, his parents' nemesis?

For fuck's sake, she thinks. Screw him. Screw him and his family. A curse on both their stupid houses. All she felt was sped and done. To top it all off, her car went and died on her too.

Had come to the service and clung to the Norwegian in spite of his failure. Watched Issy, who looked fragile, and Queenie peacocking about with her camp followers. Saw The Girl, hovering near the coffin, a bunch of flowers under an arm.

"Gov meant a great deal to that one," the Norwegian said beside her, during closing remarks from the priest.

"Who gives a shit? You blew it."

That was when the tall man looked down at her, hard and sharp, and lurched away from the party. Meaning she had to wait to be towed, long after all other guests had left.

When she finally got back to her place on the other side of the river, a fellow she didn't know—nondescript, with black hair and an appropriately bland face—was standing outside the entrance to her block. He brightened up, attached himself to her side, and says in a low voice, "Brangien! Hey, missy!"

"Do I know you?"

"Nah, nah, but cool bananas. I got a message from the boss."

Turned out he was one of the Norwegian's minions. She should hardly have been surprised. They went up to her flat together, and after small talk and a free drink (for him), he took out a pistol while Brangien remained seated on the edge of her bed, gazing along the barrel.

The man behind it is faux apologetic. "Sorry, babe. Nothin' personal. Boss don't want to leave no loose ends."

Brangien sighs. It really did figure.

This, she understands, is the sum total of her life.

Simon, Tahiti, and all that jazz.

13

ISSY

[TINTAGEL — 5:47 A.M.]

*T*hey'd been doing it for hours—stuff of legends material.

Climbing on top of him one more time, Trista shoves aside satin sheets as she settles in. No words spoken. None need to be. It's enough to read her eyes and touch her skin.

This felt so damned right.

TRISTA
[TINTAGEL — 9:13 A.M.]

*H*aving opened eyes to a new day, gazing at the man asleep beside her, Trista sighs.

This felt utterly wrong.

Very carefully, so as not to wake Issy, the woman rises.

221

Puts on a simple dress and locates her undies draped atop the lamp. She then grabs a seat by the window, taking time out over a cigarette.

Needed to work things out. Couldn't leave them unfinished.

ISSY
[TINTAGEL — 2:42 P.M.]

"*T*rista?"

Issy looked about, sleep impeding vision and a partial ache at the back of the head. Likely he'd slept too long. What time was it, anyway? The curtains of this guestroom were closed, but around the edges daylight offended.

Trista long-gone, her side of the bed cold.

Lighting a ciggie, Issy perched himself against two pillows.

Had stayed over longer than usual—and wondered if he should scuttle on back to the bridal suite (Marcella's room) post haste.

No. Fuck that.

Looked around this empty, characterless ground-floor space: Small, clean white walls, the twin bed, a humdrum desk with a blank blotter on it, sliding closets opposite the bed, and green shag carpet. At least a dozen other guestrooms at Tintagel exactly like it, according to Trista.

Yes, unlike the rest of the mansion, these rooms had little in the way of decoration—Issy imagined that some interior designer had come in and reverse-engineered the job lot, absconding with furnishings and simply slapping on a coat of paint.

Trista was the only thing of worth—and she'd vanished.

Girl is flightier than me, he decided.

TRISTA
[TINTAGEL — 10:02 A.M.]

*T*he day after Governal's funeral. Issy had been hitched to Marcella for two—yet the marriage bed remained unconsummated.

Not their doing.

Issy reported that, over the past couple of evenings, Marcey had disappeared elsewhere in this rambling place, and didn't return till the next day. No excuse, nothing in the way of apologies, any explanation dispensed with.

Which left he and Trista free to do their own carnal thing.

But doing so brought the guilt. Trista knew fully well she was betraying her aunt's trust, under the woman's own roof. Understood she had been ignoring a responsibility to bring Governal's killer to some kind of justice.

Beneath this unhappy conscience, there remained concerns.

How could she indulge in this oddity with Issy? What did the boy really mean to her? Where was Marcella over the past two nights? How to explain away those possessive glances her aunt shared with Isidor Holt, Sr., at the wedding? In God's name, why would anyone succeed in catching Governal on the hop? And what was the point of the hit, given a wedding and reconciliation between both families the very next day?

Trista mulled these issues as she stepped outside for air.

First past Holt family driver Mary, who was blathering loudly on a phone in the kitchen, and then bypassing some of Marcella's over-dressed Round Table members—they stood in the doorway of Tintagel's rear entrance, ogling the new, classless wheels parked by a six-vehicle garage: DuBois and Blanche's hot-pink Chrysler Cordoba wedding present for Marcella. They'd likely invested in this particular car because actor Ricardo Montalban endorsed it on TV.

As for the colour—well, that made more sense given Issy's recent disclosure.

Having weaved through a decked patio adjoining the house, which had black iron tables and chairs interspersed with dozens of potted plants, Trista reached the lawn and thereafter wandered the grounds. Mostly in the shade cast by a long row of junipers, past a fountain and disused pavilion. She heard the sounds of magpies in the trees and distant traffic, but barely paid attention.

Unruly impressions returned instead to Issy's mouth and the smell of him, the feeling of him between her legs.

ISSY
[TINTAGEL — 2:59 P.M.]

After getting dressed, Issy opened curtains to stare out at an enormous garden. Had a glass of Scotch in one hand, brewed strong—nothing like a hair-of-the-dog to take the edge off things.

Decided he ought to go explore this archaic Tintagel shack, get his bearings and a better gist of the lay of the new land.

Wondered (again) where Trista might be. Recalled last night. Regretted some things said. Mused over her mouth and her eyes, which made him smile.

Thought about that old cow Marcella, and felt ill.

"What's it like?" Trista had asked the night before, in a wavering tone. "Her room?"

"Pink," was all he could say.

Marcella's private quarters presented less lair than boudoir. The brass bed was shaped like a great yawning oyster. Issy surmised the intention to be that if you slept in it, you'd feel like a pearl. He wouldn't know. Had never so much as sat on the monstrosity.

It took central position, down bedding and carnation

pink pillows plumped up and looking fit for a gangland princess. Across the marble floor lay an enormous white wool rug. The drapes were salmon pink. There was an en suite housing a bath (in puce porcelain) with frameless glass shower, where the amount of territory could've easily entertained your proper Catholic family. The towels, replaced every day, were always thick, white and monogrammed. While all sat neat and orderly, Marcella's vanity plied pandemonium, knee-deep with cosmetics and a bunch of lotions with names like Crabtree & Evelyn and Chanel. Black and white framed photos of people he didn't know struggled for air behind the junk there.

Issy had claimed a small area under the bed to toss used underwear, which miraculously reappeared clean and pressed every morning.

Trista had looked surprised. "Pink? Huh."

So long as Queenie continued to keep her distance—that's what he now prayed. In a house this size, surely they wouldn't need to cross paths often.

TRISTA
[TINTAGEL — 10:35 A.M.]

*W*hen she re-entered the building, Geoffrey was standing close by the entrance, holding a black telephone receiver with an extension cord.

"Trista. You have a call."

He handed her the phone and, without further word, detoured down the hall to allow some privacy.

Nice of him.

Trista settled into the call, saying, "Hello?" followed by, "Speaking. And you are?"

Froze, once the answer came.

"Oh." Swallowed hard, pushing her tongue into the lower lip, as her mind raced. "You. Yes." More talking ensued, at the same time that she tried to restore personal order. Murmured, "Uh-huh," and then, "I know the place. Yes. I'll be there in thirty minutes. Right."

She placed down the receiver.

Stared at a wall with pictures of pastoral scenes, a wall recently invaded by a darker, more harrowing oil offering—a close-up of action and armour that had Isidor Holt's hand-written name taped to the top of the gilt frame, while across the bottom (in more professional lettering) read *Presa di Cristo nell'orto, Michelangelo Merisi da Caravaggio*.

Trista's heart hammered. Her head thought about Gov's .45.

Put a hand out to steady the old frame. Breathe, she demanded.

GEOFFREY
[TINTAGEL — 10:42 A.M.]

At some point over the past two days, probably because it recently contained a corpse afloat, the swimming pool had been drained, cleaned, and refilled.

Geoffrey very quietly came out through French doors to the place where the head of the house lay on a settee— positioned next to the cement pond—wearing a floral swimsuit, a big hat, and sunglasses. Her hair was pulled back into a bun, and she'd caked on sunscreen that blotched sagging skin on arms and legs.

She appeared to be dozing.

Having scanned the other surroundings, Geoffrey coughed softly to announce his arrival. When the woman didn't move, he spoke. "Marcella."

This caused her to stir in the sunshine and sit up, using an elbow for support. "Yes, what is it?"

"We have a technicality."

"Oh, don't tell me the freezer's on the blink again," she muttered.

"Not that I'd know. This technicality is of a more serious nature."

"Oh?" Marcella straightened up. "What, Geoffrey? You realize I hate it when you beat around the bush."

"I know."

"Well?"

"We need to discuss young Trista."

ISSY
[TINTAGEL — 3:12 P.M.]

*T*intagel had more rooms than Imelda Marcos owned shoes, but most surprising was this he'd stumbled across in the basement.

Some kind of games room—housing one mustard-yellow beanbag chair, a pristine soccer table, a tape deck with a towering set of speakers, the game 'Pong' paused on a big television screen, and a *Six Million Dollar Man* pinball machine.

Older than these accoutrements was mould flecked on wallpaper otherwise covered in tiger lillies.

Before he knew what to think, arms embraced him from behind, accompanied by the aroma of chlorine, suntan lotion, and age.

"You ruined my surprise, darling," said Marcella Cornwall, snuggling into his back.

"Surprise?" Having stiffened on contact, Issy needed to squeeze out the word. "What surprise?"

"Why, this spread—I had my people assemble it in secret yesterday. A place to call your own, with all the knickknacks that entails."

The last game on a pinball machine Issy had played was when he was sixteen, though this new one looked enticing—anything to escape the clutches of a fossil he'd been coerced to marry.

"Cool," he said.

"I want you to be at home here."

"Sure." He carefully unwound the arms and did a circle of the space. Stopped on the other side of the pool table—safer there—and looked over at Trista's aunt. Why he hadn't kicked and scratched his way out of wedlock was beyond him.

Hadn't he and Trista recently escaped a brace of bullets?

TRISTA & ISSY
[TINTAGEL — SOME TIME LATE LAST NIGHT]

*T*hey lay naked together, faces three inches apart. Cobalt eyes staring into hazel ones. Trista's hands gently holding Issy's jaw; Issy's fingers stroking Trista's bare right shoulder.

"I hate you," Trista says.

Issy hardly reacts. He's too busy fighting his own feelings. "Why?"

"Because I love you—and I have no idea why."

"Here I thought it was my charm."

"You know if anyone else said that," she muses, "I'd laugh in their face. When you say it, it breaks my heart."

"Why?" he repeats, running the hand over her cheek.

"Because I love you, and I can't have you."

Issy breaks free then, to sit up in bed. Trista can barely see him in the poor light, but she senses anger before he says a word.

"Why? Why did we let them do it?"

Reaching out, Trista's hand found the boy's hair, and she stroked the back of his head. "Because we had no choice."

He pulls further away, out of range. "That's bullshit."

Trista rises to join him seated there in the dark. Slides an arm round him before he can escape. "Yet here we are," she says.

"Why don't we just leave—together?"

"Sure."

"No, I mean it. Now. You and me. What's stopping us?"

"Responsibility. Loyalty."

These were foreign objects to Issy. "All that honour bunk? You sound like my da."

"A life without honour is a life not worth living," Trista quotes, voice grave.

"Who said that? Shakespeare?"

"Bunta Sugawara. It was in a yakuza flick I saw. Sounded better in the original Japanese, I guess."

"You *are* like my father."

Leaning close in order to see one another better, Trista's eyes hold Issy's. He witnessed so much there, most beyond an ability to understand. They twinkled, and then glistened, tearing up.

"I wish..."

"What, Trista? What do you wish?"

"I wish. That's all."

TRISTA
[FUNLAND — 11:03 A.M.]

*F*unland Fun Fair was an old amusement park on its last legs, and Trista considered that overuse of the word 'fun' probably didn't help.

Anyway, most kids these days hit video arcades or blue-light discos.

Governal used to bring her here sometimes if she shot out a bull's-eye or nailed some family-related pop quiz—usually for ice cream and a ride.

He loved the bumper cars.

Trista had come to bump skulls with the Norwegian—a man she believed had killed her foster father. God knew

229

why the bastard asked her along today, or what the point might be of meeting in this place. While close to bankruptcy, surely there were still too many witnesses to pull a swifty.

The woman paid for entrance and walked through to a dusty courtyard jammed with souvenir stalls, fast-food shops, and an ancient carousel in the middle. On this kind of cloudless day, everything would have been a bright, happy colour—thirty years ago.

The smell of overcooked hotdogs and slightly wrong popcorn hung in the air. Young children ran about helter-skelter, oblivious to the rundown nature of the venue. Their screams competed with the rides' inane, circus-like jingles and a loud, clanking sound of chains that came coutesy of the wooden rollercoaster above.

Yet from the shade of a solitary Ferris wheel, as she passed, still she heard a deep human exhalation, followed by the comment, "Our somewhat famous Trista Rivalen."

Trista stopped to stare at a rearing shadow that skulked behind the ticket booth, willing her vision to adapt to darkness there. "The more notorious Norwegian," she surmised while doing so. "Playing hide and seek."

"Uh-huh. You alone?"

"Would you believe me?"

"Not necessarily."

"So why ask? Use your eyes."

The man laughed. "The Gov was right. You do have a tongue."

Trista ignored this comment. "Give me one good reason why I should let you live—let alone trust you?"

"*Meh*—trust is overrated," replied Anders Sánchez, speaking over a cigarette in the side of his mouth when he stepped into view, and he scanned the area around. "One thing you can take from the Gov's death. There's been enough killing."

That made her bristle. "So why'd you murder him?"

"The Gov? Moi?"

"Aye—thou."

He shook his head. "Nope. You got the wrong number."

"You tried to kill me."

"Not my actual intention. Blame the boys. They get trigger-happy sometimes."

"That's convenient."

"That's the truth. Look, I don't have time to make excuses, which you'll believe is a bunch of hokum anyway—we had a job to do at St. M's, and we bungled it. More kudos to you." He saluted with two fingers. "But Governal? No."

"He was shot with a 9mm."

"So have a lot of other people." Very lazily, the Norwegian now removed his cigarette. "I didn't orchestrate the hit."

"Huh. Right. Pretend I believe you. Then—who?"

"For my money, the butler did it."

"What?"

He leaned against a wooden pole that reached up to support roller coaster railing several feet above. Put his fag back in his mouth and grinned. "You never read Agatha Christie?"

Blinking, Trista took a second to process this, quickly shook her head. "No. Only a couple of movies."

"There's a shame."

The expression made her smile, in spite of better judgment. The way in which he said it, the choice of words—so Governal. "What's your point?"

"A little birdy that trained both the Gov and me."

The Norwegian then shoved hands in his pockets. "Don't worry, I'm not packing anything in my undies— well, not what you're thinking, anyway." He nodded to her purse. "What you got in there? The same firecracker you used on Moore Holt?"

"No. I didn't bring a gun."

"For real? Christ, you live dangerous."

"Well, I wasn't exactly expecting a firefight. You know, in the middle of the day. Should I have been? Is that why we're here?"

Sánchez nodded at the Ferris wheel. "Take a ride with me."

"Why?"

"Just do it, will you?"

So they bought tickets and hopped on the Giant Wheel, like any father/daughter—even while being in close proximity to the man made Trista perspire.

As the ride ascended, he examined bystanders below. "Did the Gov ever tell you," he murmured, "much about his past? I know he was generally close-lipped, and that's okay if he didn't."

Perhaps because she had not responded, Sánchez turned to consider her.

"No?"

She shook her head.

He grinned again, said, "How unsurprising. All those years, and you know boo-hoo."

Trista looked away. "Cut the chatter and get to your point."

"Yeah, I'm getting there." The man kicked back and stretched out his arms around the gondola, like the thing was his throne.

"See all them plebs, down there? Those little people? I'd give my eyeteeth to be able to swap lives with a single shmuck. Work a day-job like watch repairs or whatever, go home to a wife and kids, paint the picket fence every summer. Never have to keep an eye over my shoulder for the next rookie trying to make a name—by whacking the Norwegian."

They'd reached the top of the wheel, and slowly began to descend.

"I never had that chance at normality, and neither did the Gov. We were picked off the street when we were kids—groomed to be assassins, pricks, whatever."

It dawned on her then. "He was your friend."

"Once. Yeah."

"What happened?"

"In our biz, mates take second-tier."

Trista nodded. "Go on."

"Sure. Well, now, the fucker who gave us this glorious career may be semi-retired, but not even I would dare go up against him. You know the cad, kiddo. Geoffrey. Queenie's proper right-hand."

Trista blanked. Barely breathed. Thought, *Oh shit*, but managed to say, "Why are you telling me this?"

"The Gov deserved better. He was still my mate, even if we did shoot at each other. You're his next-of-kin—in a manner of speaking. And I'm currently on the outer."

Sánchez, who had lit a second cigarette on the way up, took a final drag, and used the stump to light a new one.

Flicked the first out into space.

"While I was busy cleaning up loose ends—Alaina Holt washed up at Robin's Nest this morning, I hear—it turns out I'm the remaining thread they decided to prune."

"They?"

The man exhaled loudly. "The Queenie and 'Anguish'. They cooked this all up to grab back power Senior had lost. They're an item, you know. Did you know? Since way before Senior married Alaina. See, Isidor, he was a real Casanova in his day, and—"

That was when the man cocked his head.

"And, what?"

"Chill. Think I heard something." A worried look passed across his face, replaced by guarded relief as the gondola arrived at the bottom. "Anyway, think about what I said," Sánchez went on while they climbed out. "Nothing is what it seems."

Two young men were waiting their turn, standing at the front of a queue about three feet away. One wore an ill-fitting lemon *Star Wars* t-shirt, a shell necklace and Hawaiian shorts; his boyfriend was decked out in a tight brown vinyl jacket with a large-collared red short beneath, and he had a rust-coloured moustache that required desperate trimming.

Red Shirt seemed in a hurry to hop on the Ferris wheel. He pushed forward too soon, in the process bumping his shoulder into the taller Sánchez's ribcage.

"Take it easy," the Norwegian warned, annoyed.

"Oi," hissed the other boy in the lemon tee, "you Scandinavian wop!"

Before 'wop' had been completely articulated, Sánchez's chest exploded, issuing a spray of blood across Trista's face.

She fell back, loud ringing in her ears, first astonished, and then horrified.

The Norwegian, that gunsel everyone was supposed to be afraid of? Well, Sánchez tottered, mouth wide, another fag taking the long plunge to terra firma. He straight after joined it.

A shot to the head cut any twitching.

Then Trista looked up, scrabbling to clear eyes with her sleeve. The men were right before her; Red Shirt grinning madly beneath his mad mo, a snubnose .44 in one fist, while *Star Wars* had his arms crossed, his face read impassive, and he appeared bored.

"We fucking killed the Norwegian," Red Shirt shouted.

His friend deadpanned, "Groovy."

That was when Trista remembered—she'd seen the Bing and Bob routine before.

"I know you two," backing away, she stammered. "You're Geoffrey's men."

"That's right, ducky," laughed Red Shirt. His eyes glittered. "Let's go for a ride."

14

TRISTA

[OUTSIDE THE CITY — AFTERNOON]

*A*ll she knew was that Geoffrey's men were driving her on an unpaved road in the direction of Carhaix.

She thinks about the little details, the ones that Governal taught her to look for. These keep her sane right now, a little closer to the man she lost, and was likely about to reconnect with.

First up, they'd dragged her through the amusement park crowd, toward their own little version of Hell: a 1977 Dodge B200 custom disco van, pimped out with mag wheels, slots, port-hole windows and flares. The eyesore was covered in painted images of a wolf howling at the moon, a Viking fighting a sabre-toothed tiger in space, Apollo astronauts, and Bruce Lee—these on just the one side that Trista viewed.

She'd been tossed onto a lumpy L-shaped couch in the rear of the van, behind powder-blue velvet curtains. Here was velvet wall cushioning and shag-pile carpet the same colour, a red vinyl roof that clashed, a ruined bar fridge. A miniature mirror ball hung on fishing wire, forcing people to duck as they moved around.

"Welcome to the Misery Machine," said Red Shirt, pressed up against her on the left, while Star Wars—to her right, equally close—acted stoned, kept placing his head on her shoulder, and started to snore.

These two men smelled of garlic, sweat, stale beer and something else she couldn't mark. Not in this state. While vaguely knowing both fellow passengers—she'd seen them at Tintagel two or three times—Trista couldn't recall names. Governal had once pointed out that they were members of Geoffrey's private entourage. Not nice individuals. No one needs to mention this.

Killers. Pure, simple.

A moment later, the third odour occurs to her: they smelled of semen, of penises recently fired.

The second fact?

She was trussed up like a porker on its way to market, caked in the Norwegian's blood, wrists and ankles bound too tight, and an oily rag had been tied over her mouth. Guesses she kicked up such a fuss that they had little choice, but harbours no delusions they're off on a country joyride for fun.

The windows are open, yet it's baking inside—hence the sweat. She's coated in the stuff as well, along with a layer of dust courtesy of primitive roads they'd been traversing for over ninety minutes.

Third up was a doozie: They executed Sánchez in a public place, apparently unfussed by eyewitness identification. This caused her to gather they had news media, cops and the judicial system tied up—making the exercise something condoned by both major families, along with little leaguers like DuBois and 'Duke' Morgan.

Finally, they'd likely overheard or had an inkling of what the Norwegian had told her in the amusement park, about Marcella being in bed with Issy's dad.

The notion that Geoffrey had been a major player in this tomfoolery over the past couple of weeks, apparently at the behest of both Marcey and Isidor Holt, Sr., unnerved further attempts at reasoning. That he had most likely offed Governal. This all having been orchestrated with her aunt's blessing.

What the fuck was that?

Had she been living a lie these nineteen years, bankrolled by and playing loyal to a woman who had no understanding of the concept? And what of 'Anguish' Holt? What kind of man murdered his wife, and then allowed a long-term love interest to marry his son?

These hired help had their van radio turned to WEEP-AM, a Top 40 station that played a succession of grating tunes by the Eagles, Commodores, Billy Joel, Barry Manilow, Linda Ronstadt, and Olivia Newton-John. The latest was David Gates crooning the terribly fitting 'Goodbye Girl'.

Issy, she thinks. God, Issy.

Not for the first time, Trista struggles against shackles.

"Kid's a wild cat," Red Shirt grumbles, and then slaps her hard.

If she could just get word out, she'd tell Issy he'd been spot on. Responsibility and loyalty meant aught. She'd fall into his arms, hold him close, and whisper to the boy that she loved him. No caveats, nothing.

Right then, Trista hears two words from the occupant of the passenger seat in front, beside their driver. Two bits of vocabulary that kill any determination to remain calm: *Black Sails*.

The car takes a turn onto a paved road now, and heads through an entrance gate with those words curling above in wrought-iron scroll.

Oh bugger, sweeps her desperate mind.

ISIDOR
[TINTAGEL, THIS AFTERNOON]

*A*ll is grand—as it should be.

Marcella seated opposite, sipping the Hicks & Healy on ice in her glass. Elegantly dressed in a Roy Halston Frowick draped gown; both of them tuning in to (and enjoying) Perry Como songs, the LP's volume lowered to an easy listening level. A newspaper beside him (finished) and a havana between his fingers, legs crossed and muscles relaxed.

Together, away from their hoi polloi, relishing a quiet afternoon in the study.

Gazing through the window, Marcella says, "It's done."

There is an element of regret in her tone, to be sure— yet they knew that, after this, things would prove simpler. The way they ought to have been from the beginning— had power and beauty not blinded him.

"Whom did you send?" he asks, flicking ash into a pewter dish.

"Brangien."

"Issy's girl? Why her?"

The woman nods to herself. "Consider it a debt to be repaid."

MARCELLA
[TINTAGEL, THIS AFTERNOON]

*"T*he woman owes us for bumping off Sánchez's man before he could kill her," relates Marcella, still peering outside. After a moment more contemplation, she turns to her lover on the sofa. "She also has medical training. Besides—Brangien hates Trista more than she loathes me."

While stabbing out his cigar, Isidor jiggled his moustache in vaguely irritated fashion. "Valid points, I suppose."

"Well, don't get too excited."

"Oh, but I am, I am." He pats the folded broadsheet. "I saw in today's paper they found Alaina."

"All washed up?"

"Hah. Too right."

"How is your son taking it?"

"What would I know? Junior is a buffoon. He's off sulking in that playpen you gave him, TV guide in hand, watching the monkey box. And you think I care? You get that he's not mine."

"Someone needs to look after him, Is."

"He was Alaina's mistake. I wash my hands."

"But Lou's dead too.

"Well, he's your husband."

"I suppose. For now."

"Hm. So—talking up family—what *is* the plan with your niece?"

"I could never harm my own flesh and blood."

"Still."

"I know, I know. A weakness."

"Nonsense. Part of you no one else sees, but I cherish. A relief, after all I've experienced these past twenty years."

Isidor reaches over to top up Marcella's drink.

"Thank you, good sir."

"Pleasure, treasure."

"Who would have thought," the woman muses, "that either of us could be so homely?"

"Indeed." Straightening out his legs, the man nods. "Trista's being taken care of, though?—By Brangien."

"Yes. With Dr. Fulsus."

"Where?"

"B.S."

"Really?"

"Yes."

"The lunatic asylum. Lordy, she'd be better off dead."

"But at least this way I skip out on guilt—it means the girl won't cause any further waves, and I can still face my sister."

ISSY
[TINTAGEL, THIS AFTERNOON]

*H*e'd been trying to track down his cat Andred— delivered this morning to Tintagel, along with a truckload of Issy's other belongings—when he heard them talking in low voices from a room as yet unexplored.

Thought about giving a polite knock, but a life of experiencing his da's hissy fits made Issy reconsider.

A few key words made their way out the door, carried with the song 'Catch a Falling Star', while he deliberated— 'Brangien', 'debt', 'Trista', 'Put it in your pocket'—and straight away Issy edged closer.

True, he was eavesdropping. Frankly, he felt pardoned.

Thus Issy heard most everything said, starting with Isidor Senior's cool, "I see in today's paper they found Alaina," and it sounded like his father didn't give a damn.

Their chatter thereafter further dumbfounded him.

Trista.

They'd done something with Trista—seemed like they were getting Brangien to do whatever this could be on their behalf.

Panting, pushing panicked, he started to walk quickly away, quietly as possible, yet still the corridor floor conspired to echo. Issy dived behind a velvet drape just as Marcella's head popped through that doorway.

"Who's there?" she called, all irritable. "Geoffrey?"

At precisely the right point, Andred finally appeared and sauntered past the woman. Breaking into a bothered scowl, Marcella planted a swift kick, inciting the cat to race away, and then returned to her guest.

Issy lingered another minute or so, before stepping out from cover, to make his way more carefully. Passed by a few men to whom he nodded, shamming blasé.

He needed to find Trista, save the girl from whatever horrors they had planned.

Tried not to think about his mother's death, his father's apparent hand in that, or the fact the old bastard was currently playing footsies with Trista's aunt. And how about Lou? What was the meaning there?

Finally—Brangien.

How could she be involved in this mess? But then he remembered the woman was the only one who'd known of the escape attempt from hospital. He'd told her about Trista's true identity. Brangien was supposed to be the one waiting in the back alley, not that gaggle of gun-toting thugs.

His best friend'd betrayed him.

That cut his heart.

There were other allusions he could not comprehend. A lunatic asylum? B.S.? *Bullshit?*—What did these things mean? Being called a buffoon, well, that was the least of his concerns.

Before knowing where exactly he'd meandered, Issy discovered he stood in some kind of small library. Alone here—guessed that gangsters rarely stooped to reading.

Close inspection showed the top of most books were dusty, but not every one.

There were three fat tomes on a lower shelf, marked *Fidelitas usque ad mortem* (volumes one, two and three) that looked more recently wiped down.

He'd learned enough in Latin class to get the meaning: Loyalty unto death.

Issy smiled. It sounded like something from one of the yakuza flicks both Trista and his father enjoyed, so he could imagine Marcella Cornwall feeling similarly. That she'd share the same droll, smug sense of humour (and related tricks) as his da—ones Issy'd sussed out years before.

Having carefully removed the trio of books from their place—two were deceptively light, one heavy—he carried them to a small desk by the window.

Listened for a short time to ensure no one was nearby. Satisfied, the man opened the top tome and found a hollowed-out interior filled with paperwork. He stuffed all of this in his pockets, and then emptied volume two as well.

In volume one lived a small revolver.

Removing it and holding the thing away from him by the trigger-guard, Issy was about to put it back, reconsidered, and shoved the gun behind his belt.

After sliding the books home, Issy checked the hallway, listened once again, and then—satisfied no one lurked nearby—he strolled out, whistling a jaunty tune.

The fact this was the Hues Corporation's 'Rock the Boat' made it some kind of perfect.

15

ISSY

[DISCO INFERNO — NEXT DAY, LATE AFTERNOON]

*I*ssy strolled out of the club onto a busy street where the sudden shock of natural light, despite this hour, hurt his eyes.

The smell wafting over from an Indian restaurant next to the Disco Inferno—usually closed when he came here—was a mixture of onion, garlic, dried fish, pepper and spices that further assaulted his nose. He held breath a moment, squinted, considering what to do. Had no idea.

Since it was almost six o'clock in the afternoon, a horde of closing time office-workers bustled past, and while he'd finally made a decision (cross to the other side of the road), one look at traffic told Issy it was dangerous to do so—cars and motorcycles flowed past at considerable speed.

There was a black-and-white standing at the curb down further.

When he began walking again, it moved as well.

Followed Issy along this street for almost a block before the occupants flashed lights and a siren wailed all of two seconds.

People stopped to stare. While thinking about continuing on his way—what would police want with him?—a passenger window wound down and someone called his name, making Issy give up on the plan and walk over.

"What can I do for you, officers?"

"Aw, so polite." A young man with slicked-back hair, dressed in a rumpled brown suit, stepped out of the vehicle, while two uniforms remained inside. "We'd like a word. If you wouldn't mind too much, I mean."

"Is there a problem?"

"Dunno." The man swayed closer, eyes washing Issy over like he was something hardly appetizing. "Is there?"

"Look, what's this about?"

"Care to come downtown?"

Issy sized up the cop, unsure how best to act in this situation, but settled on a rather lame quip. "Now who's being polite?" After that was aired, he shrugged. "And no choice, huh?"

"Course there is. You could always cut and run."

"Why the heck would I do that?"

"Better question is why you've got a lip on you."

"You started it."

The other man laughed. "So I did. Look, no fuss. Name's Tusk." After flashing a badge, he held out a hand. "We'd just like a yack."

***

The public entrance was on a side street side away from City Hall, a low-key affair comprising two smeared glass doors that needed a hefty push. Inside, to the left, sat the dispatcher room with a large sliding window.

Issy was escorted around a corner to the right, past Street and Water Department offices, as well as the Assistant Commissioner's. Left of that door was a staircase leading to the second floor, which they took.

Turning right again fed them into a hallway that Td, past a set of restrooms. At the end of this corridor hung a big ceiling-to-floor mural depicting the Police Department's shield. On the right sat the chief's office. Across from the chief's was some kind of storage vestibule, to the left of that the squad room.

They entered the next door on, into an office with two messy desks, a cluttered pin-board covered with newspaper clippings, photos and typed pages, and a window boasting a sad-sack view of nothing noteworthy.

The place had all the charm of a broom closet.

"Take a seat," Tusk said, waving at a solitary chair on the business side of the bureau most messed up. It was just the two of them now.

Issy sat and rubbed the back of his head. Tusk settled down opposite, pushing aside junk to make space.

"Coffee?" he asked.

"No, I'm fine."

"Cocktail, then?"

Issy very nearly grinned. "Too early."

Glancing over, Tusk cast half-closed eyes. "There's a first."

"Look, pleasantries aside—why am I here?"

"We're getting there."

"Just warming me up?"

"Something of the sort." From his hip pocket, Tusk took out a small notebook and laid this out flat on the desk. Unlike most else in this place, it appeared neat and orderly. He turned several pages, and stopped.

"You want to talk about the hospital fracas, Mr. Holt?"

"What hospital fracas?"

"The one they pinned on your mother. Revenge drama, concerning her brother's killer. Your uncle—Moore Holt, I'm saying."

"I know who my uncle is."

"Was."

Issy sighed. He had a million other things he'd prefer to be doing, like tracking down Trista soon as he could, rather than raking the recent past. "Is there a point to this, Officer—?"

"Sergeant."

"Okay, sergeant. Same question."

"Yeah. There is."

Making a point of checking his watch, Issy settled back. "And?"

In answer, Tusk ducked his head. Ran a finger over more annotations in his little black book, and then said in a slow, bored tone, "Are you saying you weren't at St. Maignenn's hospital on the morning of the 14th?"

"No. I was there."

The policeman looked up. "Did you witness gunfire between parties unknown?"

"Unknown no longer. I was one of the parties."

"Do tell."

"That's what I'm doing."

"Mm-hm." Tusk flicked to another page and jotted notes.

"Why don't you just record our conversation?" Issy asked.

"I'm old school. Besides, transcribing is a bitch." He then also leaned back. "Okay, well I think we can skimp on details. We had boys outside of St. M's. They saw what went down there with the Norwegian's goons. Holt boys firing on their boss's son—something stinks in the sorry state of Ireland."

"Denmark."

"Eh?"

"It's Denmark—the Shakespeare quote you're throwing out there. Also rotten."

"What, you think I don't know that?" Eyebrows knotted, Tusk kicked his chair from behind the desk. "There is such a thing as taking the piss. Or, what, you Irish descenters don't have a sense of humour?"

Issy said nothing.

"No more Bard nuggets to lob my way?"

"Not right now."

"Alrighty. Touché. Maybe we can start to make progress. So, getting back to my point—these perps targeted you. What're we to make of that, huh?"

"They probably didn't recognize me."

"We did."

That caused Issy to think.

Tusk also lost some irritability. "Here's the thing, kid. I work directly for Commissioner Kahn. You'd know him, right? He's retiring next year, and wants books in order and a clean slate before he does, hence us aiming sights on the criminal fraternity: your families."

"I got the impression a lot of you people sat in their pockets."

"What gave you that?"

"Stuff."

"Yeah, well, your stuff isn't wrong. But not Bob—the Commish. He's had his hands tied far too long by a bunch of politicians and legal bigwigs on the take, like you said. So he set up a special division to undercut all that crap and settle things straight."

"You?"

"I'm on the team, yeah."

"Why?"

"You mean, why was I included?"

Issy nodded.

"Because my mitts're clean. Bob knows that."

"Can you be trusted?"

"I think that's the gist of what I'm trying to say." The sergeant got to his feet, walked around the desk, and sat on an edge where there was space to do so. "You want to talk, kid?"

"I don't know if it's a good idea."

"Off the record."

"Still."

"Listen, I'd be reading your rights if you were in a jam."

"Think I'll tactfully decline."

Tusk whistled briefly, fidgeted his buttocks as if trying to find a position more comfortable, and then tried on another angle for size. "They have your girlfriend."

Issy stiffened, but focused on the chaotic desk. "What?"

"Blonde girl. Very pretty." The police officer held out a straight hand. "So high."

"I don't know what you're talking about."

"Pull the other one."

That was when Issy realized he might at last get some real answers. "Okay, pretend I do know."

"Ready to play ball?"

"Maybe. So where is she?"

"Disappeared her to a hospice out of town, name of Black Sails."

Issy looked up and stared. *B.S.*

"Mean anything to you?"

"No."

"Alrighty. So, Trista Rivalen." This cop barely repressed mirth. "A sweetheart if I ever saw one. You do pick your dates, handsome. And a Cornwall too. What were you playing at—Romeo and Juliet?"

"Leave her out of this."

"Hah." Tusked grinned. "What was that about knowing nothing?"

"Fuck you. I lied."

"Language, kid. And I know."

"Leave Trista out of this bullshit."

The other man shrugged. "Hard to. See, we were lucky, or thought we were. Rivalen's surrogate dad, legal guardian, whatever, came to me after the St. Samson's debacle—you know, the one at the bar. I hear you put in an appearance there as well."

"I'm not denying that."

"Given you made a statement to police on the scene, I wouldn't either. Anyhow, seems this guy got wind of my direct line to Kahn. Man used to be a higher-up in Marcella Cornwall's crown jewels, but that was long ago. He said he was prepared to testify on a few unsolveds, so long as we offered protection to Rivalen, the kid."

"You're talking about Governal."

"I know who I'm bloody well talking about. You knew him?"

Issy lowered his head, remembering the room with the casket and a corpse in it, Trista hammered and howling and mostly naked. "No."

"Well, then our man ends up face-down in a swimming pool at the Cornwall digs, a couple of slugs in his chest. Two days later, your mother is washed up with strangulation marks round her throat. Yesterday, it's the Norwegian's turn at a fun fair, of all places. And just this morning, a punk-rocker named Destroys was found by Brittany Pier, another floater with half of him missing— fish-feed, I'd wager. The bodies are piling up. We don't know what to think."

His mother. Just another statistic in this man's business. "You make it sound like something from a rubbishy pulp novel."

"I agree." Tusk glanced away. "And I'm also sorry for your loss."

He was the first to have uttered anything of the sort. "Thank you."

"So let's turn the page."

"Why would I want to do that?"

"A certain blonde jumps to mind."

"Trista," breathed Issy.

"Trista."

"Is she safe?"

"I'd like to help you find out."

"But...?"

"But we need something in return."

"By betraying my family?"

"No, kid, by doing what's right."

Issy rubbed his fingers hard, thinking about 'Anguish', Lou, his mother, Brangien, and all that had happened this past week. Everything gleaned from the Mudbug brothers beforehand, as well as earlier today. Mostly, his thoughts kept switching back to Trista.

"All right."

"All right?"

"It's my father and Marcella Cornwall," Issy said. "Together. And I mean that—*together*."

"In bed, huh?" Tusk scribbled some more. "You people do like to keep us guessing."

"Not my people."

The police officer looked up. "Noted. Why the sudden collab?"

"I think they're making a grab for absolute power."

"You don't say?"

"I do. I overheard them."

"Yeah, well." Tapping his nose, Tusk leaned forward. "We'll need more than hearsay. Do you have any evidence?"

"I'm working on it."

"Good for you. In the meantime—how do you feel about a visit to Black Sails?"

***

At around nine a.m., Issy departed Chapelizod House.

He skipped out on Mary and drove himself—pinched

his da's prized Jaguar D-Type in order to do so.

Had been an age since he sat behind a wheel—aside from the joyride from hospital—and it felt oddly liberating. He tried not to think about the place he headed for, what might or might not be found. Whether Sergeant Tusk could be trusted to pull his weight—or if the man could be trusted at all.

No, Issy preferred to brood over what these people—family and friends—had been doing while he buried his head at parties. How they now held Trista, and it was up to Isidor Holt, Jr., to clean up his act and go rescue a damsel in distress.

Strong gusts whipped across the convertible as he left city limits. These forced Issy to stop fanaticizing and focus instead on curves ahead, on the feeling of power gunning the twenty-year-old classic auto.

Rumour said this particular example belonged, once upon a time, to actor Steve McQueen.

He could picture it.

The roads became quieter, leaves blowing across bitumen. With signage increasingly rare, our man needed to continuously consult a map on his lap.

After stopping to fill up at a one-pump service station in the middle of nowhere, Issy arrived at the institution called Black Sails just after eleven. The sky was overcast and stormy. That sat right. The huge, four-story building ahead, all concrete and worn, had been built in the 1930s and apparently never renovated since.

He parked in a strangely empty lot, and then briskly walked through to reception.

Had called ahead yesterday, from Tusk's office, to organize an appointment.

Said he was Isidor Holt and forgot to footnote which generation. If they confused the issue, the entire better. After flashing his driver's license—which also made no mention of 'junior'—Issy got escorted through the overgrown grounds of a hospice that'd swallowed up

Trista three days before, via manipulations from his father, his wife, and his best friend.

Issy's appointment was with a head quack named Credd.

The medico greeted him on a terrace that had also seen better days.

This elderly man, balding and skinny, in an oversized white lab coat, confessed he'd expected the famous Isidor Holt would be an equally advanced age—and in the next long breath gushed a string of meaningless compliments.

Listening for suitable time, wearing an expression he prayed came across beneficent (while inwardly itching to find his girl), Issy reminded the good doctor that he was a busy man, and so they set off across a lawn three inches too long, more brown than green.

Poking a hand beneath his jacket, Issy felt the wire there that Tusk and one of his men carefully set earlier.

Time for small, hopefully leading, conversation.

"So what exactly," he began, "have you done with Trista Rivalen?"

Credd let out a theatrical sigh. "Sadly? Not I."

"How do you mean?"

"No offence, Mr. Holt—but, as you know, Marcella Cornwall's physician Dr. Fulsus came up to handle the procedure."

"Ah. The procedure." Issy grimaced; gave up trying to hide that. "Um. Could you fill me in?"

"Certainly, sir. On which part?"

"On which procedure."

"Oh! Your standard transorbital lobotomy," breezed the other man. "I could easily have performed this myself, but would be first to agree that Dr. Fulsus is the guru when it comes to complications."

Issy glanced at him, heart pounding, said, "Complications?"

"Quite right."

"Please—Go on."

"Well, whilst targeting the frontal lobe, there was *accidental* damage to the temporal lobes and amygdala, as per instructions we received from Miss Cornwall's emissary."

Issy had no idea how he kept walking. "What do you mean?"

"Regarding said instructions?"

"No." He attempted to swallow, couldn't manage, and so cleared his throat. "No, I'm talking about the 'accidental damage'."

"Oh, that. It went perfectly. The young lady will not be able to turn state's evidence anytime soon. Ever, actually."

A cackle came from Credd as he trudged ahead, making Issy wrestle with himself not to seize this devil by the throat.

Plowed on instead, said, "Why? Why would that be an issue?"

The doctor feigned ignorance, a smarmy sneer slapped across his face. "I have no idea, sir—but mum's the word here at Black Sails. Always happy to help you out, Mr. Holt. You will be further pleased to note that Miss Rivalen has not spoken a single, solitary word since her operation."

Issy stopped, stared, stricken. Could not hope to pretend anymore.

"Will she—?"

"Ever speak? Oh, I doubt it." Credd was so thoroughly chuffed with himself that he had no idea his guest was on the verge of screaming. "It's a common side-effect with this sort of trauma."

"Trauma. Ah." Wiping stray snot from his nose, and then his eyes, Issy was having great difficulty recalling exactly what Tusk had asked him to say.

The doctor now narrowed eyes, inspecting his guest. Apparently, he'd clued himself in to this worrisome state. "I say—are you all right?"

From parts unknown, Issy erected a smile. "Allergies," he said.

"Oh, I see—troublesome things, what? Much like our patients!"

"Exactly." Somehow, trying desperately not to break down there on the turf, Issy remembered his task. "By the way, we need a copy of Trista's—Miss Rivalen's—medical records."

"That can be arranged. When would you like them to be sent down?"

"Today. I'll take them with me today."

It was Credd's turn to stop short, and he ogled. "That's a little short notice, isn't it?"

Having also halted, Issy glared back. "Is there a problem?"

"No, no—of course not, Mr. Holt. But you might need to stay on an hour or so."

"I'll wait." Issy tilted his head. "Now, where the hell is this patient?"

***

This patient sported two black eyes, tangled hair, and was bundled up in a yellowing hospital gown. She sat on a bench by a pond that had been emptied of water, along with any semblance of marine life, at least a decade before.

A nurse—middle-aged, solidly built—stood to welcome the doctor, smiled at their visitor, and then both physician and nurse headed quickly toward the main building. They had paperwork to complete.

Not that Issy paid much notice.

He was far too busy taking in Trista. Still, he had to wait until they were alone, and then raced over.

"Hey," he whispered, squatting to take one cool hand in his. "Jesus—You okay? I'm here now. Sorry it took so long, but I had a bugger of a time working out exactly where you were. You're not the easiest person to find."

Overhead, tied atop seven individual masts, flapped the big, faded black sails that lent this institution their name. A single raven glided between, cawing.

These things, as it turned out, had more animation than the patient on the bench.

Languidly, the girl examined Issy's hair rather than his face, while she softly hummed an abstract melody Issy did not know. There was a distant sense of something akin to curiosity, like an infant observing a butterfly never before seen.

Even so, Issy quickly began to doubt the melody belonged to any song and before long, the fragile focus in Trista's eyes leached out. She gazed instead over his shoulder. Issy looked back, and then to the girl again. Realized she was not taking in anything of note, but simply staring into space.

He tried to regain attention, said, "Hey. Look at me." Nothing. "Trista, I'm right here. It's Issy. Quit kidding round."

Reaching up, he caressed her cheek, ran two fingers along her chin and down her neck. Her reaction—being the utter lack of one—told him she felt nothing.

"Trista?"

When he left, a copy of the patient's papers under his arm—stressed and depressed and horrified as he might have been—Issy declined to drive full speed into one of the brick columns at the entrance that held up the name *Black Sails* in twisting iron script.

On the way back to the city, he almost struck oncoming traffic on four different occasions.

Had little memory of parking his car and stumbling toward the police station where Tusk was waiting. Heart ripped out and crushed underfoot by two families that destroyed everything decent in this world.

***

"The frontal lobe—that's located here at the front, obviously—is one of four principles of the cerebral cortex in the brain. It's responsible for working memory, or the ability to process transient information in the present, like reasoning and comprehension."

Issy barely heard these words spouted forth by the police physician, a Dr. Schopenhauer, who'd joined them in Tusk's disheveled office.

The doctor may have been victim of mid-life spread, but he had a mane of salt-and-pepper hair, hefty sideburns, and dressed better than your usual cop.

It was night outside, some two hours after Issy arrived back in the city with Trista's medical record. Said physician had spent one hour reviewing the notes, while Issy gulped down several tumblers of cheap whiskey, without getting anywhere near drunk. He stared at the wall, while Sergeant Tusk made a series of phone calls.

Schopenhauer now paced their little room, smoking, and occasionally pointing to parts of his own head.

"That's usually what the object is," Schopenhauer announced in a neat little conclusion, "in this kind of procedure."

Issy, seated on the window ledge, rubbed eyes with the balls of his hands, at the same time squeezing out, "A fucking lobotomy."

He heard the doctor stop walking. "They have been known to help people—though the penultimate jury's out."

"What kind of people?" asked Tusk, an unlit cigarette hanging from the side of his mouth.

"Mostly ones with symptoms of mental disorder. Schizophrenia, suicidal depression, rage, that kind of condition."

Issy lowered his fingers. "Trista had none of those things."

The doctor nodded. "I can well imagine. Our department's had its eye on Black Sails for a long time. Those people are butchers, and butchers for a price. With this information, we'll be able to shut them down for good."

"But hold on, Ray," Tusk mused, currently staring into an empty coffee cup, like it held some fascination, "I've heard of people having a lobotomy, and leading better lives."

"That can be the case," Schopenhauer agreed. "However, the real problem here, going by these case notes Mr. Holt provided, is additional tampering with the temporal lobe. That's located beneath the lateral fissure and is responsible for long-term memory, recognition memory—a subcategory of declarative memory—and the comprehension of speech and autobiographical memory. Then there's damage to the amygdala. It's a set of neurons located deep in the temporal lobe, dealing with emotional memories and, again, long-term memory."

"Speak in English, doc," Tusk complained.

"Simply put? I fear what the patient has been left with."

The sergeant exhaled loudly. "Okay. Which is?"

"Precious little."

Leaning back against the glass, Issy felt like he might go mad. He looked up to the ceiling, at an expansive cobweb in one corner, and then (somehow) composed himself. Asked, "Is it permanent?"

"I beg your pardon?"

"All this—this damage. Can it be fixed?"

The way in which the doctor glanced away, jaw set hard and choosing not to speak, was answer enough. Issy refused to believe what he saw.

"There must be a specialist—somewhere in the world."

"I'm sorry, son," Schopenhauer said in a firm voice, "no. The brain is not a toy with replacement parts."

Which finally made Issy understand. He stepped off the sill, thanked the doctor for his advice, shook Tusk's hand, collected his jacket, and headed for the door.

"Issy," Sergeant Tusk spoke up.

The other man paused, hand on the knob. "What?"

"Hang in there. We'll get these pricks, thanks to you. I

swear it. Things are now beyond their control."

Nodding slowly, Issy didn't look back, said, "Isn't everything?"

ISSY
[CHAPELIZOD HOUSE — 10:27 P.M]

*H*e inserts bullets into each individual chamber of the cylinder, closes this, spins it like they did in movies, and places the cold barrel at his right temple. With his thumb, draws back the hammer.

Easy enough.

Just pull the trigger—and *bang*!

That ought to have been the last thing heard, too, but instead all he receives is silence, with his sniffling further breaking the mood.

Shit, he didn't have the courage to kill himself.

Stands in his room dressed only in boxers, mostly cold, a two-thirds empty bottle of Chivas Regal in his left fist. Staring at a poster of Albert Einstein that he'd taped (a lifetime ago) to the back of the bedroom door—a famous one of the scientist looking old, poking out his tongue at the world.

Try again?

He puts down the Scotch, empties the gun into his left hand, and then slides the cartridges back, closes the cylinder, spins, and places a fractionally warmer barrel at his right temple.

Lowers the gun once more.

No.

Not yet.

Issy drops the pistol on the table, next to the bottle. Goes to lie atop bed covers, huddling, and he trembles. Water in the mattress made little waves, like he was really adrift, and then the sobbing starts. After that, he does try to sleep, in a stupid attempt to forget everything. Ignores a voice in the back of his skull barking a senseless "Wake up and live".

All bullshit.

When he finally rises fourteen odd hours later—without a bullet in the head—Issy gets that he can't hide any longer. Clarity slaps him out.

A decision has been made, though he does not recall its formation: he wasn't going to let them win like this. Not with honour at stake.

Trista was right.

Honour did matter.

Fool notions of outright revenge might've twisted and turned through his mind, but he slashed at such daydreams for what they truly were—dumb fantasy.

The 'Anguish' Holts and Marcella Cornwalls of the world were professional killers, Issy a pampered college twit. They'd nip into him for breakfast, any attempt at retribution ending up a quarter-baked cast off in a block of cement.

Each one of them, including his so-called da, would laugh the boy in the face before cutting his throat.

No, he had to enact this form of revenge differently—and couldn't count on Sergeant Tusk finishing the job. Too many people failed before. Tusk was one man facing a storm; this was Issy's call.

And then it really did dawn upon him—for real, this time.

How to become a thorn, and stick it (sideways) up their collective arse.

ISSY
[RESTAURANT POVEST TRYCHANE — 12.02 P.M, NEXT DAY]

After a lunch comprising lobster, six raw oysters, a side-dish of truffles, and a miniature, beautifully cooked (rare)

medallion of wagyu steak—washed down with a bottle of
Moët & Chandon Dry Imperial, bottled in 1943—Issy sat
back in the restaurant and patted one very bloated belly.

This was his da's shout, though the old man'd have no
clue he was being so thoroughly generous.

Issy had a follow-up espresso, paid the check, and went
out onto the street at a languid pace. The weather?
Pristine. There was a mailbox further down, which he
approached, carrying under his arm a large brown
envelope.

A hotted-up, pink and black Chrysler Valiant Charger
cruised past, a muscle car spewing exhaust and the bass-
heavy sounds of 'Stayin' Alive'. It caused Issy to smile.

At least disco would never die.

Having stopped before the postbox, he licked a flap,
sealed it, and dropped said package, addressed to Sergeant
William Tusk, through the slot.

Wished it luck as he walked away.

Truth being, Issy had been unable to make head-nor-
tail of the documents he'd snatched out of Tintagel, or
those from a set of similarly hollowed-out Romanian
encyclopedias at Chapelizod House.

Assumed people wouldn't hide these things unless they
meant something important, but that didn't make them
easier to understand.

He'd decided the night before Tusk would have to be
trusted—that he was more likely to know someone who
could decipher details.

Anyway, Issy had a back-up plan.

Always better to be safe—especially since he was flush
with funds rifled from his dad's. Teach the bastard to use
'MARCELLA' as a combination code.

ISSY
[DISCO INFERNO — 3:31 P.M.]

Reggie Mudbug said, "All right, now let me get this straight. You want for me to shoot you."

They were alone together in the nightclub's office, the boys having been summoned from their retreat in the basement, and then Ronnie sent on an errand to pick up more grog.

Issy raised brows, and then nodded.

"Okay," Reggie said.

"Okay? Aren't you going to try to talk me out of it?"

"Why?"

"I thought I might be asking too much."

"No worries, mate."

"Seriously?"

"Yup."

"Okay. Well, this is for you and your brother." Issy slid across a small black leather satchel. "It's possible my da might be looking down a different kind of barrel shortly, and in that case you'll see a couple of major families tumble. I'd prefer you and your brother safely away."

Having popped on spectacles, Reggie swiveled the bag, snapped it open, and peered briefly at the contents. "Mighty conscientious of you, young sir," he decided, his tone an approving one, as he closed it again. "And very much appreciated. You're a good man. Always knew that for fact."

"A favour for the many you've given—including this one."

"Killing you."

"Yes."

"Listen, old son—you have something your pater lost long ago. Integrity." Reggie sat up straight, scratched an eyebrow. "All right."

"Just one thing," Issy said. "I want it arranged that

261

evidence of the shooting leads back to Marcella Cornwall."
He then handed over the revolver he'd found at Tintagel.
"This is Queenie's. Loaded. I'm not sure if her prints are
on it, though."

"Leave that to me. We can plant the gun, put in a
friendly tip, and let the fuzz do their job. Anything else,
before we get started?"

"No, that's pretty much it. I've settled everything. Had
a king's banquet for lunch."

"Good for you." A cheeky look on his face, head tilted,
Reggie took a hip flask from inside his coat. "One for the
road?"

Issy stared at the thing for a brief moment. "Nah, I
think I've had my fill of drams in strange containers," he
laughed. "Dad has a Midleton Barry Crockett Legacy over
there."

He walked to a mini-bar beside the huge, neat
mahogany desk that also belonged to his father, in front of
a window.

"Join me, Reggie?"

"Sure. Bit of toff class never goes astray."

Having selected identical Galway Crystal tumblers, he
lifted the decanter, prised out its stopper, and poured
caramel-coloured whiskey. Took one, drank the lot in
seconds, and savoured an aftertaste commingling tobacco,
toffee, honey, vanilla, boiled sweets, and just plain good
liquor.

Refilled the glass, back to his guest.

Issy gazed through the window at the same oak tree
he'd seen a million times before. Countless lazy afternoons
he'd spent sorting through lost-and-founds, calculating
profits to counteract a hangover.

On this occasion, two small sparrows danced about in
speckled sunlight on the branch closest. He could hear
their chirping through the glass, and wondered if they were
a pair.

For a third time this week, felt the muzzle of a pistol

gently touch his head.

Closed his eyes.

ELTON
[ETHIOPIA — NINE MONTHS LATER]

*T*hey ended up settling down at a Jesuit mission near a tiny northern village in the Tigray region.

This was a dusty, dry place with abundant flies, the occasional red spitting cobra, and no running water aside from a creek that varied in width and depth dependent on the season.

The mission was one hour's drive (by death-defying unpaved track) from a larger township called Adwa—its claim to fame being the Battle of Adowa, fought in 1896 against Italian troops. The Ethiopians won, the only African nation to have thwarted European colonialism.

Elton McMurphy liked this fact, regardless that poverty, illiteracy, disease and degradation eighty years on left little else to find pride in. The current violent political atmosphere in the country's capital Addis Ababa rarely reached up so far, thankfully, although there developed an odd spat with members of a Marxist group calling itself the Tigrayan People's Liberation Front, based in Adwa.

His new friends called them *'äsha*, which he learned meant pompous fools—or more simply asses.

Aside from providing Christian faith and education, the facility taught construction, water sanitation, and ran a farm school aiming to nurture the vocational skills of a local population otherwise denied access.

The Jesuits harked from Britain, Canada, India, Malta and the United States, joined by young men from Ethiopia and Tanzania.

Since arriving, Elton assisted with teaching, at the same time that he set about trying to come to grips with the languages, Tigrinya and Amharic—one of the first phrases he properly memorized in the former tongue being "Natey hoberkeraft mulue byu basza", which roughly meant "My hovercraft is full of eels."

Elton blamed a love of the Monty Python show for one useless proverb that left listeners either baffled or in hysterics.

He also enjoyed studying regional customs, superstitions and lore. And although expected to pull his (admittedly portly) weight performing manual labour, Elton conjured up ways to avoid induction in the more physical work parties.

Several months on, he still felt uncomfortable to be greeted by other men with three kisses on the cheeks, but found these people truly miraculous for the positive way in which they confronted adversity; discovered joy in simple things others overlooked. Sometimes he felt closer to God than ever before.

The children here liked to poke his belly (*käbdi*) and watch the rolls. Though he'd shed some extra kilos, they continued to do so, but he didn't mind—it had become a running joke that crossed cultures.

And they'd embraced Trista without hesitation.

On his break this afternoon, Elton watched as women led the mute, blonde foreigner to their narrow stream. Skin already brown as coffee, peeling in places, she sat in a white cotton shift on the bank while they did laundry by hand. On the odd occasion, these ladies set aside the chore to splash water (*mai*) at one another, laughing and singing, like they were doing now.

The old life seemed an age before.

According to papers he'd read prior to departure, Issy Holt had bravely whistle-blown the criminal activities of his own family and that of the Cornwalls—and in return was murdered by Marcella Cornwall out of revenge, spite, or jilted passion, depending on the press-man you chose to believe.

A spate of arrests followed, not merely of criminal

elements but people in position of authority who should have known better. This related to leaked documents obtained by Issy that purportedly showed blackmail, bribery and extortion.

Elton had no idea of the outcome—he hadn't looked at a single newspaper in Africa that bothered with the gangland intrigues of an inconsequential western city so far afield.

Still, the man had a pet theory, and it concerned the nature of Issy's carefully orchestrated last two days. The funneling of a great deal of money to St. Michael's charities being part of that, along with delivery of incriminating information to police.

Another was Trista's arrival at the church a week later, under the watchful eye of a sergeant named Tusk, who said Issy had listed them as possible guardians for the girl. The way the police officer behaved left no doubt he felt personally responsible for Trista, and was prepared for a fight that never happened.

Why would it? How could Elton decline?

This was never a matter of how much Trista had done for the church over the past two years—actually a great deal—but more because he valued her friendship and understood the strong sense of compassion she felt for others. In her time of need, it was only right to return the favour.

Besides, Elton had not sacrificed anything precious— thanks to Issy, his relief organization inherited enough funds to run itself till doomsday.

Joining a mission on this continent, the opportunity to help those in further need, particularly the poor and the outcast, had been a calling for years. He'd mentioned this more than once to Issy over coffee, and no doubt the young man caught wind of frustration Elton felt at an inability to fulfil this dream.

Another tick in the plus column for a promising individual whose life had been tragically cut far too short.

He sipped from a cup of *atmet* (the sweet barley and oat-flour concoction which never failed to recall Christmases back home), and then sighed. At the same time he was swatting a particularly bothersome sand-fly, Elton observed Trista—over on the bank—smile at the girls frolicking before her.

A little thing, *fshkta* they called the gesture here, one easily missed. She did that of late.

In these moments, Elton forgave Isidor Holt, Jr., the sin of second-hand suicide. Reckoned our Old Fellow upstairs ought to do the same—and had decided, given the day and age, this damn well should be the case.

MEDICAL JARGON, SLANG, SCENTS, 70s-ERA MUSIC, TV, FILMS, ARTISTS, FOOD, ACTORS & MEDIEVAL EXTRAS

ABC (medical jargon): airway, breathing, circulation
ABG (medical jargon): arterial blood gas
Act the maggot (Irish slang): fool around
Agharta: Miles Davis live LP recorded in Osaka, Japan, in 1975
Ahnvee (Cajun slang): hunger
Anaïs Anaïs: first perfume from Cacharel, a floral fragrance created in 1978
Anna Karenina: novel by Leo Tolstoy, published in 1877
Another Green World: English musician Brian Eno's 1975 album
Astro Label Maker: Compact hand labeler and labeling tape
Atmet: non-alcoholic beverage, barley & oat-flour based, cooked with water, sugar & kibe (Ethiopian clarified butter) with consistency slightly thicker than egg-nog
Balenciaga, Cristóbal: Spanish designer & the founder of

Balenciaga fashion house
Bardot, Brigitte: French former actress, singer, fashion model & style icon
Bay City Rollers: Scottish pop band popular in the 1970s, esp. amongst teenage girls
Beardsley: Aubrey Beardsley, a 19th century English illustrator & author
Belmondo, Jean-Paul: French actor associated with the New Wave of the 1960s
BH Wragge: a New York ready-to-wear fashion house, run by Sydney Wragge and active from 1931 to the early '70s
Blondie: American punk/rock band founded Debbie Harry & Chris Stein
Blue (Australian slang): fight or argument
Boo (Cajun slang): honey, sweetheart
Bowsie (Irish slang): young, good-for-nothing person
Box, the: TV
Brekky: breakfast
BUN (medical jargon): blood urea nitrogen
Buñuel, Luis: Spanish-Mexican filmmaker, a leader of avant-garde surrealism
Burning Giraffe: 1937 painting by Spanish surrealist Salvador Dalí
Cabaret Voltaire: English experimental/industrial music group formed in 1973
Cadillac de Ville: the fourth generation (1971-76) of a car line started in 1949 set records for interior width
Celtic Crossing: 30% ABV liqueur made from Irish whiskey, honey & spices, created to honour the Irish immigrants who came to America
Charbaut Certificate: In the '70s, rated as the finest & most expensive champagne
Charon: In Greek mythology, the ferryman of Hades
CHiPs: U.S. TV drama about two California Highway Patrol motocycle cops
Chiseler (Dublin slang): a child

Chockers (Australian slang): crowded

Ciggie: cigarette

Cock o' the North: brand of whisky liqueur, made by the Marquis of Huntly, in Aberdeenshire, Scotland

Colcannon: traditional Irish dish of mashed potatoes with kale or cabbage

Como, Perry: American smooth baritone crooner and TV personality

Corleone, Michael: main character in the *Godfather* trilogy directed by Francis Ford Coppola

Crosby, Bing: American easy-listening singer and actor

Cross Your Heart: a famous brassiere, made by Playtex since 1954

Da (Irish slang): father

Dalí, Salvador: prominent Spanish surrealist artist

Dante: Dante Alighieri, major Italian poet of the late Middle Ages

Davis, Miles: Innovative American jazz musician

Death on the Nile: 1978 British film based on Agatha Christie's mystery novel

De Niro, Robert: American actor famous for *Taxi Driver* & *Raging Bull*

'Disco Inferno': 1976 song by The Trammps from the album of the same name

Divine Comedy: epic poem by Dante Alighieri, written circa 1308-1320

Drāno: famous drain cleaning product manufactured since 1923

Dublin Lawyer: traditional Irish dish: lobster cooked in whiskey and cream

Dunnies: toilets

Eno, Brian: English musician, principal innovator of ambient music

Extended Play: debut 1978 release by English industrial band Cabaret Voltaire

Fag: cigarette

Fedora: a felt hat with a wide brim and indented crown

Fine thing (Irish slang): good looking man or woman

Fire brigade: fire department

French barrette: hairclips providing a more secure hold, ideal for use with thick hair

Frog: French person

Fuzz: police

Galway Crystal: Irish crystal makers established in 1967

Gaynor, Gloria: American singer known for disco era hits 'I Will Survive' & 'Never Can Say Goodbye'

Gob: mouth

Godfather, The: 1972 American crime film directed by Francis Ford Coppola

Golden Treasury of Myths and Legends, The: 1959 anthology of stories such as Beowulf and Tristram & Iseult, written by Anne Terry White, with illustrations by Alice & Martin Provensen

Gould, Elliott: American actor, famous for *M*A*S*H* & *The Long Goodbye*

Guaiwei: literally 'strange/exotic taste', a seasoning mixture in Szechuan cuisine

Hagen, Nina: German actress/singer, often dubbed the godmother of punk

Havana: cigar

Hicks & Healey: 7-year-old Cornish single malt whiskey, £150 for a half-litre

Historia Calamitatum: 12th century autobiographical work by Peter Abelard, a medieval pioneer of scholastic philosophy

Homburg: formal felt hat characterized by a single dent running down the center of the crown & a stiff brim shaped in a 'kettle curl'

'How Deep is Your Love': 1977 Bee Gees song from the *Saturday Night Fever* soundtrack

'I Feel Love': famed 1977 Donna Summer song, written by Summer with Giorgio Moroder & Pete Bellotte

Illycaffè: Italian company specializing in espresso, founded by Francesco Illy in 1933

Imperial Leather: Soap created in the early 1900s by England's Cusson's

Jaguar D-Type: sports racing car produced by Jaguar between 1954 and 1957

Josie and the Pussycats: animated U.S. TV series based upon the Archie comic book series, produced by Hanna-Barbera in 1970-71

Keitel, Harvey: American actor, famous for *Taxi Driver* & *Pulp Fiction*

Kip: sleep

Knappogue Castle: single malt Irish whiskey named for a castle in County Clare, Ireland

Korev: Cornish lager beer

Kumichō: family head of a Japanese yakuza group

Layla and Other Assorted Love Songs: 1970 LP. 'Layla' was inspired by 12th century Persian poet Niá°"āmī's version of Laylá and Majnūn, which Lord Byron once dubbed the 'Romeo and Juliet of the East'

Lansbury, Angela: British-American actress, born 1925

Loo: toilet

LP: long-playing 12 or 10 inch vinyl record that spins at 33⅓ rpm

Mabinogion: earliest prose literature of Britain, with stories compiled in the 12th-13th century from earlier oral traditions by medieval Welsh authors

Madame Bovary: Gustave Flaubert's debut 1856 novel

Mam (Irish slang): mother

Marie de France: medieval poet probably born in France & lived in England during the late 12th century. Wrote about Tristan & Iseult in *Chevrefoil*

M*A*S*H: 1970 film directed by Robert Altman, based on fiction of Richard Hooker

McGoohan, Patrick: American-born Anglo-Irish actor, writer and director

McMillan & Wife: lighthearted U.S. TV police procedural starring Rock Hudson & Susan Saint James

McQueen, Steve: actor, starred in *The Great Escape*, *The*

Sand Pebbles & *Bullitt*

Mengele, Josef: notorious German SS officer and physician in Auschwitz concentration camp during World War II

Midleton Barry Crockett Legacy: $200+ Irish pot still whiskey

Miyako Maki: shōjo manga artist, designer of Licca-chan, & wife of Leiji Matsumoto

Mona Bone Jakon: 1970 album by British singer-songwriter Cat Stevens

Monty Python: British surreal comedy group, est. 1969

Moroder, Giorgio: Italian record producer, songwriter, performer and DJ often credited with pioneering synth-disco and electronic music

Muir Èireann: the Irish Sea

My hovercraft is full of eels: part of a a sketch about a badly translated English-Hungarian phrasebook from the British TV comedy show, *Monty Python's Flying Circus*

Mystère: oriental fragrance for women launched in 1978

Nineteen Eighty-Four: 1949 novel by George Orwell

Old lady (Irish slang): mother

Old Spice: American brand of male aftershave founded in 1934 by William Lightfoot Schultz

Pacino, Al: American actor, famous for *The Godfather* & *Scarface*

Patek Philippe: expensive square-shaped, white-gold 1970s watch, said to be an inspiration for the Apple Watch

Pater: Latin for father

PBX: private branch exchange, a telephone exchange or switching system

Perv (Australian slang): to gaze lustfully or lecherously

Peter the Hermit: a priest, emotional revivalist, rabble-rouser & key figure during the 11th century First Crusade

Ponch: Officer Francis Llewellyn 'Ponch' Poncherello in TV show *CHiPs*

Porkpie: hats popular since 19th century, bearing resemblance to a culinary pork pie dish

Presa di Cristo nell'orto: Caravaggio's *The Taking of Christ* (1602), a painting showing the dramatic betrayal and arrest of Jesus

Prisoner, The: iconic 1967-68 British sci-fi/spy series

Quatro, Suzi: American singer-songwriter, & first female bass player to become a major rock star

Queen Mab: fairy referred to in Shakespeare's *Romeo and Juliet*, described as a miniature creature who drives her chariot into the noses and into the brains of sleeping people to compel them to experience dreams of wish-fulfillment

Rathbone, Basil: South African-born English actor famous for villainous roles

Rhodesia: the old name for Zimbabwe in Africa

Rin Tin Tin: Hollywood canine star of 27 films; later name of 1950s TV show

Salem: introduced in 1956 - the first filter-tipped menthol cigarette

Schifrin, Lalo: Argentine musician/composer best known for scores for the films *Mission: Impossible*, *Bullitt* & *Dirty Harry*

Scrowled pilchards: traditional Cornish dish, grilled over fire on an iron plate

Serling, Rod: American screenwriter & narrator famous for his sci-fi anthology TV series, *The Twilight Zone*

Sex Pistols, the: English punk rock band formed in London in 1975

Shiv: knife

Singlet: tanktop

Sloe gin fizz: made with sloe gin, regular gin &lemon juice, topped off with club soda

Small Change: 1976 Tom Waits album

"Something is rotten in the state of Denmark": *Hamlet*, Act I, Scene 4

Spingo: strong beer in Old English, generic name for beers brewed solely in Helston, Cornwall

Stargazy pie: Cornish dish in which fish such as sardines are arranged in pie crust with heads pointing upward outside the crust, so they appear to be looking up at the sky.

Starsky & Hutch: 1970s TV cop series, with David Soul & Paul Michael Glaser

Status Quo: English rock band, originated in The Spectres, founded in 1962

'Stayin' Alive': 1977 disco song by the Bee Gees, from the *Saturday Night Fever* soundtrack

Steptoe and Son: British TV comedy airing from 1962, starring Harry H. Corbett

Stevens, Cat: British singer-songwriter

Stewart, Rod: rock singer-songwriter-crooner of Scottish and English ancestry, one of the best-selling music artists of all time

Sugawara, Bunta: Japanese actor, famous for his yakuza gangster roles such as in *Battles Without Honor and Humanity*

Sutherland, Donald: Canadian actor, famous for *M*A*S*H* and *Klute*

Summer, Donna: American singer, songwriter, and painter, prominent during the disco era

10CC: English art rock band famous in the 1970s

Theatre of Cruelty: 1940s theatre style by Antonin Artaud: the effects of expressing through the body as opposed to 'socially-conditioned thought'

Third Man, The: 1949 British-American film noir, directed by Carol Reed and starring Joseph Cotten, Alida Valli, Orson Welles and Trevor Howard

Tjader, Cal: American Latin jazz musician, linked to the development of Latin rock and acid jazz

Townsend, Pete: English musician best known as lead guitarist & songwriter for the rock band The Who

Trammps, The: Based in Philadelphia, and one of the first disco bands

'Trelawney': a.k.a 'The Song of the Western Men', a Cornish patriotic song written in modern form by Robert Stephen Hawker in 1824, but with roots in older folk songs

Trilby: gentleman's fedora—a soft felt hat with narrow brim and indented crown

Twilight Zone, The: Vital American TV anthology series screened from 1959, created by Rod Serling

Tzara, Tristan: Romanian/French avant-garde poet, essayist & performance artist—one of the founders & central figures of the anti-establishment Dada movement

Undies: underpants

Vatican II: from 1962 the Second Vatican Council addressed relations between the Roman Catholic Church & the modern world

Village People, the: American disco group well known for their on-stage costumes depicting American masculine cultural stereotypes

Waits, Tom: American singer-songwriter, composer, and actor

Weatherboard: clapboard

Well of Loneliness, The: 1928 lesbian novel by British author Radclyffe Hall

West Side Story: musical by Leonard Bernstein, Stephen Sondheim & Jerome Robbins

Who, The: English rock band that formed in 1964

Wuthering Heights: Emily Brontë's 1947 novel

Yakuza: transnational organized crime syndicates originating in Japan

Yatagan: men's fragrance, named for curved Turkish sabre, made by Caron from 1976

'You Are My Lucky Star': written by Nacio Herb Brown & Arthur Freed, sung by Gene Kelly & Debbie Reynolds in *Singin' in the Rain* (1952)

ACKNOWLEDGEMENTS

*I*f you haven't previously acquainted yourself with the
medieval story of Tristan and Isolde, or Tristram and
Iseult (sources vary on the correct spelling), there are a
wild amount of "takes"—including an Icelandic deviation
called *Tristrams saga ok Ísöndar*, and an 1850s-produced
opera by Richard Wagner.

Most famous, probably, is the one (literary, not choral)
by Béroul, a Norman poet of the 12th century, but we
could pen an entire tome here on possible origins and
offspring

More simply put, this legend has been called source
material from which sprang the tragic romances of both
King Arthur and Guinevere and Romeo and Juliet.

My first brush with the tale occurred in primary school.
Dad picked up a second-hand copy of the Paul Hamlyn-
published *Myths and Legends* (1959), written by Anne Terry
White and beautifully illustrated by Alice and Martin
Provensen. This book kick-started my fascination with

characters like Roland and his horn, Beowulf and Grendel, Pluto and Persephone, Sigurd the Volsung, and Tristram and Iseult (as our young lovers were named there).

Let's call them T&I from here on, if only for brevity's sake.

I already loved ancient history, so livening it up with these mythic feats of heroic derring-do (and related tragedy) was always going to be a bout of synchronicity.

By high school, as an early form of adult cynicism began to settle in, so too did my entanglement with classic film noir and hardboiled literature. Here think, in particular, writers Raymond Chandler, Graham Greene, Ross Macdonald and Dashiell Hammett, directors like Carol Reed, John Huston, Akira Kurosawa and Orson Welles. It cannot be overstated here how much impact had the in-print and celluloid versions of *The Maltese Falcon*, *The Big Sleep*, *The Long Goodbye*, *The Thin Man*, and *The Third Man*.

It's been a lasting romance.

Tied to these are more contemporary influences like authors Nicholas Christopher, Richard Matheson, Angela Carter, Fuminori Nakamura, Patrick deWitt and James Ellroy, comic book writers Ed Brubaker and Matt Fraction, and filmmakers Martin Scorsese, Satoshi Kon, Quentin Tarantino, John Woo, Joss Whedon, the Coen and Russo brothers, and Christopher Nolan.

I had the whim to rewrite the legend of T&I ever since I scribbled my first novel in high school, but the ideas changed over ensuing years—from a faithful period piece to one set in the distant past, using modern vernacular. Elements of the tale had a direct impact on my second novel *One Hundred Years of Vicissitude* (2012), and Kohana from that book gets to make a cameo here.

In late 2014, I decided to approach the tale again, with it set in a noir-drenched 1940s, but within a week swapped that to the 1970s, and reversed the sexes of our key two protagonists. Having grown up as a child of that decade—

through elements as diverse as the *Godfather* films, *Star Wars*, *Saturday Night Fever*, *Chinatown*, Robert Altman's *The Long Goodbye*, TV shows such as *Starsky and Hutch*, *The Rockford Files* and *CHiPs*, not to mention the disco, flares, glaring fashion and mesmerizing hairstyles—I felt I had a better handle on proceedings, no matter that they might have been faded memories.

By New Year's Eve in 2014, I'd finished the first two pages of what would become a fifteen-issue comic book series I wrote and illustrated last year titled *Trista & Holt*. I was fortunate to receive instructive feedback initially from fellow writers Lori Alden Holuta and Renee Asher Pickup. Renee went on to script #7—Trista's "origin" tale—which pushed so damned good that I recycled and expanded upon it here.

Thereafter proceeding with the novel was, for me, the logical next step as I felt there remained more to say, and like to believe writing is something I'm better at than artwork.

This long-player introduces new characters, goes further in depth, the finale is completely different, and it toys more earnestly with the Ireland vs. Cornwall slant of the original material, including food, culture and music.

On the side, I do like to play with monikers, doff the hat, pay homage, and name-drop anything that I feel relates to a story, or the influences themselves.

Hence, for example, the integral Muir Èireann river, which splits our fictional city between the Holts and the Cornwalls—it's Gaelic for the Irish Sea, which separates Ireland and England.

Police officers Lode, Tusk, and O'Dar are a wink at Dashiell Hammett's recurring Continental Op coppers Thode, Lusk, and O'Gar.

The Holt family mansion, Chapelizod House, is named after a village preserved within the city of Dublin called Chapelizod (in Irish, Séipéal Iosóid, meaning 'Iseult's Chapel'). This village is associated with Iseult of Ireland

and the location of her actual chapel.

The original builder of Marcella's Tintagel Apartments, Conan Merry, is a play on Conan Meriadoc, or Conan the Merry, a 4th century king of Dumnonia—which preceded Cornwall.

Why the character name Norman 'Berry' Béroul? Well, Béroul (that person most famous for the T&I legend, remember?) harked from Normandy in France. Boom, boom.

Also, Governal's house is called 'Morrois Duff' for a reason. The Forest of Morrois is where Tristan and Iseult were sent into exile, accompanied by Tristan's constant companion and childhood tutor Governal. As a noun, 'Duff' has various meanings, from "to whisk, smoke, darken, obscure" and "decaying vegetable matter on a forest floor", to being beaten up. Other interpretations? "Bits left in the bottom of the bag after the booty has been consumed, like crumbs", "To disguise something to make it look new", and "Something spurious or fake; a counterfeit, a worthless thing." As an adjective, think "Worthless; not working properly, defective." I'll leave it to your imagination which one(s) apply.

There's a lot more where these supposed nuggets came from, but I need to leave in some breadcrumbs for the can-be-bothered to bird-dog.

By the way, you might have noticed that the city in *Black Sails, Disco Inferno* remains unnamed. It could easily be Heropa, from my book *Who is Killing the Great Capes of Heropa?*—the police commissioner Bob Kahn, who we never meet, shares the same name as police detective Robert Kahn in that earlier story, and a young iteration of washed-up racketeer Solomon Brodsky and his French femme fatale might have stalked the pages of spin-off comic *Bullet Gal*—but chalk these up (for now) as coincidental.

Finally, living in Japan these past fifteen years has had an obvious impact. I'm an overbearing fan of the cinema of Akira Kurosawa, actors Toshiro Mifune and Takashi Shimura (Shimura-san in this novel), and 1970s yakuza crime flicks—notably those starring Bunta Sugawara. My daughter Cocoa collected Licca-chan dolls up until a couple of years ago, and I wrote an article about their history and cultural impact for *GEEK Magazine* in the U.S., while just last year I suffered through an untranslated bout of bunraku puppet theatre.

Anyway, I'm going to close here with a word of gratitude to my publishers at Open Books—indulgent enough to allow me to run with this revisionist yarn—and Australian artist Frantz Kantor (with whom I work on the strip *Magpie*) for the pitch-perfect cover painting. Arigato to Kim for checking my Irish slang, Brian for bringing the Cajun Chef to life over drinks, along with friends and family—forever supportive. And to you, the reader of these words, let's keep things deceptively simple: thank you.

—Andrez, Tokyo, Japan

*F*or Trista's origin story, what I got stuck on was this idea of a relationship between her and Governal that would play out in reality. A young girl whose life is in turmoil, taken from her family and raised by a man whose experience is based around crime—what does that look like? As I played with how they would interact, and the way in which their roles would change as Trista took her place in the 'business', the story unfolded before me. There is love there, some tenderness, but a distance created by both necessity and circumstance. I'm ever grateful to Andrez for letting me fly as freely as I wanted to regarding how that relationship developed and the ways in which it affected things going forward.

There are so many people I want to acknowledge and thank, but of course I'm crippled by the fear I'll leave someone out. Many thanks go to my husband, Jon, without whom I'd never have a moment's peace to write, and who is always willing to shove me when I need to get back to work. The crew at LitReactor, especially Rob Hart; my once-partner in crime, Jessica Leonard, who co-hosted Books and Booze with me (which led to Andrez and I meeting); my *Dirge* Fam; my actual family, and Dale Fellows, who supported my writing at a time when most kids have stories about teachers making them feel as though something was wrong with them for what they wrote. If I missed you, and you feel you should be thanked here—you probably ought to have been, and I apologize!

—Renee, Murrieta, CA, U.S.A.

AUTHORS PROFILE

Andrez Bergen is an expat Australian writer, journalist, DJ, artist and ad hoc saké connoisseur who's been entrenched in Tokyo, Japan, for the past 15 years.

Bergen has written for publications such as *Mixmag*, *The Age*, *Australian Style*, *Remix*, and the *Yomiuri Shinbun*. He has published five novels, wrote and illustrated two graphic novels, and published three comic book series.

Bergen's fiction previously appeared through Crime Factory, Shotgun Honey, Snubnose Press, All Due Respect, Perfect Edge Books, Roundfire Fiction, and Another Sky Press, and he occasionally adapts scripts for feature films by the likes of Mamoru Oshii (*Ghost in the Shell*) for Production I.G in Japan.

He also makes music as Little Nobody and Funk Gadget, and ran groundbreaking Melbourne record label IF? for over a decade.

Renee Asher Pickup is a mellowed-out punk rocker living in Southern California. She is senior editor at *Dirge Magazine*, class facilitator at LitReactor, and is one of the hosts of the Unprintable Podcast. Renee writes fiction about bad things happening to flawed people—and stands by the statement that *From Dusk Till Dawn* changed her life